Favorite Harlequin Historica̶l̶ brings you a brand-new trilogy:

Heirs in Waiting

One day these Oxford gentlemen will inherit estates, titles and wealth.

But for now, they're forging their own paths in life...and love!

With great titles will come great power and responsibility, for which they must prepare. But waiting in the wings isn't easy for these daring gentlemen, so they're forging ahead on their own paths, where they'll encounter three exceptional women who would never be found at a *ton* ball...

Let's meet them in

Book 1: *The Bluestocking Duchess*

And coming soon

Book 2: *The Railway Countess*

Book 3: *The Explorer Baroness*

Author Note

It is difficult for us to appreciate how restricted opportunities were for nineteenth-century women. Females weren't believed to have the intellectual capacity to benefit from "formal" education. Even genteel ladies were seldom taught more than music, dancing, French and a bit of literature or geography—skills to make them good hostesses able to entertain guests.

Jocelyn Sudderfield defies the norm. Raised by a scholarly father, working first as his scribe, she has now become the real author of their translations of ancient Greek literature. She has no desire to give up the work that fulfills her to take on a husband.

The only man who tempts her is Alex Cheverton, estate agent for the duke who sponsors her father. But not even to Alex does she dare reveal her true role, for neither the duke nor the scholarly community would accept translations made by a female.

For Alex, the daughter of the duke's librarian has suddenly transformed from pesky annoyance to alluring woman. He's struggling to control his attraction when he unexpectedly finds himself heir to the dukedom. It's now his duty to find a highborn, wealthy lady for his duchess. Certainly not a bluestocking who disdains marriage.

Circumstances sweep them both to London, where Alex struggles to master his new role while resisting the attraction that keeps pulling him back to Jocelyn. Learning to accept the gift of love will prove the most valuable lesson for them both.

I hope you'll enjoy their journey!

JULIA JUSTISS

—

The Bluestocking Duchess

HARLEQUIN

HISTORICAL

Recycling programs
for this product may
not exist in your area.

ISBN-13: 978-1-335-50606-1

The Bluestocking Duchess

Copyright © 2021 by Janet Justiss

This edition published by arrangement with Harlequin Books S.A.

For questions and comments about the quality of this book,
please contact us at CustomerService@Harlequin.com.

Harlequin Enterprises ULC
22 Adelaide St. West, 40th Floor
Toronto, Ontario M5H 4E3, Canada
www.Harlequin.com

Printed in U.S.A.

Julia Justiss wrote her first ideas for Nancy Drew stories in her third-grade notebook and has been writing ever since. After publishing poetry in college, she turned to novels. Her Regency historicals have won or placed in contests by the Romance Writers of America, *RT Book Reviews*, National Readers' Choice and Daphne du Maurier Award. She lives with her husband in Texas. For news and contests, visit juliajustiss.com.

Books by Julia Justiss

Harlequin Historical

Heirs in Waiting

The Bluestocking Duchess

The Cinderella Spinsters

The Awakening of Miss Henley
The Tempting of the Governess
The Enticing of Miss Standish

Sisters of Scandal

A Most Unsuitable Match
The Earl's Inconvenient Wife

Hadley's Hellions

Forbidden Nights with the Viscount
Stolen Encounters with the Duchess
Convenient Proposal to the Lady
Secret Lessons with the Rake

Visit the Author Profile page
at Harlequin.com for more titles.

To the determined women of every age
who will settle for nothing less than achieving
what they are capable of doing.

Chapter One

West Sussex—late February 1834

If his Oxford friends could see him now...they might not think so highly of his choice of profession. Not that he'd really had one.

With a sigh of annoyance, Alex Cheverton, estate manager of Edge Hall, the Duke of Farisdeen's principal country property, got down on his hands and knees and crawled under his desk to retrieve his waistcoat button. Castigating himself for putting off the task of repairing it, he backed out carefully, not wanting to compound his annoyance by banging his head on the desk.

Rising back to his feet, he stared at the offending button. Might as well leave the correspondence on his desk and tend to it now. Besides, he'd been craving a hot cup of tea since returning to his office after the chill of inspecting the stable block and the State Rooms the staff had just finished cleaning.

Button in hand, he walked out of his office and headed down the corridor to another of the smaller, private family rooms located, like his office, in a separate wing that backed on to and mirrored the U-shaped formal entry wing of Edge Hall. A moment later, he reached the sitting room, appreciating as he entered the warmth emanating from the fire on the hearth and the sunlight streaming through the window.

He shared this pleasant space with a handful of staff whose birth, like his, elevated them above congregating in the servants' hall, yet was not sufficiently grand to entitle them to use the State Apartments or the sumptuous salons, bedchambers and anterooms reserved for the Duke. Soon after taking up his post, he'd had a small stove added to the fireplace in the room so that he could prepare tea for himself whenever he wished, without having to send to the kitchen. With wine in the decanter on the sideboard, a tin beside it containing the bread and cheese Cook sent up daily with his breakfast, he had sustenance to keep him going throughout the day.

The sideboard also contained an assortment of everyday necessities like needles, thread, scissors and thimbles.

He'd made the tea, taken a seat at the long table before the hearth, threaded a needle and bent over to begin his chore when a disturbance in the air of the room, followed by the wafting of rose perfume, announced a new arrival. *Jocelyn*, he thought, his senses stirring.

'Ah, you've heated the kettle, I see,' the newcomer said.

'Yes. There should be enough hot water left to make tea for you and your brother, if you'd like.' Distracted by her presence, he looked up to smile at her—and jabbed himself in the thumb.

Giving an undignified yelp, he rubbed at the spot of blood on his finger, not wanting to drip it on to the waistcoat.

'What's this? Have you injured yourself?' she asked, walking over to the table. 'Let me see.'

'I think I'll live,' he said, holding up the finger for her inspection.

She took a handkerchief from her sleeve and wiped off his finger.

The pain of the pinprick forgotten, he savoured the touch of her hands, acutely sensitive to the brush of fabric over his finger, the subtle scent of roses that clung to her. Guiltily aware that he shouldn't be noticing it.

'Yes, you'll do,' she said, releasing his hand. 'Speaking of "do", whatever were you attempting here?' She peered down at the thread, scissors and waistcoat laid before him on the table. 'Sewing on a button?'

'How very acute you are.'

'It's my superior education. It allows me to rapidly evaluate a situation and discern the most salient points,' she tossed back, her beautiful dark eyes dancing.

He could stare into them for ever, Alex thought. But of course, he wouldn't. Trading barbs with Jocelyn Sudderfeld, the lovely, intelligent sister of the Duke's librarian, who over the six years he'd worked here had grown from exuberant youngster to desirable young lady almost before he noticed it, was all he would allow himself. Especially now that he could no longer ignore how attractive her tall, graceful figure, gamin face and fascinating eyes had become.

Fortunately, even if she didn't view him merely as another pesky older brother, she was promised to another—or as close to promised as made no difference.

'Which begs the point,' she was saying, 'of why the lofty estate manager of Edge Hall, cousin to the Duke of Farisdeen himself, is lowering himself to perform such a mundane task. Any number of housemaids could do it for you. Mary, in particular, would be delighted to be of assistance.'

'Which, if your understanding were as acute as you seem to think it, you would realise is exactly why I did *not* ask her—or any of the others.'

'Oh, my—has she turned lovesick, too? Well, what can a gentleman like you expect, when he is handsome, charming, intelligent—and cousin to a duke?'

'He expects to tread a very careful path *away* from lovesick housemaids,' Alex said with asperity, drawing a laugh from Jocelyn. 'Although a little more respect from the sister of His Grace's librarian wouldn't come amiss.'

'Ah, but I'm not a lovesick housemaid.'

'No, you're just an outspoken bluestocking whom I vainly hoped would have matured from the mannerless brat I encountered when I arrived six years ago.'

'Perhaps, but a *talented*, outspoken mannerless brat,' she returned. 'In fact, despite your cruel aspersions, which would have me bursting into tears, had I any sensibility, which fortunately I do not, I am still magnanimous enough to sew on that button for you. Can't have you bleeding all over the parlour. If you'll hand me the waistcoat and thread?'

Saying that, she seated herself at the table and held out her hand.

Quite happy to turn the task over to someone whom he didn't have to worry about trying to sneak into his bed—much as he might welcome such a shocking but highly unlikely invasion from *her*—he offered her the threaded needle and handed over the waistcoat. 'Are you sure you are able to sew on a button? Writing down your brother's Greek translations all day doesn't exactly qualify you as a seamstress.'

'Perhaps not, but since both he and Papa seem to shed buttons as freely as dogs do their winter coats in spring, I've plenty of practice doing that, too. You might cease insulting me and make me a cup of tea instead, while I mend your button. Preparing tea, I know you are competent to handle. Despite your lack of expertise with needle and thread, you're not entirely the useless, idle cousin of the Duke you were when you first arrived.'

'I'll be happy to make you a cup, if you will cease the "cousin of the Duke" harassment. Since I am, as you very well know, merely the son of a country gentleman, just as you are the daughter of one. Only my father was content to occupy himself on his modest estate, rather than embrace scholarship, as your father and brother have.'

'If it earns me a hot cup of tea, I suppose I can desist.' Abandoning her teasing for a more normal tone, she asked, 'How are the repairs going on the stable block?'

'Slowly,' he replied as he extracted tea leaves from the tin, put them into a pot and poured simmering water over them. 'Although the local stone used in the original construction is a beautiful colour, it doesn't last well. There is chipping and cracking on almost every one of the carved cornices. Now that we're reasonably sure there will be no further frost to exacerbate the cracks, the mason thinks he can start on it. But he expects it will be a lengthy and extensive project.'

'No riding for you, then,' she said, pausing to accept a steaming cup.

'No, alas. I enjoy it when I can, though it's not often.'

'And the Duke's hunters do require exercise.'

'They do indeed. In fact, I'm planning to make a circuit of the tenant farms on the west side of the estate tomorrow, to inspect for any winter damage to cottages and barns and make sure the farmers have sufficient equipment and seed. All the weather indications promise it will be a fine, sunny day. Would you and Miss Morrison like to ride with me?'

'Emily is still tending her papa as he recovers from a putrid cold, but I'll send a note and ask her. Speaking for myself, I'd be delighted to ride. As long as I can choose which of the Duke's hunters I get to exercise.'

'Knowing you, it will be the most skittish and ungovernable one in the stable,' Alex said.

'No, just the fastest. After all, the hunters do need to be galloped to keep up their stamina. So they can give the Duke and his guests a good run, if he should bring a party down to hunt. Do you think he will?'

'Since he's waited this late, I doubt he'll come now. He's been attending a house party in the north with some political associates, and with Parliament to reconvene soon, I don't think he'll come all the way to Sussex before heading back to London. All is in readiness, of course, if he should turn up. I just looked through the State Rooms and they are immaculate—not that I expected anything less. Still, I told Simmons to pass my compliments on to the staff.'

'They have all been working like Trojans, getting the house ready. Farisdeen usually does come to Edge Hall to hunt before Parliament reconvenes. I imagine some will be disappointed to miss having the excitement of a grand party visit the house. You, I expect, will not.'

Alex laughed. 'Disappointed not to add the work of housing, feeding and entertaining the Duke and a hunting party of anywhere from ten to fifty guests for several weeks, while at the same time helping the tenants prepare for spring planting and supervising the never-ending task of repairs and upkeep on the Hall, the stables, all the other outbuildings, and the tenant cottages? Not one bit. Though I expect that means I shall receive instructions shortly to meet the Duke in London and give him my spring report there.'

'Papa will be disappointed. He'd hoped to show His Grace all the progress Virgil and I—well, Virgil—have made on the translation of the Euripides tragedies. With the Duke of Portland having commissioned a new set of Aristotle translations from his chaplain, Reverend Owen, Papa knew Farisdeen hoped to have Virgil complete his work first.'

'Winning the first-to-the-finish competition among patrons sponsoring the translation of Greek classics into English?'

'Something like that. Just as well that His Grace won't descend on us. Virgil is much happier with his nose buried in Greek text than he is presenting a report to the Duke—a prospect which always sends him into a state of high anxiety.'

'Speaking with Farisdeen often has that effect on people,' Alex said drily. 'If Virgil is in such a hurry to finish, will he allow you to ride tomorrow?'

Jocelyn laughed, a delightful tinkling sound that always made Alex smile. 'You must realise that "finish" is a relative term. I doubt either Virgil—or the Duke of Portland's chaplain—have any expectation of completing their projects for years yet. I think my brother can spare having me here to record his pristine words for an afternoon. Besides, I can tell him I'll be helping Reverend Morrison by checking on his parishioners while he is laid up.' She angled her head up at him, her dark eyes dancing. 'Despite being mounted on the Duke's fastest hunter, I promise not to outrace you…too often.'

'Only if you also promise not to sulk if I outrace *you*.'

'Easily done—since there's little chance of that happening.'

Alex laughed, as she meant him to. Sometimes, when she challenged him to a gallop or to a game of chess, she seemed once again the vibrant, saucy girl who'd shocked him when he'd first arrived by riding the feistiest horse in the Duke's stables—clad in her brother's breeches. Unconventional, outspoken, endlessly curious about everything around her.

Her manners had improved—and she no longer rode about in breeches. But sometimes he'd catch a whiff of her rose perfume...or a glimpse of her in profile, her lushly rounded figure definitely no longer that of a child.

It had certainly been easier when he could think of her only as an engaging brat. But despite the temptation she presented, even if it were possible, he wasn't sure he'd opt to return her to her girlish state of six years ago—and thereby forfeit the pleasure of appreciating the beauty and allure that both enticed and bedeviled him.

Fortunately for the maintenance of his control and good character, she lived with her little family in the Dower House. No chance of running into her in her night rail as she came down to the kitchen to prepare her wakeful father a glass of warm milk. He saw her only in the public rooms at Edge Hall, or out riding and walking the fields and farms, often with her friend Miss Morrison, the vicar's daughter, accompanying them.

Tomorrow, he could rely on her desire to outrace him and her delight in meeting with the tenants, as well as the presence of Miss Morrison, to reinforce his control over the annoying amorous impulses she seemed to inspire in him of late.

Not that he really needed any help to avoid crossing the lines of propriety. After the searing experience in his late teens that had seen him secretly engaged and then summarily rejected by the young lady's father, he'd become very good at reining in both unruly emotions and amorous impulses.

Besides which, though they might both be offspring of obscure country gentlemen, lowly members of the gentry whom the *ton* in London might consider beneath notice, he was a gentleman, and she was a lady. He liked and respected her too much to abuse her trust.

No matter how much her beauty and spirit might speak to him.

'There!' she said, pulling him from his thoughts as she held up his waistcoat. 'Button firmly reattached. With, I'll have you note, perfect, fine, even stitches of which even your mama would approve.'

He took the garment, a shock of awareness flashing through him as, for a moment, their fingers touched.

Maybe it *would* be better if she were to regress to being a saucy sixteen-year-old, he thought with a sigh.

'Very fine stitchery,' he said, recovering his wits. 'My mama, a notable needlewoman, would approve.'

'Mine was, too,' Jocelyn said, her teasing look fading and a distant expression coming over her face. 'She was so patient, teaching me, restless and irritated as I often was with the lessons. She knew I'd far rather be with Papa in his study, learning Greek and Latin and French and Italian, than sewing samplers and practising embroidery.'

'She despaired of having so unnatural a daughter?' he teased.

'No, she was proud of Papa's scholarship, proud enough to defy her family and marry him in the teeth of their disapproval. A Randall of Innisbrook should have done much better for herself than to wed a former Oxford don whose chief goal in life was finding a patron to support his translation projects. She was pleased that I shared his interests, pleased that my aptitude for languages allowed me to assist him.'

'You copied out the translations for him, even before you began doing it for your brother, didn't you?'

'Yes. It began as an exercise, when he was teaching me Greek. Then, when he developed rheumatism in his hands and writing became difficult, he found that I was able to take down his words as quickly and accurately as he could dictate them. So I was already quite accomplished by the time he passed the work on to my brother.'

'Still an unusual occupation for a female.'

She grinned. 'Ah, but I am a very unusual female. Now, if I am to go riding tomorrow, I'd better get that tea for my brother and get back to work. Shall we meet at the stables around one? Emily can meet us there.'

'One would be fine. I need to work on the ledgers in the morning.'

'I'll have the Dower House cook make us up some provisions,' she said as she added more tea leaves to the pot and poured in some additional hot water. 'If the tenants don't press too much food and drink upon us, we can picnic on top of Trethfort Hill. If it is as fine and sunny as you claim it will be, we'll get a wonderful view over the South Downs, from Edge Hall village all the way to Charlton.'

Extracting a tray from a drawer in the sideboard, she put her cup and saucer on it, added another set and the teapot, then poured a bit of milk into the cups. 'I'll see you tomorrow, then.'

'Shall I carry the tray to the library for you?'

'Thank you, but I can manage. You'd better get back to your reports. Besides, it wouldn't do to have his Magnificence, the Duke's cousin, carrying a tea tray like a lackey.'

'Minx!' he threw at her as, laughing, she hefted the tray and walked out of the room.

She was set to marry a curate, a friend of her brother's from university, once the young man secured a living sufficient to support her, he knew. Alex wondered how this lively, intelligent, unusual lady who loved galloping hunters and spending her days transcribing ancient Greek would fare as a vicar's wife serving a small rural parish. Where hunters, and scholarship, were likely to be thin on the ground.

He would certainly miss her when she did marry. That liveliness and intelligence and her always unexpected view of the world brightened his days as much as her beauty attracted him. Her brother was polite enough, but not even his doting sister would describe him as 'lively', and her father, though a fine gentleman, was rather garrulous, with a tendency to ramble on and on about his work. Except when the Duke was in residence, bringing along his secretary, like Alex a gentleman from a modest but respected family, Alex had no other company of his station.

He knew he was welcome to visit the Squire and the handful of gentry families who lived in the area. But as a bachelor—the Duke had made Alex's remaining unwed for at least ten years a condition of his employment—he couldn't return the hospitality. Though at the time he'd thought the requirement rather odd, after his previous unpleasant brush with matrimony Alex was quite content to comply. And since that stricture was not generally known, he didn't wish to visit any of the local families with marriageable daughters with enough frequency as to give rise to any marital expectations.

Should he be foolish enough to wed, thereby forfeiting his position, the small competence he had thus far managed to save from the salary the Duke paid him wouldn't allow him to support an independent household. While he knew his mother would receive him and his bride back at Wynborne, he'd witnessed first-hand with his younger sister's marriage how unpleasant it could be to have a wife and a mother-in-law under the same roof. Nor did he want to add to his family's burdens the necessity of supporting both him and a wife. With his mother fully experienced in running the small estate he'd inherited upon his father's death years ago, being able to earn cash to supplement the family income had been the main reason he'd accepted the estate manager's job to begin with.

All of which meant he attended only the celebratory events or holidays for which the whole neighbourhood was invited. Dinner or cards with the Sudderfelds provided the majority of his evening entertainment, and with Jocelyn the most dynamic member of her family, life after she married and left Edge Hall would lose much of its sparkle.

For now, he thought as he doffed his coat, shrugged on his repaired waistcoat, then replaced the outer garment, he would continue to enjoy her company—and hope that her vicar took his time finding a living.

Chapter Two

The next afternoon, attired in her riding habit, Jocelyn paced the stable forecourt, waiting for Alex Cherverton.

She'd purposefully arrived early, so she might have a few extra minutes in which to arm herself against the spike in her pulse and tingle in her nerves that inevitably happened when she met Alex.

It really was ridiculous, she thought with a sigh. She should have long ago outgrown the *tendre* she'd conceived the moment she'd set eyes on the handsome, intense, green-eyed, golden-brown-haired cousin of the Duke that unforgettable afternoon six years ago, when he came to the Dower House to introduce himself to her father. After all, she was a woman now, no longer a child to indulge foolish romantic dreams.

She'd been just the coltish, awkward, outspoken brat he'd accused her of being when she'd first met him. But even though she hadn't really understood what was happening to her nerves and her body, she'd instinctively known she must hide her reaction to him, a response that a man of his birth and education would surely find at best unseemly, at worst outright ridiculous.

They'd soon fallen into an easy, teasing friendship,

trading taunts as they competed at riding or chess or solving the word puzzles her father liked to create, challenging each other's knowledge and opinions when they conversed over the dinners he often joined them for at the Dower House. Over the intervening years, his hold over her hadn't diminished a bit, her initial awe becoming overlaid both with liking and a simmering, uncomfortable, edgy physical attraction.

She really should make more of an effort to overcome her feelings for him. If and when the cousin of a duke married, it would be at the direction and for the benefit of his family. The daughter of a minor member of the gentry, who did not possess a large dowry to compensate for her unremarkable birth, would never be considered a suitable candidate.

Not that she could marry him, even in the unlikely event that he wanted her. Marriage to anyone other than her clerical suitor would mean the end of her work with Virgil, work she had no intention of giving up. Work she was determined to find a way to continue, even after the Euripides was completed.

If she meant to conquer her annoyingly persistent attraction to Alex, she should probably avoid him, rather than agree to spend additional time in his company—like indulging herself with this ride. But avoiding him now, after years of meeting him daily in the library or their shared sitting room at Edge Hall, or at dinner at the Dower House, would not only be difficult to manage, it would be so striking a deviation from their normal routine as to invite a curiosity and speculation she'd rather not arouse.

Sighing, she shook her head. Having once again found no effective solution to the thorny problem of how to stamp out her attraction to him, for now, she would go on as they had been and not worry about the future.

Alex...whose smile as he walked towards her down the lane to the stables sent that irresistible wave of awareness through her.

'You are the most unusual female,' he said as he reached her side. 'Not just punctual, but early.'

Always happy to see you, she thought. 'Always eager for a good gallop,' she said. 'Thompson has the horses ready. Shall we go?'

'Are we not waiting for Miss Morrison?'

'She wrote to me explaining that she wasn't sure she could get away, but if she could, she would join us at Mr Allen's. You do intend to call on him today, don't you?'

'Yes. He will likely be our first stop.'

At that moment, the grooms led the horses out. 'Black Flash,' Alex said, shaking his head at the mount being brought to her. 'I should have known. You realise the head groom believes this gelding isn't well disciplined enough yet to hunt.'

'He also says Flash is the fastest horse in the stable. How is the poor lad to become disciplined unless someone takes him out? Riding in company with only one other horse will be good practice for him—not enough commotion to distract and excite him, but enough to continue teaching him how to move and behave around other riders.'

Since that logic was, as she knew, unanswerable, Alex said nothing, only shaking his head again as he swung up into the saddle of his own gelding. Her head grateful and her body regretful that it was the groom, not Alex, giving her a hand up, Jocelyn took her position on the side saddle.

'Let's take them down to the lane and turn them loose,' he suggested.

'And see just how fast Flash is,' she agreed, urging her mount into motion.

After proceeding from the stable down the lane that led from the rear of Edge Hall to the country road that traversed the ridge, they gave the horses their heads.

Apparently as anxious for the exercise as she was, as soon as she touched her heels to the gelding, Black Flash took off like Congreve rocket. Within seconds, he was racing down the lane at a full-out gallop, taking Jocelyn on the fastest ride she'd ever experienced. They soon left Alex and his mount far behind.

After letting the gelding run at will for long, wonderful, exhilarating minutes, Jocelyn pulled back on the reins, not wanting to get too far ahead of Alex. But the horse had other ideas, resisting her efforts to curb him. Enjoying the wild ride too much to fight him, and curious just how long he could maintain his speed, Jocelyn hung on and let him race.

His stamina was remarkable, especially as it had been quite some time since the horse had been given such hard exercise. Not until he started to flag did she attempt to slow him, this time able to school him from the gallop to a canter, then a trot, and finally to a walk.

Patting his neck and telling him what a wonderful racer he was, she turned him to walk back in the direction from which they came. Even so, it was several more minutes before she spied Alex, guiding his mount at a trot towards them.

'That was impressive,' he said. 'Diamond is no slug and you left us in the dust. How long did he maintain a gallop?'

'For almost three miles! Much further than I expected. The Duke is going to be very pleased with this one! He does need schooling, though. He refused to obey initially when I signalled him to slow. I have every admiration for a horse who loves to run, but he'll need to be much more responsive to command before he can be trusted to ride out in the raucous atmosphere of a hunt, with milling horses and chattering riders and barking hounds. We'll get you another race later before we head home, won't we, my handsome fellow?' she said, bending down to pat Flash's neck. 'But now, we must take care of the master's business.' Looking back up at Alex, she said, 'Shall we go see Mr Allen?'

'Yes. Your magnificent gelding probably took you almost all the way to his farm on your gallop.'

'Indeed he did. How is Mr Allen?'

'Doing fairly well, considering his age. He insists he will plant grain on the same number of acres this year.'

Jocelyn sighed. 'I wish his son and daughter-in-law hadn't decided to look for work in London. It's been awfully lonely for him since Mrs Allen died, with just his milk cow and a few chickens for company. We aren't in too great a rush, are we?'

'Why do you ask?'

'I thought we could linger for a bit, have a longer chat with him.'

Alex nodded. 'Excellent suggestion. We'll make time for it.'

With the horses proceeding at an easy trot, they soon arrived at a lane that branched off from the main track. They followed it as it wound through the grain fields towards a small copse of beechwood that sheltered the elderly farmer's thatched cottage. He must have spied them approaching, for as they neared the house, he walked out to wave at them.

'Good day to you, Mr Cheverton. And to you, Miss Sudderfeld.'

'Has Miss Morrison arrived yet, Mr Allen? She hoped to stop by as well.'

The old farmer shook his head. 'She sent the boy that helps in their garden out with a message. The Reverend seems a bit worse today, so she's stayed home with him. Sorry it is I'll not get to see her.'

'Indeed it is!' Alex said. 'Sorry, too, to hear the Reverend hasn't yet recovered. But how are you today, Mr Allen?'

'Tolerable, tolerable. I've my aches, like any man my age, but I will get the seed in, Mr Cheverton, see if I don't. But now, won't you come in and have a glass of cider with me?'

'Thank you, sir, we'd be pleased to,' Alex said.

They dismounted, Jocelyn taking her provisions parcel from the cantle bag before Alex took the reins and led both horses into the small enclosure beside the cottage.

'Have a seat by the hearth, Miss Sudderfeld, Mr Cheverton,' the farmer said as they followed him into the cottage. 'I'll pour us some cider.'

'Let me, if you would,' Jocelyn said. 'Mr Cheverton will want to chat with you about the spring planting. Just in case Miss Morrison wasn't able to accompany us, I brought a loaf of bread and a jar of their housekeeper's gooseberry jam that you like so much. To thank you for the honey you sent them. Now, you won't distress us by turning them down, I trust?'

'I suppose that wouldn't be neighbourly,' he said after a moment's hesitation. 'The cider's in the jug on the table. Sit yourself by the fire, Mr Cheverton. Not near enough to spring weather yet! These old bones appreciate a good warming.'

'My bones do, too,' Alex told him, taking a stool near the hearth. 'So, how are you set for the spring planting? Have you sufficient seed? Does the thatch on the shed roof need any repairs?'

While Alex kept the old man talking about the state of his buildings and equipment, Jocelyn poured cider into wooden mugs, sliced some of the bread and ladled a healthy spoon of jam on to each slice. She also added several slices of ham and a chunk of cheese she'd brought along to the plates before carrying them over to the men.

At the look Mr Allen gave her, she said, 'There was ham and cheese in the parcel as well. I've sliced some, but you must keep the rest. You know Mrs Reynolds would ring a peal over me if I brought back any of what she'd put up for you.'

The farmer remained silent, obviously considering. But then, as Jocelyn had hoped, he nodded. 'Very well, I'll keep it. Wouldn't want to get you into trouble with that woman. Got a sharp tongue in her head! And doesn't my son Jeremy know it. The daughter's just like the mother.'

'Sharp-tongued she may be, but she has a good heart. And she makes wonderful jam!'

'Aye, she does,' Allen agreed. 'A good cook all around. Don't you think that's how her daughter tempted my son to marry her!'

'Have you heard how they are faring in the city?' Jocelyn asked.

For another half an hour, they chatted with the farmer. Then, after giving Alex a significant nod, Jocelyn had him keep the old man talking while she quietly tidied up the kitchen, put the bread, cheese and ham in the larder and swept the floor.

Her tasks complete, she nodded again to Alex, who brought the conversation to a close. As they walked out, she said, 'Thank you for spending time with us, Mr Allen. It's always such a pleasure to talk with you.'

'Don't I know that it's ye giving me the pleasure, taking the time to visit with an old man.'

'I'll stop by again in a week or so,' Alex said. 'I'd like to bring the horse and plough from Jameson's farm, so you can get that field prepared in a hurry.'

'You think I'm not up to ploughing by hand?'

Alex laughed. 'I think you could plough rings around me! But opening the ground with the horse-drawn plough will go much faster. You'll be able to finish and then get seed sown all in a short time. You know spring weather! Best to get it finished up quick, or you might get caught out by a week of downpours.'

'Aye, that's true enough. Very well, I'll use the horse, if Jameson can spare him.'

'Thank you, I'd appreciate it. It's a help to me to have all the farmers get their seed in at roughly the same time. Makes it easier to check on the progress of the crops and co-ordinate the harvest.'

Allen walked them out, waiting while they mounted, Alex giving her a hand up. Savouring the contact, Jocelyn took as much time to settle herself on to the side saddle as she thought she could get away with, without it becoming obvious she was dawdling.

And felt bereft when he took his steadying hand away. Silently shaking her head at herself as he walked over to swing up on to his own horse, she told herself it was time to stop tempting herself with his touch and use a mounting block.

'Thank you again,' Mr Allen was saying. 'Give the vicar my best wishes for his recovery and to Miss Morrison and Mrs Reynolds, too. And thank you, miss. You might think I wasn't noticing, but I appreciate the help.'

'We're all neighbours, Mr Allen,' she replied. 'We help each other.'

After bidding the farmer goodbye, they rode off.

'I hope the longer visit with Mr Allen didn't put you too far behind in finishing what you need to accomplish today,' Jocelyn said when they reached the country lane.

'All signs say the good weather should hold for several more days. If I don't make it to all the western farms today, I'll finish up tomorrow.'

'I'm afraid I left Mr Allen most of our provisions. But Emily and I worry that, living alone as he does, he doesn't eat as he should.'

'So the victuals didn't come from the vicar's household. I thought as much. I don't normally approve of prevarication, but a few white lies to preserve the old man's pride are excusable.'

'I didn't lie! I may have *implied* that Emily and the housekeeper prepared the provisions, but if you'll recall, what I actually said was that *I* had brought the bread and jam, jam Mrs Reynolds did make—for me. There was ham and cheese also in the packet, just as I said. And Mrs Reynolds *would* ring a peal over me if she'd given me something to deliver and I failed to do so. Perhaps stringing those sentences together in such a manner might have led to an…erroneous conclusion, but I certainly didn't *lie* to Mr Allen.'

Alex rode silently for a moment, apparently reviewing the conversation in his head. 'So you did not! I withdraw the charge of prevarication. How clever you are! Quite the wordsmith.'

'I should be! After all, I am daughter and sister of master translators!' Belatedly realising that wasn't an observation she wanted him to think overmuch about, she switched to a teasing tone. 'I should like to see you toiling in the field with a hand plough! I've no doubt Mr Allen *could* plough rings around you.'

'True, but not fair. He was bred up to it and has decades of practice. I do not.'

'You are doing much better at estate work, though. The tenants no longer talk of revolt and the staff has decided it might be useful to keep you around after all.'

'I'm so glad to hear it,' he said acerbically. 'Now, why did I invite you to ride with me today?'

'To exercise the hunters.'

'Ah, yes. I thought I must have had some better reason than offering you my character to shred.'

'I'm sometimes brutal, I allow. But always honest.'

'Brutal, certainly. I'd reply in kind, but that wouldn't be gentlemanly.'

Laughing, Jocelyn said, 'Pax, then! Where do we ride next?'

'Are you sure you want to continue on with me—now that Miss Morrison was unable to join us?'

She stared at him for a moment. 'Surely you are not worried about my reputation? Heavens, we've ridden out together innumerable times over the years! Perhaps in London it might raise some eyebrows, but here, where we are both so well known? Most of the county consider you like another elder brother to me!' Not wanting to have their time together cut short—even though it would be wiser—she went on, 'No, I am not at all worried about continuing without her and neither should you be.'

He shook his head, and for a moment, she thought he might overrule her. But then he sighed. 'An elder brother indeed. To a little sister even peskier than the one related to me by blood. Very well, let's continue on to Jameson's farm. And, yes, you may gallop Flash on the way.'

'Excellent!' she replied, suppressing a sigh of relief. 'If I can keep him reined in, I might be able to let you win.'

'A laudable aim, but I doubt you'll bring yourself to do it.'

'Forgiveness in advance! Then I shall not have to feel guilty about leaving you in the dust again.'

With that, she signalled her mount to a gallop, smiling as the pound of galloping hoofbeats behind her grew fainter and fainter.

Chapter Three

Several hours later, having visited all the farms on Alex's itinerary, they rode at an easy pace—Flash having already been treated to three runs—to the flat plateau crowning the highest point on Trethfort Hill. As they reined in, Jocelyn scanned the vista from left to right, her spirits lifting as they always did at viewing such an expanse of Nature's beauty spread out before her.

Even better that she got to share such loveliness with Alex.

'Isn't it magnificent?' she said, turning to him. 'I know the city has its delights, but I can't imagine wanting to live anywhere else.'

'It is beautiful. Do you intend for us to pause and take some refreshment? Or did Mr Allen receive the whole of your bounty?'

'I'd anticipated leaving provisions for Mr Allen, but I kept back enough for us to have a bite. That fallen log over there should make a good bench. And please do tell me you are not going to go on again about how it might be improper for us to picnic together.'

He hesitated a moment, then smiled. 'I probably

should, but I won't. It's too lovely a day and having time to pause for a picnic at a view this magnificent is too rare for me to object.'

'I commend your wisdom—older brother.' She chuckled as this time he *did* grimace—even as she wryly acknowledged the irony to herself. Her feelings for Alex Cheverton had not from the first moment she'd seen him been 'sisterly'. How fortunate for her determination to remain a scholar that *he* had never treated *her* with anything other than brotherly fondness.

They dismounted, Alex taking the reins to wrap around a convenient tree branch. 'You really are good with the tenants. You talk easily with just about anyone,' he said as she took the provisions out of her cantle bag and walked with him to the log.

'Well, I have known most of them for most of my life,' she said, settling on the log a companionable distance from him and starting to unpack their repast. 'We've been living at the Dower House since the summer I turned five years old. You've become much better at conversing with them, too. Without lessening that air of authority that conveys who's in charge, you give the impression that you are concerned for their welfare and respectful of their opinions.'

'I should hope so! Since I *am* concerned for their welfare and respectful of their opinions,' he said, taking the chunk of cheese she handed him and pouring them each a cup from the flask of wine.

Jocelyn laughed. 'When I recall the first few times Emily and I accompanied you on your visits... My, what a difference! You scarcely had a word to say to anyone and kept looking our way, silently pleadingly with us to keep the conversations going.'

'I did not!'

'Indeed, you did!'

'Well, I may have appreciated how easily the two of you interacted with them. But I most definitely did not "plead" for your assistance. As I got to know the farmers, and understood better the requirements of my job, working with them became...easier.'

'You weren't trained to estate management by your father? I've always wondered about that.'

'Of course, before he died when I was hardly in my teens, he began to instruct me in performing the chores required to oversee a small estate. But the whole of Wynborne is hardly bigger than one of Edge Hall's larger farms and we have only a handful of tenants. After Mama insisted that I continue with my plans and attend Oxford, when Farisdeen offered me the opportunity to become manager here—at a salary that would enable me to add coin to the family coffers—even she agreed that I really couldn't turn him down.'

'But eventually, you will leave Edge Hall and return to Wynborn?'

'Yes. Although, after years of overseeing the work here, returning to such a small estate may leave me with a great deal of time on my hands.'

'You could always do what most of the gentry do—spend the Season in London and let a manager handle the day-to-day needs of Wynborne.'

'I might do that and continue on here. There is the inducement of continuing to earn that handsome wage. Besides, after initially feeling woefully unprepared—and I would appreciate no comment on that frank admission—I now enjoy the work and the challenge. I sometimes have the sense of being a sort of circus acrobat, always juggling five or six equally pressing tasks at once, knowing there could be a minor disaster if I drop one of them.'

'You really have grown into the job. Now, wasn't that a *handsome* admission?'

His green eyes widening, Alex brought a hand to his throat. 'It's a good thing I wasn't sipping the wine. Shock would have had me choking on it.'

'Remember, I'm brutal—but also honest.'

'Well, being brutal and honest, though I admit at times I've had my doubts, I'm beginning to think that you may make a superior vicar's wife. You've had excellent practice, assisting Miss Morrison, and you do seem to have a knack for talking with people. A sensitivity, too. Like realising Mr Allen would appreciate having his visitors linger. I'm not sure that would have occurred to me. I certainly would never have thought to bring him extra provisions—or worded their delivery so cleverly, he was almost guaranteed to accept them.'

'Coming from you, he would have seen it as charity— and a young man judging an older man to be no longer as capable as he once was. But the vicar's daughter is well known for bringing gifts to her father's parishioners.'

'Exactly. You shall know just how to go about it when you are tending the people of your husband's parish.'

Jocelyn made a face. 'I enjoy visiting people, just as I enjoy a good gallop. But after an outing, I'm always ready to get back to the library and get to work again.'

'Transcribing ancient documents? Come now, answer honestly. Doesn't it get…boring, sometimes?'

'Never! First, the stories themselves are so interesting. To think, they were written thousands of years ago, yet the situations, the difficulties, the emotions, are so real and fresh! Then there's the challenge of the words themselves, teasing out the true meaning of a language that hasn't been spoken in a millennium.'

'Aren't there reliable dictionaries that can tell you such and such a phrase means "He wandered down the path"?'

'There are some. But as in our own language, there is almost always more than one word that could work. Did he walk or wander or meander or trudge? And once you've looked carefully at the context clues and chosen the words that seem to best convey the sense, you need to consider whether the phrase itself is literal, or whether it might have a figurative meaning. Does "wander down the path" mean only that, or could it be an idiom for being foolish, or lost, or indolent? If so, you must translate not the literal words, but an expression in English that better conveys that meaning.'

'Goodness! It's a much more complicated business than I imagined.'

Enthused to talk about the work that so delighted her, she shook her head in agreement. 'It's like having this large, complex, fascinating puzzle to solve. You must figure out what each piece is and how best to put together the whole. And the words you choose must also be rhythmic and lovely—we are talking about translating lyrical drama, after all—if you want to best capture not just the meaning, but the spirit, of the original.'

'I begin to have a renewed respect for your father and brother.'

'So you should! Even with best efforts, it's really a guess. The French have a phrase for it—*traduire, c'est trahir.* To translate is to betray. But since it's unlikely that the majority of the literate British public will ever be fluent enough in ancient Greek to read the originals, one must do one's best, lest those beautiful, fascinating works remain inaccessible for ever.'

'And do you, your father's oh-so-apt pupil of languages, ever suggest possible meanings?'

'Oh, of course I—' Abruptly catching herself, she switched her tone from ardent to teasing, and said, 'Of course, passionate as I am about everything literary, I may *occasionally* offer an opinion on Virgil's word choice.'

Alex laughed, as she'd hoped he would. 'Only "occasionally"?'

Relieved to have successfully diverted him, she laughed, too. 'Very well, I shall make another handsome admission and allow that his ability at translation is far superior to mine.'

He made an exaggerated expression of shock. 'Do my ears deceive me? I didn't think I'd ever hear you admit you could be bested at anything.'

'Heavens, what a conceited beast you make me sound!' she protested. 'I freely admit I am not superior to everyone at *everything*, but I do have my talents. Riding, for example. I shall have to beat you again on the way back, just to remind you.'

'You might be better served practising modesty,' he tossed back with a grin. 'I understand your clerical suitor will be visiting soon and I'm sure *that* virtue is one he will appreciate in his future wife.'

He would bring up the one topic that must depress her spirits. Sighing, Jocelyn said, 'Yes, Mr Finley is to come to see us at the Dower House next week.'

His teasing look fading, Alex cocked his head and studied her. 'You don't seem all that...enthusiastic about an imminent visit from your intended.'

'Charles Finley is...an old and good friend. He's amiable, learned and willing to let me continue helping Virgil after we marry.'

'You don't sound particularly anxious for the wedding. I thought all ladies were eager to marry.'

If he were someone who attracts me as much as you do, I might be. Although I would have a better chance of continuing the scholarly work I adore if I were able to avoid marriage altogether. But she wasn't going to be brutally honest—or foolish—enough to admit that.

'I suppose some girls are eager for a household of their own to run,' she said instead, 'but I already have that. And work that I enjoy doing and consider important. If one is a lady of modest birth and little fortune, one makes the best of the…limited marriage possibilities available. So I am not in any great hurry to enter the wedded state. And what of you? You have your own property, even if Wynborne is only a "small" estate. Is your mama not nattering at you to choose a bride?'

He opened his lips to begin, then closed them. 'My… circumstances are such that I have no intention of marrying for quite some time,' he said after a moment. 'The Duke prefers his estate agent to remain unmarried and I believe a husband should be able to support his wife in proper style—something I don't yet have the means to do without the additional income I earn from managing Edge Hall. Happily, my sister Margaret has already provided Mama with a quiverful of grandchildren to occupy her.'

'So are you a romantic, waiting to fall in love?'

Once he thought he had and what a horrible mistake that had been. 'Certainly not!' he said contemptuously. 'Irresponsible poets may celebrate it, but if and when I marry, I shall choose a bride based on much more practical reasons than fleeting emotion.'

'I expect Farisdeen will also want a say in the matter of whom his cousin marries.'

Alex gave a wry smile. 'The Duke seldom deigns to speak to me of anything personal, but one of the few things he has recommended is that when I do marry, I choose a bride who brings a substantial dowry to increase the value of my estate, as befits my distinguished lineage.'

'He wants you to marry a wealthy cit's daughter?'

'I'm not sure quite what he intended. He must know, despite our connection, that my position is not elevated enough for me to entice a high-born heiress. Or to persuade her family to agree to her choice, if she did choose me.'

'Unless she fell in love with you. Although I don't envisage it happening to me, I do believe people can fall in love. My parents did, leading my mother to marry my father, whom everyone in her family believed far beneath the granddaughter of an earl. She defied everyone to marry him and claim what she knew would make her happy. I so admire her for that.'

'Well, yes, I suppose there's always the possibility of truly falling in love. Just as there is of lightning striking us on this log where we sit.'

'And we've been talking together so amicably! I've hardly insulted you for ten minutes running.'

While she gazed up at him, smiling, an odd expression came over his face. 'A most unusual situation. Which leads to...the strangest feelings. As if one might actually have been struck by lightning.'

Suddenly, Jocelyn was intensely conscious of his nearness, sitting barely more than a hand's breadth away from her. As she watched his eyes darken, she felt a flash of physical connection between them, sending a wash of heat through her.

Surely that couldn't be...*desire* she saw in his eyes?

With a prickly awareness sparking in every nerve, she stuttered, 'I... I think I know...what you mean.'

She should move away. But captivated by the intensity of his gaze, she could hardly breathe, much less move. And then he was bending down, touching his lips to hers...

Shock gave way almost immediately to response. When he would have pulled back, she put a hand on his neck, holding him in place, urging him with a murmur to continue the exquisite, unparalleled sensations set off by the brush of his lips against hers.

When he finally did break away some moments later, she gazed at him numbly, bringing a hand to her tingling lips.

Before she could assemble her scattered wits to form words, he'd jumped up from the log and paced an agitated distance away. 'I'm so sorry, Jocelyn! I didn't intend to insult you. I am not the sort of man to trifle with another man's intended! Pray, forgive me!'

'I'm not insulted,' she replied, finally recovering speech. 'Not at all. I'm...delighted,' she blurted and almost clapped a hand over her mouth. Good heavens, why in the world had she admitted that?

Looking as shocked as she still felt—as if she'd indeed been touched by lightning—he repeated blankly, 'Delighted?'

Nothing to do now but brazen it out. 'I'm brutally honest, remember? Which forces me to admit... I've always wanted you to kiss me.'

'You have?'

That ought to scare him off for good, she thought

ruefully. But at least she now had a kiss—his kiss!—to remember. 'Yes. And thank you for it. Before you begin to think me wanton, or lacking in respect for my future husband, you must know that Charles is no more passionately attached to me than I am to him. Our union will be a marriage of convenience on both sides. But… now, before I am obliged to marry a man who truly *is* no more than a brother to me, I know what it's like to kiss a man who attracts me.'

She held up a hand, needing to stop him speaking until she'd finished what she had to say. 'Before you overcome your shock and decide you've compromised me, or some such rot, be assured that I will never reveal what just passed between us. Our…indiscretion was witnessed only by the cows on the adjacent hillside. It was a…a delightful moment, never to be repeated, as I'm sure we will both work to ensure. So you may be easy.'

After another long moment of silence, Alex said, 'I can hardly be "easy", but if you accept my apology, I… I will not insist on overturning your existing arrangements. I can pledge to guarantee such a lapse never occurs again. We should probably ride back now.'

'Yes. We both need to get back to work.'

Hoping the unexpected but thrilling moment hadn't destroyed their long friendship—though destroying it might be for the best—Jocelyn quickly packed up the remains of their simple repast, while Alex went to retrieve the horses.

The unusual, fraught silence between them continued as she returned the provisions to the cantle bag, then prudently used the log as a mounting block, rather than asking Alex for a hand up.

Silent still, Alex mounted his gelding. In unspoken

accord, they signalled their mounts to a trot and headed back on to the track leading to Edge Hall.

During the transit, Alex made no attempt to converse, instead gazing fixedly into the distance.

He looked as though he was having grim and serious thoughts. She didn't want him entertaining grim and serious thoughts. But for the first time in their long association, Jocelyn couldn't think of a single teasing remark to draw him out of his abstraction.

Not until they'd reached the stables, turned their mounts over to a groom and he fell in step beside her as they walked back to the Hall, did he finally break his silence.

'I just wanted to assure you again that I meant no disrespect. You know I have a very high regard for you.'

That he apparently found her attractive was even more thrilling, she thought. Even now, she could feel that edgy physical tension simmering between them— a pull, she realised, that had existed between them for quite some time. Something she'd been so certain he couldn't feel for her, she hadn't believed it could be mutual.

'I know,' she said at last. 'Just as I have a great respect and a high regard for you—even if my remarks do not always reflect that.'

To her relief, that did provoke a glimmer of a smile. 'I wouldn't have you turn complimentary. I'm not sure my heart could withstand the shock. Still, I don't take what happened today…lightly. Are you certain you want to continue with your future plans as they are?'

'If you are offering to sacrifice yourself on the altar of propriety, there's no need. And, yes, I think it best if we both proceed in the direction we intended…before today.'

Before that glorious, wonderful, exciting taste of passion I shall treasure for ever.

As they reached the Dower House, Jocelyn halted. 'I'll leave you here. I should go check on Papa.'

'You are *sure* you want nothing to change?'

'Absolutely. I should be very grateful if we could return to the easy friendship we shared before this ride.'

She knew that would prove impossible, even as she said it. From the look on his face, he knew it, too.

None the less, he nodded. 'I will try my best. I would be loath to lose your friendship.'

'As I would be to lose yours. So… I will see you later, your Magnificence.'

Shaking a warning finger at her, Alex turned to continue down the drive towards the looming towers of Edge Hall.

Skirting the Dower House entrance, Jocelyn walked on into the gardens. Despite what she'd told Alex, she wasn't quite ready to meet her father—yet.

She needed a bit of solitude to completely regain her composure.

Not that she doubted the wisdom of putting this episode behind them and continuing with the plans they'd previously made for their lives.

Even if the idea of marrying Charles Finley had never seemed less appealing.

She needed to concentrate with single-minded purpose on the goal of completing the translations, a project which, as she'd told Alex, would require years more work. She couldn't abandon it—and strip her brother of his position—just because her unruly senses and turbulent emotions had her longing for Alex Cheverton.

He would never be hers. The work *was* her.

Which was why she needed to be much more discreet. Bad enough to have admitted she'd wanted his kiss. But beguiled by his nearness, enthused by explaining the intricacies of the work she loved, she'd almost given herself away.

Which simply must not happen. It had taken her almost a year to convince her father she possessed the talent to fashion his Greek concepts into an English prose superior to his own. The process of teasing out the best, clearest meaning from the original and then rendering it, not just accurately, but in elegant, descriptive English, was a process she loved with as much passion and dedication as her father and brother. Their collaboration would be terminated were her true part in it ever to be discovered.

The only reason she'd agreed to marry Virgil's good friend Charles Finley was that his admiration for her brother's scholarship was great enough that he'd agreed he would allow her to continue 'recording' Virgil's translations, during periodic visits back to Edge Hall while they completed the Euripides, and perhaps after that, if she could persuade Virgil to undertake new projects.

Not even Charles suspected just how great her role in translation actually was. And she meant to keep that secret. Even from Alex Cheverton.

Alex was a friend and she knew he would never knowingly harm her. But he was a *man*. Which meant he would first be sceptical of a female's ability to perform such a task and if convinced the work were truly hers, would most likely discount the accuracy and worth of the translations.

She shuddered to think how the Duke of Farisdeen

would react were he to learn that the true author of the most recent works in the extensive translation project he was sponsoring was a female.

He'd probably be furious. He'd likely end his patronage, discharge Virgil and evict them from the Dower House, the only home she remembered. Her father and brother would be humiliated, respect for their lifelong body of work destroyed. The disgrace would make it difficult for her brother to find another position, despite his excellence as a scholar. It would probably kill her father.

It would be just as devastating for her. As long as she could remember, it had been words and their meanings and their interplay that fascinated and energised her. If she were stripped of that activity, barred from working with Virgil, what would be left to her? What would be left *of* her?

Knowing her family would press her to marry eventually, she'd seized upon marrying Charles as the best way to be able to continue the work that defined who she was. She must not let her lingering attraction to Alex Cheverton put that future at risk.

She would just have to be much more careful around Edge Hall's far too distracting estate manager.

Chapter Four

A week later, after having responded to the expected summons to confer with the Duke of Farisdeen in London, Alex left his appointment at the Duke's sumptuous town house in Grosvenor Square to head to a far more convivial meeting—a rendezvous with his Oxford friends, Gregory Lattimar and Crispin d'Aubignon, Viscount Dellamont.

He felt fortunate to be able to catch both friends in town during his brief stay. Gregory was often in Northumberland, dealing with estate business for his father at their family's main country estate, and Dellamont travelled a good deal, inspecting proposed routes for various railroad bills pending before Parliament.

After spending several hours with the Duke, who had the personal warmth of a breeze off the North Sea in the dead of winter, Alex was really looking forward to a night of fine dining, good wine and interesting conversation.

As he hailed a hackney to convey him from the Duke's residence to the comfortable suite of rooms Dellamont occupied in Jasmin Street, Alex found his thoughts drifting back—as they so often had this last week—to Jocelyn Sudderfeld.

He'd been more shaken than he wanted to admit by the kiss he'd let himself be lured into giving her that sunny afternoon on Trethfort Hill. Her unexpected response—innocent but enthusiastic—had so engaged him, it had taken all his considerable willpower not to deepen and prolong it. Only when the shrieking of a brain warning of danger finally penetrated through the delirium of desire and delight, was he finally able to break away from her.

And had immediately felt appalled. After the traumatic and humiliating experience he'd endured when he'd rashly pursued Eliza all those years ago, he'd thought himself too mature and careful to be carried away by passion. Even his relief at discovering that Jocelyn did not consider herself compromised, mercifully avoiding a repetition of that awful episode in his life, only marginally reduced his distress at discovering that comforting assumption was apparently false.

Her frank avowal immediately after that she'd *wanted* him to kiss her was just as concerning. Knowing that she found him as attractive as he found her alarmed him—even as it excited him. By blowing out of the water his certainty that she considered him simply another annoying older brother, he'd lost one of the protections that had buttressed his ability to resist his increasing desire for her.

After that episode, he knew he would have to tread much more carefully around her.

Still, he was also troubled by her admission of just how unenthusiastically she viewed her upcoming engagement. He hated to think of her liveliness and passion wasted on a man she didn't really want, her exuberance gradually snuffed out by being trapped in a union with someone who didn't admire or appreciate her.

Given that neither of them looked to find some rapturous love match, should he try to convince her to hold out for a marriage partner for whom she had real enthusiasm?

But he had no right to interfere in the arrangements made for her by her family, arrangements to which she had long since agreed. Arrangements that, when driven by honour to hint that he would offer for her himself, if she felt he'd compromised her, she had confirmed she'd rather maintain.

And given his appalling lack of control at Trethfort Hill, he probably ought to avoid any têtes-à-têtes that might lead them into equally compromising circumstances. Especially after the exasperating girl blithely announced that, although she had no intention of changing her current wedding plans, she had none the less welcomed his kiss.

He knew she was neither wanton nor a tease. She had certainly, though, thrown his carefully controlled emotions into disarray—an unexpected reaction he needed to look upon as a warning.

He'd found the Duke's summons in the post the butler had left on his desk when he'd returned from their afternoon ride. Knowing he would be leaving for London and unsure exactly how to act around her after the picnic, he'd deliberately avoided Jocelyn for the few days before his departure. A task less difficult than it would normally have been, since preparing a comprehensive report for the Duke obliged him to ride out to all the farms for one final inspection.

After a week apart, his mind and senses remained

unsettled—and despite all the chiding he'd given himself, his attraction to her remained undimmed. Knowing now that she also sensed the strong undercurrent of connection that hummed between them, how was he to ensure he could resist the insidious temptation to kiss her again? And after all that had transpired, how in the world was he supposed to return to Edge Hall and restore their friendship to the same teasing, uncomplicated one they'd shared before, as he'd promised her he would?

By the time he'd gone one more time through the same circular round of thoughts and questions that had dogged him all week, the hackney was halting at Dellamont's lodging. And having once again come to the end of them without reaching any useful conclusions, he shook his head in disgust.

At least he'd have tonight with his friends to distract him. And a long drive back to West Sussex to hopefully get his thoughts in order and come up with a reasonable plan.

Half an hour later, the three friends were sitting in Dellamont's small parlour, glasses of wine in hand. 'Shall we start with our host?' Alex asked, inclining his glass towards Dellamont. 'How goes the investing? Has all that riding about the countryside provided you with sufficient clues about which of the pending railroad ventures might prove most profitable?'

'I doubt that any of them will match the returns of the Liverpool & Manchester,' Dellamont said. 'But there are two that look quite promising. And riding about the countryside does keep me away from Montwell Glen and my father's carping.'

'The Earl can't be too critical, considering how much

blunt you've made on your first two railroad investment ventures,' Gregory Lattimar said.

'If you think that, you don't know Comeryn,' Dellamont said acidly. 'I'm not sure what annoys him the most: that I refused to remain at Montwell Glen under his thumb, to receive his daily corrections and admonishments, or that despite his prediction that I'd be wasting my aunt's bequest on my "wild schemes", I've actually done well.'

'The horror of earning filthy lucre in a most ungentlemanly fashion?' Alex said drily.

'Exactly. After all, a gentleman's income should derive from his lands, his gaming skill, with perhaps a bit allowable if he invests on the Change,' Dellamont said.

Alex laughed. 'Ah, the joys of being among the lower gentry. By contrast, my family was happy to give their blessing to my working for Farisdeen and earning filthy lucre that helps buttress the small income earned by my own estate.'

'Exactly. As Gregory and I told you when you left Oxford to take up the post,' Dellamont said, 'you are luckier than both of us.'

'Lucky not to one day inherit a grand title—' Alex gestured towards Dellamont '—or fabulous wealth?' he said, indicating Gregory. 'Not that I'm discontented with my lot. But few would agree that I'm the luckiest of us three.'

'But you are!' Dellamont argued. 'You're not saddled with one day inheriting a large estate your controlling father refuses to allow you to practise running—or at least, refuses to allow you to run without such a continual barrage of oversight, criticism and complaint as to inspire you only with the desire to escape the place. After you've earned as much as you want, you can leave Edge Hall whenever you like, with no further obligation.'

'Nor do you have the opposite problem,' Gregory said. 'The headache of trying to run a vast estate you do not yet legally possess. Hardly ever able to force a decision out of the man who is supposed to run it, but who has no interest in anything outside his collections.'

'Hasn't the puzzle of his continual acquisitions eased somewhat, now that your sister Prudence and her husband are abroad, finding objects for him?' Alex asked.

Gregory sighed. 'That has helped, certainly. But Papa still obtains things from other sources. It's not that I mind the blunt he spends—it is *his* blunt, after all, and he has plenty of it. It's that he orders objects and curiosities from dealers other than Pru and Johnny while I'm buried away in Northumberland, running Entremer. Since neither the cost nor the provenance is of any interest to him, he either doesn't obtain invoices to begin with, or tosses them wherever they happen to land. Every time I return to London, I have to waste an appalling amount of time trying to sort out bills from various merchants and match them to goods he has ordered.' Gregory laughed wryly. 'How am I supposed to know the difference between an Abyssinian dagger and an Ethiopian knife? It's a situation ripe for fraud, which is what keeps me awake at night.'

'Then there's that sword of Damocles hanging over every heir—the eventual necessity of marriage,' said Dellamont. 'Though after your lucky escape years ago and Farisdeen's strictures on your marrying while managing his estate, you won't have to deal with that problem any time soon. When you eventually do consider it, I suspect Farisdeen will have some recommendations, but you are under no obligation to follow them. Nor will you have to worry about choosing a bride whom your family and society consider suitable to become the next Countess of Comeryn.'

Gregory nodded. 'Or in my case, worry about finding a bride whose family is so eminently respectable, your union will persuade society to forget that your mother is infamous and one of your sisters married an adventurer.'

'Temperance married an earl,' Alex objected. 'That should have helped redeem the family's image of respectability.'

'True, but before she married, she shocked or offended most of society,' Gregory said ruefully.

'The prospect of having their daughter become the wife of the wealthiest baron in England should erase the reservations most society mamas might have about their darling making an alliance with one of the Vraux Miscellany,' Dellamont said drily.

'I have no doubt that potential wealth will trump a stainless family reputation,' Alex agreed. 'And you're both correct. With my estate giving me the status of no more than a modest country gentleman, I don't have to worry about finding a lady I can envisage marrying who also possesses high birth, or one celebrated as a paragon of virtue.'

Pushing away the image of Jocelyn Sudderfeld, which this talk of marriage brought back to mind, Alex said, 'But since none of us expects to marry for years, enough of this discussion. How about more of Dellamont's excellent wine and a few cut-throat hands of cards before dinner?'

'An excellent idea,' Dellamont said, rising to retrieve a deck of cards from the sideboard, along with the decanter of wine to refill their glasses. 'But first, you must tell us how things go at Edge Hall. Are you still enjoying running it? Did your exalted cousin, the Duke, have any words of instruction for you during your meeting today?'

'As usual, he listened to my report in silence, his face so expressionless that had I not become accustomed to his manner, I would have been tempted to place a candle in front of his lips to make sure he was still breathing.'

'Better than having him castigate you for some perceived error,' Dellamont said with feeling.

'Which would be impossible, since I don't make any,' Alex joked. 'I do admit, seeing him still makes my stomach churn, but after surviving his criticism for some errors made in my early days, I face him now with much more confidence. And, yes, I am still enjoying the job. There's a real sense of doing something important, knowing your work not only keeps the estate profitable, but provides a livelihood for many and ensures that their farms prosper, too,' he concluded, smiling as he recalled the visit with Mr Allen during which he'd persuaded the old farmer to use a horse-drawn plough to tend his acres.

'Does the Duke never invite you to take tea or stay for dinner?' Gregory asked.

Alex laughed out loud. 'Lord, no! For all that we are distant cousins, I'm very much the "hired help". Which his austere manner reinforces whenever he summons me to a meeting. And his son Penlowe reinforces in more annoying terms.'

'What's his Indolent Lordship, the Marquess of Penlowe, up to now?' Dellamont asked. 'Intolerable fellow! So acutely conscious of his high birth, even I, as a future earl, rate barely a nod from him when I encounter him at White's. Not that I'd seek out his company. What a worthless fribble! He seems to have no interest beyond swanning about the clubs with his sycophant friends in tow, gaming away as much of his inheritance as possible in every hell in London while trying to drink his companions under the table and pressing his attentions on any Cyprian unlucky to catch his eye. I should think he is the despair of his father.'

'As high in the instep as the Duke is, he probably considers such self-indulgent, self-centred behaviour quite suitable for a duke's heir,' Gregory said.

Alex grimaced. 'Penlowe seems to take a special delight in trying to ram home my inferior status whenever I have the mischance to encounter him, as I did this afternoon in Grosvenor Square.' He laughed without humour. 'He always adds some little dig, like reminding me today, in case his father might have forgotten, to make sure the hunters at Edge Hall have been re-shoed and that their feed is adequate. As if I were the groom in charge of them.'

Dellamont gave a snort of disgust. 'I'm astounded he had any idea what taking care of a horse entails! He's probably never performed a practical task in his entire life.'

Like sewing on a button? Alex thought, Dellamont's comment recalling the incident with Jocelyn. The memory of their exchange made him grin wryly.

'Everything all right, Alex?' Gregory asked. 'You just had the oddest expression.'

Alex jerked his gaze back to Gregory, feeling his face flush. The last thing he wanted was for these friends— among the few who knew of his previous romantic disaster—to suspect some new amorous complication. They would then bedevil him without ceasing until they teased or tricked the whole story out of him.

Besides, with Jocelyn soon to marry, that story was about to end. Which ought to fill him with relief. So why did he feel a pang almost of…regret?

Shaking his head to rid himself of that perverse reaction, he said, 'I'm fine. Just distracted, picturing Penlowe this afternoon. He did look as if he'd only recently returned from a serious episode of carousing. Unsteady on his feet and pale as this table linen.'

'Did you detect the odour of spirits?' Dellamont asked. 'If you encountered him when you arrived at the Duke's this morning, he'd probably just arrived home after a night of dissipation.'

'Perhaps. But if it spares me associating with someone like that, I do count my "modest birth" as lucky! Now, shall you cut the cards, or shall I?'

Three days later, his London business for the estate concluded, Alex rode back towards Edge Hall. Further reflection had not clarified his thoughts on how he should proceed upon meeting Jocelyn again, other than a vague notion of limiting their meetings—however unpalatable the thought—and maintaining a tight control over his attraction to her, which was absolutely essential.

How he was to do both and try to regain a semblance of the easy, teasing friendship they'd enjoyed 'before', he still hadn't figured out.

And so, rather than arrive back at Edge Hall in midafternoon, and perhaps encounter Jocelyn fixing tea for herself and her brother, he dawdled, stopping to look in at some of the outlying farms. Telling himself it would be kind to spare Cook having to provide him with dinner, he decided to make another halt at Edge Hall Village and take advantage of the innkeeper's excellent roast.

As he rode into the village, he spotted Miss Morrison, the vicar's daughter, walking from the direction of the village green, and reined in.

'Miss Morrison, well met! I'm just back from London, and wanted to stop by and see how your father is doing. Under your loving care, completely recovered from his late illness, I trust?'

To his alarm, rather than return his smile, her eyes filled with tears. 'Oh, Mr Cheverton! The most awful thing has happened!'

'Has your father taken a turn for the worse?' he cried, truly concerned now. 'Has the apothecary seen him? Should we send to Chichester for a physician?'

'No, no, Papa is fine! Completely recovered. It's… something else entirely. You haven't been back to Edge Hall yet, have you?'

'Not yet.'

'I didn't think so. Have you time to stop by the parsonage now? I can offer you tea and tell you…what's happened.'

So the problem must be at Edge Hall. His alarm spiralling up a notch, Alex said, 'Is there illness among the staff at the Hall? Surely there is nothing amiss with Reverend Sudderfeld, his son or J—Miss Sudderfeld, is there?'

'Have patience for a few moments and I'll tell you the whole. But I don't wish to do so in the street, where anyone might overhear.'

Jumping down from the saddle, Alex caught up his reins. 'Lead on, then.'

Half an hour later, sipping the tea Miss Morrison's maid brought him, Alex shook his head. 'I can hardly believe it.'

Miss Morrison nodded, her large grey eyes filling with tears again. 'Infamous behaviour! Reverend Finley seemed like such a kind, caring gentleman. An admirer of scholarship, too, which made him such a good match for Miss Sudderfeld.'

'You're telling me he…jilted her? Is this certain?'

'Oh, yes. Jocelyn came by to tell me yesterday, so I might know not to say anything to anyone. As if I'd gossip about my best friend! It seems that a bishop with a fine living in his gift also has a daughter who took a fancy to Reverend Finley.'

'So the award of the living was dependent on his offering for the daughter?'

'Yes. It's all well and good for Jocelyn to say a young man must look out for his best interests—but what of hers? Who is she to wed now, stuck away as she is at Edge Hall, never seeing anyone but her brother? It's too, too distressing.'

While Miss Morrison struggled to control her emotions, Alex's thoughts whirled around in his head like dice rattling in a cup. Outrage on Jocelyn's behalf, concern for her future, a guilty relief that she would now not be married any time soon, all rolled around a regrettable but undeniable excitement.

Create problems resisting her it might—but he was none the less glad that she would be at Edge Hall, complicating his life, for a while longer.

As he tried to order his thoughts, Miss Morrison patted her eyes. 'Sorry, I don't mean to distress you by giving in to tears. It's just that I know you see Jocelyn almost daily, that the two of you have been dear friends for years and that you would be very concerned for her. I thought it would be easier if you already knew what had happened before you arrive back, so that she would be spared the distress of having to tell you about it.'

'She must be distraught,' he said. *Or maybe not.* 'As her best friend, how would you advise me to react to her? I don't want to compound her distress.'

'Tell her I've already told you what happened, so she doesn't need to go through it all again. I think that will make it easier for her to preserve her dignity—and her composure.'

Or maybe she would be distraught. Eager now to get back to Edge Hall and find out, Alex finished the last of his tea. 'Thank you for letting me know. I will try to be as supportive as I can. If you can think of anything I might do to make it easier for her, I would appreciate it.'

'After you acknowledge that you're aware of her… change in status, try to go on as much as possible with your normal routine. I think falling back into that is what will help her the most. Jocelyn has always been devoted to the work of her father and brother, and I think she will try to truly lose herself in it now. Although I wouldn't wish to see her immure herself for ever, perhaps for a few months, while she recovers from this crushing blow, it would be a good thing. And the kindness of a long-time friend, who shows he appreciates her many fine qualities, might go a long way to restoring her confidence, which cannot help but have been wounded by Finley's infamous betrayal.'

'I will try to lend my quiet support and keep the household routine as close to normal as I can,' Alex promised as he set down his cup and rose to his feet.

'Thank you, Mr Cheverton. Though some men might be duplicitous, I knew you would stand her friend.'

'Hers and yours always, Miss Morrison. I'd better get back to Edge Hall. Thank you again for warning me.'

Her eyes sheening again with tears, the vicar's daughter walked him to the door. 'Be kind to her, Mr Cheverton.'

'I certainly will be. Good day to you, Miss Morrison.'

Thoughtful, Alex mounted his gelding for the short ride back to Edge Hall. By now it was late enough that Jocelyn and her brother would probably have returned to the Dower House for the evening. That would give him some time to work out the best way to approach her.

Though she hadn't been enthusiastic about the match, she must still be feeling hurt and abandoned. Despite knowing she must be upset, Alex couldn't quite make himself regret that her plans to wed Charles Finley were ended for good.

Chapter Five

The next morning, Jocelyn left the Dower House while her father and brother were still at breakfast. She'd heard from the servants' gossip that Alex had returned from London last night. She wanted to intercept him and inform him of her changed status before anyone else did—certainly before he happened to encounter her brother in the sitting room or the library.

Not that her change in status would make any difference between them. Except, perhaps, make Alex feel less guilty about kissing her.

She smiled. That kiss was something she was never going to regret or feel guilty about—no matter how unwise it had been and no matter how stringently she must guard against it happening again.

She entered through the back doorway to the private family wing, intending to seek Alex out in his office. She was halfway down the hallway when she spied him on his way to the library, along the corridor where the two U-shaped wings, one formal, one private, backed up to each other.

As always, her heart rate quickened and a flush of awareness tingled her nerves.

She halted, acknowledging her unfortunate response with a sigh.

Apparently the cancellation of her unofficial engagement, which ought to have signalled the need for her to redouble her efforts to resist his appeal, had not managed to curb her automatic response to him. No longer protected by having to behave with the propriety of an engaged lady, lest she shame her family—or embarrass Alex—she would have to tread even more carefully around him.

Then he turned, saw her and smiled. Delight brought an answering smile to her lips. *Maybe there could be something between them after all* flashed into her head before she could squelch the thought.

No, there could not, she reminded herself sternly. She had speculated about this too many times already and always reached the same conclusion. Did she truly want to be foolish enough to risk the future of scholarship she'd worked and planned for, which might now be within her grasp, possibly even without the necessity of marriage?

Please, let her be wise enough to keep that prospect uppermost in her mind—no matter how much the beguiling Alex might tempt her.

By now, Alex had approached within greeting distance. 'Good morning, Jocelyn! You're at Edge Hall early. I was just heading to the library, hoping to catch you when you came in.'

'You are early, too,' Jocelyn said as he walked up to join her...and drat it, his nearness set off that simmering awareness in the pit of her stomach. 'As it happens, I was just heading to your office to try to catch you.'

'Why don't we go to the sitting room instead? We

can have a cup of tea before your brother arrives and puts you to work.'

Meeting him in the sitting room where Virgil might walk in at any minute, rather than alone in his office, ought to help her curb any amorous impulses. And it might be easier to have this first conversation since their...interlude, and to convey her upsetting news, over the soothing ritual of serving tea.

'Yes, I'd like that. So, was your journey to London pleasant?' she asked as they turned and walked towards the sitting room. 'Were you able to meet your Oxford friends? Did the Duke have any particular tasks for you?'

'The weather held, so the ride was pleasant. I was fortunate enough to find both Mr Lattimar and Viscount Dellamont in town. The Duke received my report in his usual fashion.'

Jocelyn chuckled. 'With the warmth of an icicle and the encouraging response of a stone wall?'

Alex laughed. 'About that. He did seem interested in the project we're doing, draining the south pastures. And he wanted further details on the progress of the young hunters. He actually produced what, in him, amounted almost to a smile when I related how fast Black Flash can go.'

'Fast, but ill disciplined.'

'Since he confirmed he will not be coming down to hunt, I didn't tell him that. I have complete faith in Jerry Thompson. He'll bring Flash up to snuff before the next hunting season begins. Now, why don't you have a seat on the sofa and I'll make some tea? I left the kettle on to simmer after my breakfast, so it will only take a moment.'

Nodding her agreement, Jocelyn walked over to sit

on the small sofa that faced the window and the pleasant view of the rose garden beyond. Time to put on her best impertinent little sister guise and break the news.

How would he take it? she wondered. Angry on her behalf, as Virgil was? Concerned, now that there was no longer an engagement to protect *him* from the attraction she'd admitted?

She must reassure him again that he could rest easy; despite the oh-so-wonderful kiss they'd shared, she truly had no designs on him.

He brought over a tray with teapot and cups. For a few moments longer, the ritual of pouring tea delayed the revelation she had to make.

Finally, though, there was no putting it off any longer.

'Actually,' she began in an even, conversational tone, 'I came in early expressly to see you before Virgil arrives. There's something... I think I must let you know.'

Alex sighed, a troubled look on his face as he fixed his gaze on her. 'If it's what I think it is, I already know about it. I encountered Emily Morrison when I rode into the village yesterday afternoon.'

Jocelyn felt her face flush. For all that she was indifferent to Charles Finley, he *had* rejected her, which couldn't help but sting. 'If you saw Emily, then I'm sure you do know.'

'You mustn't think she was carrying tales! But she knows I care about you and that I'd be concerned about anything that affects your future. She wanted to warn me, so I wouldn't inadvertently say something to upset you. Or require you to relate again a turn of events which you must have found distressing.'

Before she could reply, he put a hand on hers—effectively paralysing, for the moment, her powers of speech.

'I'm so very sorry. I'm afraid I agree with her in finding Mr Finley's behaviour shocking and unforgivable.'

Fortunately, after that brief contact, Alex moved his hand away, allowing her brain to resume functioning.

'That's the main reason I wanted to speak with you before you encountered my brother. Virgil is still livid. I've never seen my scholarly sibling, who normally has his nose too far buried in ancient texts to notice anything around him, get so angry.'

'I can't blame him, when the matter involves ruining the future of a beloved sister.'

'I think he sees it, not as only that, but as a personal betrayal of their friendship. Whereas, I think he's being too harsh on poor Mr Finley. The bishop's offer of a prime living put him in a very difficult situation.'

'If he was able to reconcile breaking a sacred promise for personal gain, I doubt his suitability to become a spiritual advisor to his new flock,' Alex said acidly.

'What would you have him do? I've already told you that ours wouldn't have been a love match, merely an arrangement convenient to both parties. He needed someone suitable to become a pastor's wife and who more suitable than a pastor's daughter? Whereas his admiration for Virgil's scholarship was high enough that he was willing to let me continue my work here even after our marriage—something of utmost importance to me. By contrast, choosing a lady who not only understands the role of a vicar's wife, but also gains him a living substantial enough that he and his eventual family will prosper, rather than struggle, was a sensible choice. A courageous one, too, as he had to know that breaking our informal agreement would offend my brother.

'He was honourable enough to come to Edge Hall and inform us both personally before anything was made public—even though he knew that Virgil would likely be furious with him. And demonstrated both courage and humility by standing quietly, making no excuses, while Virgil abused him.'

'If he had half a brain, he had to have been expecting that.'

She smiled. 'It was Virgil's reaction that concerned him most, I think. He probably expected I would take the news calmly enough.'

'And were you not…devastated? Or at least disappointed?' he asked, his keen gaze inspecting her face.

'Emily thought I should be.' She chuckled. 'I suppose I did display a bit more emotion when I told her the news, since I know she expected it. Oh, of course I felt a bit…humiliated. Rejection is rejection, after all. But if I call upon that brutal honesty I know you expect from me, I think more than anything I'm…relieved.'

'Relieved?' he repeated, his brows winging upwards in surprise. 'Truly?'

She nodded. 'The closer we came to making the engagement official, the more I dreaded the prospect. In all honesty, I was beginning to think I would be making a bargain I wasn't sure I could keep. I had, still have, a fondness for Mr Finley, but frankly, he's not the intellectual equal of my father or Virgil. He often fails to understand the sallies we trade and is hopeless at the word games Papa so enjoys. I find myself growing impatient with him at times. I feared, as the years went by, I would begin to find him…tiresome.

'He's so very earnest and takes everything so very seriously! As a fine, honest, principled Christian gentleman, he deserves better than ending up with a wife who merely…tolerates him. And as he lived with me and came to know better my lack of interest in most womanly chores, I think he, too, might have begun to believe he'd made a bad bargain.'

'What about how bad a bargain it would be for you, settling for a man you don't love and just admitted you never could?'

'Very true. I think Emily is most upset because Finley represented the best, perhaps my only, marriage prospect. She herself is counting on a promising young man still at university. For most women, there is no other meaningful path in life except marriage. But more and more, I'm coming to believe that path is not meant for me.'

'Not marriage?' he echoed, surprised. 'What do you see as your path, then?'

'I expect to work with Virgil until he finishes this project. Which, as I told you last week, will likely take years. After that—perhaps he will take on other projects. And I will continue to assist him.'

'But at some point he will marry and your father will pass on. Surely you can't look with equanimity upon the prospect of becoming a hanger-on in your brother's household.'

'No, I should need to leave once he married. There cannot be two mistresses in the same household and I've been in charge of ours too long to easily cede the position to another. I have a small competence from my mother's aunt, but it's not enough to enable me to live on my own. I expect I shall end up looking for some elderly bluestocking who needs a companion to accompany her to the theatre and museums. To read aloud to her from scientific texts and scandalous novels. From time to time, we could visit Virgil's household so I may assist him in his ongoing translation work. Which would still be possible, as long as I do not have the impediment of trying to fit in such visits around a husband's wishes.

'After all, most gentlemen would expect their wives to focus on taking care of their households and, eventually, their children, not ones who want to keeping running off to immerse themselves in ancient Greek texts.'

Alex shuddered. 'What a dreary vision of the future, reading to old ladies, no household to run, no lively conversation and no hunters to gallop! Don't you wish for more? After working closely with your father and brother for so many years, would you not miss having the daily companionship of gentlemen?'

She would certainly long for the company of *this* gentleman. But over the long term, that wouldn't be possible, so best to focus on trying to set herself up to do the work she knew would fulfil her.

'I'm sure I would. But you must remember, for a lady of modest birth and small dowry who lives on a grand estate in a country neighbourhood with virtually no marriage prospects, the possibility of finding compatible male companionship—by which I assume you mean a marriage partner—is rather slim. Quite honestly, I'm rather glad that's true.'

'So you would never wish to marry?'

She almost told him marriage was likely impossible if she wanted to continue her work, but that might bring up questions she wasn't prepared to answer. Instead, she said carefully, 'If I could find a gentleman who was amenable to my assisting Virgil indefinitely, I might consider it. But even were my pool of prospects larger, the likelihood of finding such a gentleman is doubtful, and here in the country, virtually impossible. My chances of ending up as a companion are far greater. Truly, I am content with that.'

And now for the more difficult part of the conversation. Abandoning her serious tone for a bantering one, she said, 'But let me relieve you immediately of what may be your most troubling concern. Though I am now free of obligations, you still need not fear any consequences from the...indiscretion we shared. I promise I shall never set my sights on you.'

Just mentioning that 'indiscretion' had her simmering senses on the alert again. Did he feel it too, that constant, low hum of attraction? Something they both might wordlessly acknowledge but must determinedly ignore?

As he looked away, apparently trying to decide how to respond, she studied his expression. She thought it was relief she glimpsed on his face—but also, a bit of...pique?

'Ever the brutally honest,' he said drily. 'But, yes, I am reassured. And I promise to make sure there are no further...indiscretions. With me not in a position to marry and you not wishing to, we must avoid any situations that would have others...compel us to wed.'

'With the way we are always at odds, could there be any union less propitious than one between the two of us?' she teased.

'We'd probably murder each other within a month of the nuptials,' he agreed with a smile.

She could think of a lot of things more exciting than doing him bodily harm, if they were married, she thought with a sigh. Like kissing and more... Dragging her thoughts from that fruitless topic, she nodded. 'Very likely. What a scandal for the county!'

'Indeed. So for now, we should attempt to rub along together in our usual harmony.'

'Or dissonance,' she corrected with a smile.

His own teasing expression fading, he said quietly,

'I know you are putting the best face on what has to be an unhappy situation. If…if I can do anything to make your adjustment easier, please let me know.'

Touched, she studied him for a moment. 'Thank you, Alex. That's very kind.'

'We began as, and ever shall remain, good friends, I trust.'

Despite that undercurrent between them, perhaps they *could* restore that friendship—if they both were determined and careful enough. Immensely cheered by the prospect, she said, 'I shall be very glad to continue as friends', and impulsively reached over to clasp his hand.

She felt the jolt of contact all the way to her toes.

For a moment, they both froze. Then, while his eyes widened in alarm, she hastily pulled her hand away.

'Perhaps continuing our friendship would be easier if we refrain from…any physical gestures,' he said, his voice sounding strained.

'Agreed. I shall be more on my guard in future.'

'As will I.'

Before she could assemble her scattered wits to say anything more, he rose. 'I'm glad that's settled. Do call on me if you think I can help in any way.' With a nod, he strode out of the room.

Jocelyn stared down at her tingling hand. Oh, could she think of a way he could help assuage her 'disappointment'! Like giving her more kisses to satisfy the appetite his first one had only whetted. But thinking down that path led to disaster, and she must not go there. No matter how much the prospect of his kisses tempted her.

Instead of indulging in foolish thoughts like kissing, she should concentrate on her relief that their friendship was restored…mostly. And put her mind to making the latest round of translations as excellent as they could be, while she worked on deciding the best way to ensure she could continue indefinitely the work that defined her.

The fact that her broken engagement made it likely that she would be at Edge Hall for some considerable time—where she would encounter Alex Cheverton daily—was both a blessing and a curse.

She'd be able to indulge herself in Alex's company—but only if she was very, very careful not to do anything to jeopardise either their friendship or their respective futures.

Chapter Six

Later that day, as afternoon turned into evening, Alex was in his office updating the estate books when Simmons, the butler, knocked at his door. 'There's a dispatch rider arrived from London to see you, sir,' he said after Alex bid him enter. 'He says it's urgent.'

The rider must have been sent by the Duke. He couldn't imagine anyone else needing to contact him who would stand the expense of hiring a rider, rather than sending something by post, or riding down himself. That said, he had no idea what could have prompted so extraordinary a gesture.

'You'd better send him in at once, then.'

'He's waiting in the hallway just outside. I'll fetch him in.'

Simmons bowed himself out, his exit followed immediately by the entrance of a man whose weary face and mud-spattered garments spoke of a hard ride with little rest. 'You are Mr Cheverton?'

'Yes, I'm Alex Cheverton,' Alex said, rising to return the man's bow. 'You have urgent news for me?'

The man nodded. 'The Duke of Farisdeen sent me, sir. I'm to tell you there is pressing and confidential business that requires you to ride to London immediately.'

'What sort of confidential business?'

'He did not tell me, Mr Cheverton. Only that it was extremely urgent and that I was to press you to ride out as soon as possible after I delivered you the message. He needs you in London at once.'

Alex frowned, wondering what could have happened in the two days since he'd left London that would demand his immediate recall. Coming up with one possibility, he asked, 'Did the Duke appear ill?'

'No, sir. He's a right forbidding gent, but he didn't look poorly.'

'And he gave you no written message for me?'

'No, sir.'

If the Duke wasn't ill, then what? But there was no point making further enquiries; the rider had brought no written instructions and obviously knew nothing more than what he'd already imparted.

With all that needed to be done in the next few weeks to prepare Edge Hall's farms for spring planting, Alex wasn't thrilled at the prospect of having to abandon his tasks here. But the hired help was the hired help. It wasn't his place to decide what was important enough to require his recall to London. He just followed orders.

'Very well, I'll make plans to leave at once.' He walked over to ring the bell-pull. 'I'll have Simmons show you where you can get a meal and some rest. It's too late in the day for you to start back for London tonight.'

'Will *you* leave tonight, sir? The Duke was quite insistent.'

'Not tonight. There are details I must arrange for the

estate first, in case the Duke detains me in London. I'll leave at first light tomorrow.'

'Very good, sir. I've done all he wished, then, and will receive the rest of my pay when I get back to London.'

A flicker of a smile creased Alex's lips. How like the Duke to withhold full payment until he was certain the rider had completed the task to his satisfaction.

At that moment, the butler appeared. 'Simmons, will you see that Mr...' Pausing, Alex looked at the rider.

'Frank Jones, sir.'

'Mr Jones gets a hot meal and a bed for the night? And let Cook know I won't be back for dinner. Ask her to send a tray to the sitting room for me to have later.'

'Is something amiss, sir?'

Knowing the butler, to say nothing of the rest of the staff, was bound to be curious and perhaps alarmed by the sudden appearance of a dispatch rider, Alex said, 'Mr Jones informed me that the Duke requires my presence in London as soon as I can get there. That's all I—or he—know. I must visit the tenants tonight and make sure all is in train for spring planting before I leave tomorrow. If I discover in London that the matter concerns something that must be done at Edge Hall, I'll send you word.'

'Very good, sir. I'll see Cook has wine and some victuals brought up for you, so you may dine whenever you return. Should I let the stable know you'll need a carriage tomorrow?'

'No, I'll ride—it will be faster. I'll tell Jerry to get a horse ready when I see him at the stables. I could possibly travel faster by hiring horses along the way, but the quality can vary so much, I'd rather take my own gelding. He can manage the journey in a day.' Turning to the rider, Alex said, 'Goodbye, Mr Jones. I wish you a safe journey back to London.'

'And a quick one, too, sir.' Giving Alex a respectful nod, the rider followed Simmons out of the office.

Nodding absently in return, Alex sat back at his desk to close up the ledgers and store all the papers and invoices where he could find them again later. As he left the office and ran up to his chamber to get a heavier coat—the weather would turn much chillier once daylight began to fade—he ran a number of possible scenarios through his head. By the time he'd shrugged on a heavy outer garment and set off for the stables, he still couldn't imagine what emergency would have prompted the Duke to send for him.

As he mounted his horse, he put any further questions out of his mind. No sense speculating. He'd have a hard ride tomorrow and hopefully learn at the end of it what had prompted his recall.

The following evening, after a long day's ride through a rain-spattered countryside, Alex walked his spent horse into the mews behind the Duke's Grosvenor Square mansion. He'd turn his tired mount over to the head groom, tell the butler to notify the Duke he'd arrived and get a wash and a quick meal, in case the Duke summoned him tonight. Which, since the hour wasn't yet too advanced, His Grace might well do, if he were at home and not attending some entertainment.

At least, that had been his intention. To Alex's shock—he would have bet the Duke had never set foot on the upper floor where the smaller bedchambers were located—he'd barely had time to remove his coat and toss some water on his face when a knock at the door was followed by the appearance on his doorstep of Farisdeen himself.

'Your Grace!' Alex stammered, startled. 'I have only just arrived and was trying to clean off the dirt of the road.'

'Do you mind if I come in?'

Alex shook his head, not entirely sure he wasn't dreaming. He would never have imagined that the Duke would call on *him* in his bedchamber—or ask permission to enter a room in his own house. 'Of—of course. Will you take a chair?' He gestured towards the armchair near the hearth.

'Thank you, I'd rather stand. I'm sure you are wondering what could have happened that prompted me to issue such an urgent summons.' As Alex nodded, the Duke continued, 'It's Penlowe. He's very ill.'

'I'm sorry to hear it! Are there tasks you would like me to take over, while you oversee his care?'

'I'm afraid it's beyond that. This information is not to leave this room, but the physician is reasonably sure that this time Penlowe is dying.'

Completely shocked, Alex echoed, 'Dying? The physician is certain?'

The Duke nodded, his lined face looking weary. 'Yes. He wasn't sure he'd even last until you arrived.'

'Again, I'm so very sorry. How can I be of assistance?'

'I would like you to remain here, for the time being. Until Penlowe's illness is resolved, one way or another.'

Alex nodded. 'Certainly, if that is your wish.'

'By remaining here, I mean here, within the house. I don't want you to visit a club or see friends or have anyone know you are in London. That sounds unusual, I know, but I have my reasons. In any event, I don't think your isolation will be necessary for long. I'll let you know when I have further need of you and make sure food and refreshment is sent up from the kitchen. Ask Thurgood,' he continued, naming the butler, 'and Thurgood only, if you require anything else. That will be all for tonight. If that is understood?'

Totally mystified now, Alex made him a bow. 'Yes, Your Grace. I am, as always, at your service.'

'Good.' Giving Alex a nod, the Duke turned and walked out.

Shaking his head again, Alex walked over to the basin to finish washing his face. He would bathe and change into clean garments, then summon the butler to send for some food.

As he thought about the odd events of the last twenty-four hours, the sense of dream-like unreality intensified. A summons by dispatch rider, followed by a long, chilly slog through rain and mud to reach London. Then, the Duke himself calling on Alex in his chamber, charging him not to leave the house or let anyone know he was in London—and instructing him to have the butler to wait on him. None of it made sense.

Suddenly he recalled one of the Duke's comments— *Penlowe is dying.*

Alex recalled how pale and unsteady the Viscount had appeared when he'd seen him a few days ago. He'd thought the pallor induced by a long night of dissipation. Penlowe must have already been taken ill. Perhaps he'd been ill for some time.

The Duke had no other living sons, having lost two babes as infants, and Penlowe had not yet married. Perhaps the Duke needed him to help arrange matters while the College of Arms examined the claims of whichever uncle or cousin of the male line now stood next to inherit the dukedom.

Though the Duke had a secretary to do that.

So why was *he* here?

It was sad that the Duke was apparently going to lose his one remaining son and Alex did feel sympathy for him. Although Farisdeen had betrayed not a trace of emotion while discussing the imminent death of his son, it couldn't be less than a crushing blow. Alex's own dealings with Penlowe were not cordial enough for him to feel more than regret at the prospect of a life cut tragically short.

Whatever role the Duke had brought him back here to play, he wasn't likely to discover it tonight. He'd find a book in the library, enjoy a meal prepared by the Duke's excellent chef and settle in to read with a glass of what would doubtless be a superior wine.

Early the following rainy morning, Alex was sitting by the fire in his chamber, finishing the breakfast the butler had brought up and sipping his coffee over the morning paper when once again, there was a tap at the door, followed by the appearance of the Duke.

Rising, Alex studied the man's face before bowing to him—but could discern nothing from his expression, which was as inscrutable as ever. 'Good morning, Your Grace. Is there…news?'

'Penlowe died in the early hours of this morning.'

This time, Alex did feel a pang of sorrow for the Duke. Though he never displayed more visible emotion than a granite statue, deep down, the man must be grieving. 'My condolences, Your Grace. What would you like me to do for you?'

Farisdeen sighed. 'This time, I will take a chair, if you would.'

'Of course,' Alex said, rising to wave the Duke to the chair he'd just vacated and walking to the hearth. 'Shall I ring for more coffee?'

'No. What I have to impart is simple, though the carrying out of it is likely to be very complex.'

'The process of locating and validating the claim of the new heir?' Alex guessed.

'That part was done long ago, when I first learned of Penlowe's...condition. Locating the new heir is easy—he is standing right in front of me. You, Alexander Cheverton, will be the next Duke of Farisdeen.'

In the early afternoon two days later, Alex rode back into the stables at Edge Hall, still suspended in a state of shock and disbelief. He, to some day become the Duke of Farisdeen? He still couldn't believe it.

The Duke had sent him back to Edge Hall, granting him two weeks to adjust to his radical change of status while Farisdeen found someone to take over as estate manager. At which time he was to report back to His Grace in London and begin to be groomed for the grand position he would one day occupy.

He was allowed to inform the staff of his changed position and he would—eventually. But first, he wanted to savour a few moments of normalcy before life as he'd known it these last six years at Edge Hall was radically altered.

And break the news to Jocelyn.

He couldn't imagine what she would have to say, but her perspective on the matter should prove interesting. He was going to be sad to bid the staff goodbye, regret leaving a job he'd found fascinating and fulfilling. Although he intended after returning to London to try to persuade the Duke to let him take up managing Edge Hall again, whatever training Farisdeen felt necessary for his new heir to undergo in London might preclude that, at least for the present.

He was also honest enough to admit that he would greatly miss Jocelyn Sudderfeld. Removing himself from Edge Hall would be a relief for a self-control that had been increasingly tested by his desire for her. But while it would end the tension—and worry about the consequences, were his control to slip again—the cost of that peace of mind would be the loss of one of his most engaging friends.

Probably for good. Though he had not discussed anything relating to his future with Farisdeen before departing, both of them tacitly acknowledging that there would be time for detailed discussions when he returned, after the shock of losing his heir Alex felt sure one of Farisdeen's first objects once he arrived in the metropolis would be to introduce him into the Marriage Mart. The Duke almost certainly regretted now that he hadn't pushed his own son harder to do that most essential part of an heir's duty—to marry and breed sons to secure the succession. He would be anxious not to repeat that mistake with Alex. So even if he were allowed to return to Edge Hall, he would probably do so as a married man.

Thereby altering, and very likely ending, his long friendship with Jocelyn for ever.

Something deep within him protested at that assessment, but he squelched the reaction. After the disaster of his youthful brush with excessive emotion, taking a well-bred, well-born wife whom he could respect and for whom he felt only a fond affection would be a wise

as well as a convenient choice. Even if he could not yet
summon up much enthusiasm for the prospect.

But it was foolish to wish that he could go back to
being simply the Duke's estate manager who also owned
a small property of his own. He'd have to use the two
weeks the Duke was allowing him to reconcile himself
to his new responsibilities—and the necessity of leaving behind a position, and people, he'd grown to care
deeply about.

At least he would have two weeks to savour more
than he ever had before being around the estate, the
tenants and the staff. And arm himself to say goodbye
to Jocelyn Sudderfeld.

Turning his horse over to a groom, Alex strode to
the house and slipped in a side door, wanting to avoid
encountering Simmons or anyone else from the household staff, who were bound to immediately ask him
what had transpired in London.

He went first to the library where, as he expected,
he found Jocelyn seated at the desk, writing, while her
brother paced the room, his gaze on the book he held.

Virgil, as usual, was oblivious, but Jocelyn looked
up at once as he entered. 'Alex, you are back! And earlier than any of us expected. I hope the circumstances
that led the Duke to summon you to London turned out
not to be too dire.'

'They were…most unusual. I've just this moment arrived and I could do with some tea. Virgil, could you
spare half an hour for a cup?'

'I think we can stop now,' Jocelyn said. 'My brother
is still puzzling over the proper wording of this next
section. Will you join us, Virgil, or would you prefer
me to bring your tea back to the library?'

Fortunately, as Alex had hoped so he might have

that private conversation he craved with Jocelyn, Virgil said, 'I really don't want to have my concentration interrupted just as I'm beginning to get a better feel for the passage. Bring me back a cup, if you would, please, Jocelyn. Oh—and welcome back, Alex.'

'Thank you. I'll wish you well in ferreting out the precise meaning of your passage.'

Giving Alex an absent nod, Virgil looked back to his text and resumed his pacing.

After carefully storing her pen, Jocelyn rose and walked out of the library with Alex. Once they were in the hallway, far enough away not to disturb her brother's ruminations, she said, 'We've reached a thorny spot, which always frustrates Virgil. Sometimes the best meaning of ancient Greek can be hard to pin down. But it's always so gratifying when the puzzle finally falls into place. I imagine he will be smiling with delight by the time I bring back his tea.'

Now that he was moments away from speaking with her, Alex wasn't sure exactly how to begin. Before he could say anything, she continued, 'So, what fell into place for you in London? Something that will have *you* smiling with delight?'

'Not exactly,' he said drily. 'Let's make the tea first and I'll tell you everything.'

Though the silence as they walked to the sitting room was companionable, Alex was supremely conscious of the attraction that set his nerves on edge and made him acutely aware of her walking beside him a mere foot away, her rose perfume filling his senses.

That odd conflicted feeling arose in him again—an impossible mix of resentment that he was going to lose her mingled with relief that he would no longer have to resist her.

As they entered the sitting room, she said, 'Why don't you take a seat on the sofa? You must be tired after riding back and forth to London twice in less than a week—elderly gentleman that you are. I'll make the tea.'

'Yes, let me rest my ancient bones while you serve. And get used to it. You will be doing a great deal of that in future.'

'Waiting on you?' she asked with a smile. 'Not for some years, I expect. You may be my elder, but you're not yet in your dotage. So, what of London? Everyone at Edge Hall has been agog with curiosity. Hopefully His Grace didn't discover you'd been filching his best wine and sack you.'

He waited for her to bring the tea over and pour him a cup. 'That's not exactly what happened. Although I am going to lose my position.'

About to seat herself on the adjacent wing chair—regrettably but prudently not on the sofa beside him—she jerked her gaze to him, her eyes widening.

'You're going to lose it? You can't be serious! I know I tease you constantly about your competence, but truly, of late, you have been doing an excellent job with Edge Hall. Both staff and tenants hold you in esteem!'

Alex grinned wryly. 'It's almost worth losing the job to hear you pay me such extravagant compliments. But it's true; His Grace intends to replace me.'

'But why?' she cried. 'Surely he can't imagine he can find someone who would do a better job!'

'More on that in a moment. The Duke summoned me to London because his son, the Marquess of Penlowe, was very ill. So ill, in fact, that he died the night of my arrival.'

'Good heavens! How terrible for the Duke! Not that

I have never seen him display much emotion, but he must be devastated.'

'I suppose so too, though you are right; it is difficult to tell.'

After taking a pensive sip of her tea, Jocelyn said, 'Penlowe was the Duke's only surviving son. How bitter it must be for him to contemplate having to turn his estate and his title over to someone else. Probably a rather distant relation, if memory serves. I don't believe the current Duke has any surviving brothers, or nephews, either.'

'He does not. The new heir is quite a distant cousin. In fact, the new heir...is me.'

Once again, Jocelyn's startled gaze swung up to his face. Then she burst out laughing.

Chapter Seven

She was so relieved, Jocelyn had a hard time bringing her mirth under control. But after a breath-stealing instant of unpleasant shock at the prospect of Alex being dismissed, leaving Edge Hall—leaving *her*—his grandiose announcement was a joke simply too absurd to resist.

'Well, you got me on that one,' she said, wiping her eyes before taking another sip of tea. 'Discharged, indeed! You had me halfway to believing you, you wretch! Now, tell me what *really* happened in London.'

Only then, as she looked back up at him, did she realise he hadn't joined in her mirth, or smiled, or even pointed a triumphant finger at having successfully humbugged her.

He was, in fact, studying her with a disconcertingly solemn expression. 'It might not be politic for you to find the prospect of me as your brother's eventual employer quite so amusing.'

Her breath caught and her stomach swooped like it had when she'd fallen out of an apple tree at the age of seven. As she studied his serious face, she said, 'You—

you *weren't* joking? You *will* be the next Duke of Faris-deen?'

He nodded. 'Alas, it's true.'

'I'm so very sorry!'

That did make him smile. 'Trust you to react as probably no one else would. I'm no happier about it than you are.'

'It's certain?'

'Unfortunately, yes. I assure you, I didn't want to believe it! After the Duke broke the news and released me, I went at once to his solicitor's office. But the man confirmed it. He even showed me the very document the College of Arms prepared for the Duke over ten years ago.'

'Farisdeen knew ten years ago that you stood in line after his son? And never told you?'

'I'm sure he'd hoped he'd never have to. That Penlowe would marry, have a son and the succession would pass down through the senior line. But apparently he's known for some time that Penlowe suffered from the same weakness of the heart as his mother, the late Duchess. It seems the Marquess had his first attack when he was in his teens and several of increasing severity since then. So Farisdeen had the lineage traced, just in case. Turns out, my great-grandfather was the second son of the Fifth Duke. His heir, the Sixth Duke, had two brothers, one who died as a child and another who had a son, but both died before the Sixth Duke. The Sixth Duke's heir—the Seventh Duke—had several daughters but only one son who survived infancy—the Eighth and current Duke. And, as you pointed out, Penlowe was the current Duke's only surviving son. As the eldest son of the grandson of the Fifth Duke's next-oldest son, I'm the nearest descendant in an unbroken male line.'

Trying to wrap her mind around the news, Jocelyn said, 'It sounds as if the research was thorough. So there's no escaping it?'

'I only wish there were. But the tracing of the lineage is certain enough that the College of Arms verified it and they are the authority on such things. After the current Duke's death, assuming he predeceases me without taking a new wife and begetting another son, I could refuse the writ of summons from Parliament to take up the title and let the dukedom pass into abeyance. But I would still be legally the owner of all the entailed property, with a host of people dependent upon my exercising that ownership prudently—not just those here at Edge Hall, but also tenants on half a dozen other properties. Without claiming the inheritance, I wouldn't have the means to hire managers to ensure they were all being properly tended. Nor could I in good conscience ignore the Duke of Farisdeen's responsibility to attend the Lords and help oversee the government of the nation, simply because I don't want to shoulder the task.'

She nodded. 'You could not leave the tenants at all the Duke's properties to fend for themselves. Or avoid the titleholder's duty to Parliament. So I suppose there is no way out.'

Alex shook his head. 'I always wondered why the Duke chose to look me up after I graduated from Oxford, when the previous Dukes had never before had any dealings with my junior branch of the family. Not that he explained himself when he summoned me from Oxford to offer me the estate manager's position, or when he broke this news two days ago in London. I'm guessing he wanted to keep me close and know what I was doing, maybe even make sure I was trained to run a large estate—just in case. It also explains why he insisted I not marry. If I ended up inheriting, he wanted to have a say in making sure the woman I wed was suitable to become the next Duchess of Farisdeen.'

Keen to know what his sudden elevation would mean for their long friendship, she said, 'So what are your plans now? Will you remain at Edge Hall, with a new estate manager working for you?'

'That would certainly be what I would prefer. That is not what Farisdeen wants. I've already proven I know how to run an estate, he said. What I must master now is how to be…a duke. I am to return to London so he may introduce me to society as his heir, become a member of all clubs he considers suitable and be schooled by him and his associates in what I will need to know to eventually enter Parliament. Fortunately, the family will officially be in mourning, so I'll be spared becoming the prime exhibit at society balls and soirées. *Un*-fortunately, that will still allow the Duke to be able to kit me out, trot me out to private dinners and introduce me to all the people he considers important. So that I may, to quote His Grace, "be taught to conduct myself as a man of importance".'

Shaking his head again, Alex gave a short laugh. 'I don't wonder at your amusement when I made my dramatic announcement. When my horse set hoof on Edge Hall land today and the knowledge struck me that this estate I've been tending the last six years will eventually *belong* to me, I started laughing. So hysterically, had anyone been present to observe me, I'd probably now be in a cart, a gag in my mouth and my hands tied behind my back, on my way to Bedlam.'

'It does seem…impossible. No, not impossible—you are quite capable of being a duke. But standing so far

from the succession and then inheriting…it's such an
unlikely a turn of events!'

'Unlikely, and frankly, unwanted. *Tending* this land,
and later my own small estate, was all I ever envisaged.
All I wanted. Not this.'

His return to London *would* mark the end of their
friendship. Stifling a painfully strong pang of protest,
she said, 'It will be a vast increase in responsibility.
You've done an excellent job looking after the well-
being of the people of Edge Hall. But the Duke has
several other large properties, does he not? As well
as those responsibilities in Parliament you mentioned.
Your life…will no longer be your own. No, I can well
understand why you don't want this.'

'Sadly, inheritance takes no account of wanting.'

And now, what was for her the most important question. 'How long do you have before…before you must
leave?'

'Two weeks.'

Jocelyn sucked in a breath. *So little time.* All that
was left to her now was to enjoy his company as often
as she could before he began his 'training' as a duke.
Unable to come up with anything encouraging to reply,
she said faintly, 'Just…two weeks.'

'Yes,' he said shortly, his tone grim. 'I… I hope you
will believe me when I say there is no one at Edge Hall
I will regret leaving more than you, Jocelyn. How I will
miss your good sense and intelligent comments in London! I always appreciate your well-considered point of
view—even though you usually also take me down a
peg while you're giving it.'

London. Suddenly she recalled the recent change
to her plans that his shocking news had sent clear out
of her head and a flash of hope staved off her grow-

ing dismay and sadness. There might be a possibility of hanging on to his friendship a little longer after all.

'As it happens, I have some news, too. Not nearly as dramatic as yours, of course.'

'Indeed? Good news, I hope. I could use some good news.'

She had to laugh at the absurdity of it. 'Listen to us! Probably the only two lunatics in the British Isles who would consider the unexpected inheritance of a dukedom to be a misfortune!'

'Maybe they'd better send a cart from Bedlam to pick you up, too,' he said, at least smiling a little now. 'So, what is your news?'

'You may remember I told you that my mother's family washed their hands of Mama for having the bad judgement to wed a simple country scholar. But apparently they were still watching out for news about us. A few days ago, I had a letter from my mother's formidable Aunt Elizabeth, Lady Bellingame, a very grand dame who married a wealthy viscount. Somehow, she was informed of my recent, ah, disappointment— I suspect by Reverend Morrison. Apparently she was incensed on my behalf by this slight to her kinswoman by a young man of no particular wealth or family. She wrote to summon me to London, where she proposed to go about finding me a suitable husband. Of course, I wrote back telling her I couldn't possibly leave my brother in the middle of his project.'

'Not even for the laudable goal of finding a husband who could support and care for you? Couldn't Virgil recruit someone else to be his scribe—a recent graduate from Oxford, perhaps?'

'I'm far more than just a humble scribe!' she protested. Then, catching herself before she said anything even more indiscreet, she continued in a teasing tone, 'Not just *anyone* would do! As you may remember, after many years of working with my father, *I* have the expertise to offer suggestions.'

'Pardon me!' Alex said, smiling. 'I didn't mean to minimise the importance of your *esteemed* experience.'

'I should certainly hope not. At any rate, upon receiving my reply, my aunt wrote back again immediately. From the tone of her letter, she was shocked that I'd turned down her magnanimous offer, although I hope I conveyed how appreciative I was that she'd made it. After a grave warning that I ought to be more concerned about my future, she concluded by stating she considered it imperative enough for me to be established in a home of my own that she was prepared to allow Virgil and Papa to accompany me to London. Quite a concession, considering she blames my father for luring my mother away from a more advantageous match!'

'Quite a concession,' Alex agreed, smiling. 'Do you think she would be able to swallow her discontent enough to treat them as politely as you would wish them to be, if they become guests under her roof?'

Jocelyn laughed. 'She must know me better than I suspected, for she assured me on just that score! In the next line after penning their invitation, she added that I might be assured that, despite the bad feelings between them in the past, she was prepared to receive them cordially in order to do what was best for my future. Although I still didn't think I'd be accepting her offer.'

'Why not? It seems a most handsome one.'

'Oh, it was. But I didn't think either Papa or Virgil would have any desire to leave Edge Hall. You know how Virgil hates to have his concentration interrupted and it's bound to be noisier and more distracting in the city! However, to my surprise, they both said they'd entertain the idea of a short sojourn in London. Not that I expect to find in London any prospective suitor I could envisage accepting.' *Because I couldn't risk taking a husband who might discover my secret.* 'So we will be relocating to London in a few weeks, too. I just hope my aunt won't be too disappointed when I end the visit unmarried.'

To her gratification, his face lit. 'All of you, going to London! That's excellent news! Perhaps we will still be able to see each other! I could call on your aunt. Everything all correct and proper.'

'Yes. You could complain to me of all the blunt you're having to spend, buying smart new garments and carriages and high-spirited horses to draw them. The ennui of being surrounded by the most eminent politicians in the realm and being entertained by the highest-ranking members of society. I could provide you a levelling dose of your lost normality.'

'It sounds wonderful. Perhaps I could dance with you at some evening entertainment, or escort you to dinner at some musicale.'

Laughing, she shook her head. 'I hardly think the daughter of a country vicar and the heir of a duke will be invited to the same entertainments. Especially since, as you will be in mourning, you will attend very few and all of them quite select.'

Nor was she sure she would want to be present. The unmarried heir to a dukedom was a coveted matrimonial prize. Every high-born mother with an eligible daughter who could contrive an invitation—or issue one—to any of the private soirées to which the Duke would bring him would be thrusting her girl under his nose. Farisdeen would doubtless be pressing him to wed, too. Much as she sincerely wished Alex the best, she wasn't sure she wanted to witness the spectacle of him choosing a wife. Firmly she forced out of her mind the distressing image of him kissing someone else.

'Perhaps it could be arranged,' he was saying. 'It is certain, then, that you will go to London? Your aunt has already made arrangements?'

'They haven't been finalised yet, but we should know the details soon.' She'd been mildly enthusiastic about going to the metropolis to visit the museums, shops and theatres. Then it had occurred to her, while her aunt tried to introduce her to prospective husbands, *she* could look about for suitable wealthy and intellectually-minded widows who might at some point need an intelligent, well-read and scholarly companion.

Knowing Alex would be in London, too, made the prospect of a visit even more appealing. She might be able to eke out a few more days or weeks of companionship with her oldest friend, before the Duke proceeded far enough in Alex's training to convince him he was above maintaining a relationship with mere Miss Sudderfeld—and focused his time and attention firmly on the daughters of marquesses, earls and viscounts.

'When do you expect your family will leave for London?'

'Not before your two weeks are up, probably. There are still many details to be arranged.'

He seized her hand, surprising her enough to make her breath catch. 'I tell you truly, the only thing that makes facing this change easier is knowing you and your family will be in London. It's selfish, I grant. But it's likely both my closest friends will be away, Lattimar in Northumberland, tending his family's acres, and Dellamont off investigating some new railroad project.

Knowing I will have at least one friendly, familiar face I can actually look forward to seeing... One person who knows me for who I truly am, before I must put on the camouflage of rank I never wanted. It makes what I cannot escape seem at least tolerable.'

As he spoke, he looked down at her, holding her motionless with the power of his gaze. All other thoughts fell away, leaving only one...an ardent wish that he would kiss her again, give her one more sweet memory of him to hold for ever before the world took him away.

His eyes darkened, his gaze intensifying before he bent his head. A thrill spiralling through her, she lifted her chin as her eyes drifted shut.

Just before his lips touched hers, a knock sounded at the door. As they hastily moved apart, Simmons entered the room.

'Mr Cheverton, Eddie in the stables told me you'd returned. How was your journey? Is there any news from London you are able to convey?'

Her hand still tingled with warmth where he'd clasped it. Rubbing the skin, she regretted his loss. Though she must arm herself to get used to it.

Still, she fiercely resented Simmons for cheating her of that one last kiss.

Suppressing her desire and pushing away the resentment, she found a light tone. 'Well, Mr Cheverton? Are you ready to break the news?'

Shaking his head at her, Alex sighed. 'I suppose I shall have to.'

'You must. Families in the country with ties in London are bound to hear about it quickly. You wouldn't want gossip to reach the staff before you told them yourself.'

'No, that wouldn't be right.'

'Or shall I do the honours?'

He waved a hand at her. 'Oh, by all means.'

Turning to the butler, Jocelyn said, 'You must make your bow even more deferential, Simmons. You're now standing before your eventual employer, the future Ninth Duke of Farisdeen.'

To her amusement, the butler looked almost as shocked as she had been.

Standing, she patted Alex's arm before going to the sideboard to load up a teapot and cups. 'I'll leave you to explain. By now, Virgil will have sorted out that passage and be impatient for his tea.'

'We'll talk later?'

'Of course. Would you like to come to dinner at the Dower House tonight? I'm sure both my father and brother will be delighted to hear your news.'

'Yes, I'd like that.'

'Until tonight then… Your Future Grace.'

Though she smiled as she said it, the smile faded as soon as she exited the room. The future Duke of Farisdeen would continue to be called 'master' by all in this household.

But soon, she would no longer be able to even call him 'friend'.

She'd finish the day's translating with Virgil, then return to the Dower House and write to her aunt to settle the final details of their visit to London.

Where she would, for a few more days or weeks, have the possibility of Alex's company. Before his destiny and hers propelled each of them in different directions.

Chapter Eight

Since the dinner at the Dower House the night of his return from London, when Alex had revealed his change in status to Reverend Sudderfeld and his son, he hadn't seen much of Jocelyn. With so many details to settle at the manor house before the start of spring planting, in addition to making sure all the tenants had adequate seed, assisting with repairs to ploughs and equipment, and riding into Chichester to secure new items for those beyond repair, he'd not been at Edge Hall often during the day and sometimes did not arrive back at the Hall until late evening.

But when he came into his office early this morning, ten days after his return, he'd found a note from Jocelyn propped in the centre of his desk. Informing him that her family would be leaving for London in two days, she asked if he could join them for dinner one last time at the Dower House—'since, if and when you return to Edge Hall, your elevated status will put you far above taking a meal with the family of a lowly librarian.'

He'd smiled as he read it. Typical Jocelyn, to tweak him about the 'elevated status' she well knew he'd neither desired nor appreciated receiving.

He'd missed her, much as he'd tried not to. Not that he'd been deliberately avoiding her, but with their paths about to diverge, he'd realised with some alarm that deep within, he harboured a strong resentment that his elevation would likely mean the end of a friendship he was only now realising how much he truly valued. That understanding had only intensified his smouldering desire. Not sure he could trust himself to control it, he'd deliberately limited the time they spent together to short episodes of taking tea, always with her brother present.

At least he still had her friendship to look forward to in London. That would have to be enough. And calling on her there, under the careful chaperonage of her great-aunt, would curtail the possibility of any dangerous interludes—like that one in the sitting room the day of his return, when he'd almost kissed her.

How easily the magic of her attraction seemed to disarm his self-control! Bad as it had been to succumb to the temptation of kissing her that day on Trethfort Hill, when she was nearly affianced, kissing her now—when she was available, as he was not—would be worse. It would verge on toying with her, an unspeakable offence against a girl he liked and admired so much.

If he wanted to be worthy of her friendship, he needed to do a much better job of resisting her.

Knowing it might be the last time they spent a whole evening together, he'd rearranged today's schedule to ensure he would be back in time for dinner, dressed with more than usual care and, knowing Reverend Sudderfeld appreciated punctuality, arrived on the doorstep of the Dower House precisely on time.

The maid-of-all-work answered his knock and informed him the family was presently in the drawing room. Telling the girl he would announce himself, he walked down the hallway.

As he paused on the sitting room's threshold, he noted Virgil in the wing chair before the fire, reading, Reverend Sudderfeld sitting on sofa, watching his daughter, and Jocelyn at the pianoforte, playing. Her attention fixed on the music, she didn't notice him slip in—which gave him a rare opportunity to study her.

She was looking especially pretty—or was it that, having not seen her for some days, he'd forgotten how lovely she was? A faint smile lit her face as she gazed down at the music—a complicated Mozart concerto, he realised. Her dusky hair was worn up for evening in an attractive knot of curls, leaving her neck bare. The dinner gown's low neckline displayed the graceful curve of her neck and bared shoulders and emphasised the voluptuous curve of her breasts. As his gaze traced her figure, his mouth went dry and he gritted his teeth against the inevitable reaction of body.

You must curb this and think only of spending a pleasant evening among friends, he reproved himself, redoubling his efforts to concentrate on the music. When the piece came to an end, he clapped. Looking up in surprise, Jocelyn exclaimed, 'Alex! How ungenteel of you to slip in unannounced!' Smiling, she shook a disapproving finger at him. 'Farisdeen would definitely not approve. A duke's heir mustn't *creep in*, he must be announced with suitable pomp and then make a grand entrance.'

She hadn't wasted any time teasing him again, he thought with smile. As much as he'd missed her physical attractiveness, he'd also missed that clever wit.

'You're probably correct. Let me rectify that.' He backed out of the doorway, then turned and paused on the threshold. Chin elevated, he surveyed the room, then proceeded with self-important strides to the middle of the space, where he halted and gave them an exaggerated bow. 'Miss Sudderfeld, Reverend and Mr Sudderfeld, good evening. How kind of you to invite me to dine.'

While her father gazed at him with mild surprise and Virgil looked up from his book, blinking, Jocelyn laughed and clapped her hands. 'Much better! You should have had a quizzing glass to properly scan the room, but otherwise, I think Farisdeen would deem that entrance much improved. Not quite *important* enough yet, of course, but I'm sure the Duke will give you lots of additional practice.'

Alex groaned. 'I fear you are right. But for one more evening, I can be simply Mr Cheverton, estate manager for Edge Hall.'

'Come, have a seat,' Jocelyn invited. 'Dinner will be served in half an hour. Virgil, would you pour us all some wine?'

Alex walked over to bow again to Reverend Sudderfeld before taking a seat beside him on sofa, while Jocelyn left the piano bench to take the wing chair adjacent. 'That was a pretty piece you were playing— Mozart, wasn't it?' Alex asked.

'Yes. The Duke will approve your musical erudition.'

Ignoring that provocation, Alex said, 'You must have been practising. I don't remember that you used to play so competently.'

'How unhandsome!' she protested, swatting him on his sleeve with her fan. 'Are you practising remarks designed to repel presumptuous young ladies? However, my usual brutal honesty compels me to admit you right. I know we will attend some musical evenings while in

London and I'll doubtless be called upon to play. Not wanting to disgrace my aunt, I *have* been practising.'

'Your efforts have been rewarded. The piece was quite pleasant to listen to. I didn't have to grit my teeth over wrong or discordant notes once.'

'Why, thank you!' Jocelyn said drily. 'High praise indeed.'

They paused in their mutual harassment to accept a glass of wine from Virgil, who took the other wing chair in front of the fire.

Switching to a more polite tone, Alex addressed her father. 'Reverend Sudderfeld, you indicated when we last dined together that you were in the process of compiling a list of places you would like to visit while you are in London. Have you succeeded in finding enough to keep you busy while your wife's aunt drags, um, escorts Jocelyn to various social gatherings? Or have you changed your mind and decided to attend those with her?'

With an expression of distaste, the Reverend shook his head. 'Certainly not! I've never enjoyed idle social events. When forced to attend one, I always looked for a quiet corner to wait in until I could politely make my escape. It's how Jocelyn's mother found me,' he added, smiling at his daughter. 'Retreated into a corner, inspecting the rather mediocre art on the wall. She came over to interrupt my scrutiny and said I must be a scholar, if I could spend so much time studying what was an entirely unremarkable painting.'

Jocelyn nodded. 'Mama said she was intrigued by this handsome young man who seemed completely indifferent to all the lovely ladies parading about the room, trying unsuccessfully to catch his attention. So, to the horror of her mama, she boldly walked up and addressed him.'

'And were you, sir, equally taken with her?' Alex asked.

The Reverend's eyes grew soft. 'I fell in love with her the moment I saw her and she felt the same.' He chuckled. 'Her mama—and her whole family—were even more horrified by *that*. To my wonderment, though she could have done much better than settle for a dreaming scholar, and despite everything her family tried to do to discourage her, she refused to give me up.'

'In the end, Mama threatened to elope to Gretna Green if my grandfather continued to refuse permission for them to marry,' Jocelyn told him. 'Since her two older sisters had already made splendid matches, at length, the family relented.' Turning to her father, she added, 'Mama held fast to what she knew would make her happy. And never for a moment regretted her choice.'

As he watched them, father and daughter gazing at each other with deep affection, Alex felt an ache in his chest. When he was young, he'd expected that eventually, when inclination and his circumstances allowed him to marry, he would find a relationship as satisfying as the one they'd just described. At the very least, a pairing of compatible and affectionate individuals, and if he were truly lucky, a partnership with someone he loved so deeply, neither of them would ever regret their choice of each other.

Then had come the devastation of his impetuous pursuit of Eliza, her equally impetuous acceptance and the humiliating refusal of her father to even consider him.

Unwilling to defy her father, Eliza had been left heartbroken—his fault, he thought with a muted wave of the guilt that had consumed him then. But her father had been right. He *had* been a presumptuous boy with no income of his own to provide for a wife.

Even worse, his rapturous regard for Eliza hadn't outlasted for very long the termination of their affair, which wouldn't have boded well for the success of their marriage, had they been permitted to wed.

The whole distasteful episode had left him vowing never to fall victim to such turbulent emotions again.

He still believed a match based on suitable lineage and fortune, the sort of marriage the Duke would doubtless urge him to seek, was the wisest arrangement. Somehow, though, the warmth with which Jocelyn spoke of her parents' devotion made him long, just a little, for a relationship that might be...more.

'So, Papa, since you've no intention of accompanying me on the social rounds my aunt will insist upon,' Jocelyn was saying, 'tell Mr Cheverton what you *are* looking forward to.'

'I've been happily employed at Edge Hall near on twenty years, buried in the beauty of scholarship. Even these last three years, after my fading eyesight forced me to turn my project over to my son, I've been able to continue study, though I've had to limit my reading. But now I find the prospect of interrupting that study with a sojourn in London quite exciting.'

'I can well imagine!' Alex said. 'Are you much acquainted with the city?'

'A little, though since my last visit occurred just after I left Oxford in 1802, I'm sure much as changed. Certainly, over the intervening years there have been major additions to the antiquity collections at the British Museum. I was fortunate enough upon my last London visit to obtain a personal tour from Mr Townley of the statues and vases he had on display at his home in Pall Mall and also to see Mr Hope's collection at his home on Duchess Street. Both are now at the Museum. I'm particularly keen to take Virgil, who has not seen either, to view them and the other objects obtained from Sir William Hamilton, Sir John Soane and John Spencer Stanhope. And of course, the Elgin Marbles.'

At that moment, the maid appeared at the door. 'Excuse me, Reverend Sudderfeld, but Cook says dinner is ready.'

'Shall we continue this conversation at table?' Alex asked.

Standing, Jocelyn said, 'I should probably have Mr Cheverton lead me in, as he is soon to be the highest ranking among us.'

Alex gave her a thin smile. 'I think for one last time, we can keep to the old ways and have you go in on your father's arm.'

'How *gracious* of you, Your Almost Grace,' she said in mock-obsequious tones. 'One more time, then.'

'Enough, Jocelyn!' Alex warned. 'More of that and you will provoke me to practise delivering a very ducal set-down.'

'I suppose a duke can say whatever he likes to lowly persons who annoy him.'

'Like suggesting to her father that an impertinent miss be sent to bed without supper?'

'Since it's to be a very fine dinner I should not like to miss, I suppose I shall have to behave myself.'

Long inured to their banter, the Reverend simply shook his head at them. 'I require you both to be serious at least long enough for me to say grace.'

After taking their seats and giving properly respectful thanks to the Almighty, Alex turned to Jocelyn's brother. 'Are you as eager as your father to visit the British Museum, Virgil?'

'Absolutely!' he replied with enthusiasm. 'I'm looking forward to viewing the Greek collection, of course, but I'm even more excited at the prospect of examining the Rosetta Stone. For any serious linguist, the chance to study the key that unlocked our understanding of an ancient language previously lost to mankind cannot be less than thrilling! And then, to be able to compare its ancient Greek text to the Egyptian and perhaps gain enough understanding of the hieroglyphic symbols to be able to read the inscriptions on the other Egyptian objects in the collection—how exciting! Not that I intend to abandon work on my own project, of course, but I will spend some time studying there.'

'The Museum also houses the books from the King's library and several other manuscript collections. Virgil and I intend to request permission from Sir Thomas Grenville, one of the Museum trustees, to view his extensive personal library, which includes some excellent early volumes of Homer,' Reverend Sudderfeld said.

'The Museum's collection contains the volume that first inspired Papa to become a student of ancient Greek,' Jocelyn said.

'Truly? And what volume was that?' Alex asked, genuinely curious about what could so fascinate a man, it would inspire him to devote the better part of his adult life to penetrating the mysteries of a language that hadn't been spoken for a thousand years.

'The *editio princeps* of Homer's *Iliad* and *Odyssey*,' Reverend Sudderfeld said with a fond smile. 'The first printed edition in the world of an ancient Greek work in the original language, made in Florence in 1488. Reverend Clayton Mordaunt Cracherode obtained the volume as part of his extensive manuscript collection. Upon his death, although he left most of his volumes to the British Museum, he left the *editio princeps* to Reverend Cyril Johnson, then Dean of Christ Church, Oxford. My tutor, as it turns out. Using that work as the text, he conveyed his love of the language to me and, well, here we are.'

'Here we both are,' Virgil corrected. 'I'm eager to see Papa's inspiration for myself.'

'And what of you, Jocelyn?' Alex asked. 'Will you be partaking of scholarship, too, or do you intend to devote yourself entirely to frivolity?'

'Like most mindless females?' she shot back. 'In deference to my aunt's kind invitation, I shall accompany her to whatever social events as she wishes us to attend. But since my great-aunt is not an early riser and I understand the events of the *beau monde* are not known for starting early—a breakfast *champêtre*, I'm told, begins at four in the afternoon!—I expect to have time in the mornings for exploration. At the British Museum, certainly, but I should also like to tour the National Gallery, and if we remain in London until May, view the Royal Academy's summer exhibition. The theatre, of course, and concerts of ancient music at the Hanover Square Rooms. Then there is Hatchard's bookshop, and Gunter's for tea and ices, and all the shops! Quite a giddy prospect for a country girl.'

'Yes, I expect the shopping will be irresistible. I imagine you shall acquire trunks full of new gowns, slippers, spencers, reticules and assorted feminine fripperies.'

'Oh, I dare say, as the Duke's heir, the new wardrobe *you* acquire will be far larger than mine,' she tossed back, and then laughed as Alex levelled a frown at her in warning.

'What role does the Duke play in politics?' Virgil asked. 'Is he active in Parliament? Will he expect you to support his positions, or perhaps even stand for Parliament to represent his interests?'

'He is rather active—he just returned from a meeting in the north. But since the passing of the Reform Bill eliminated most pocket boroughs, I don't think he has any intention of having me stand for Parliament.'

'Have you followed the reform movement?' Reverend Sudderfeld asked.

'Not particularly,' Alex admitted. 'I've mostly kept my head down and tried to learn how to run Edge Hall as efficiently and profitably as I could.'

'Quite interesting developments,' the Reverend said. 'I read very little about politics while I was working on my translations, but since my retirement, I've become more interested in the changes recently brought about.'

'Most of what I know concerns the bills brought forward for railroad development, since my good friend, Viscount Dellamont, has been an investor. The brother-in-law of another friend, Mr Lattimar is a reform MP.' Alex sighed. 'The current state of Parliamentary politics is another area about which I expect the Duke will shortly begin schooling me.'

'Would you like a quick summary of the major reform bills?' Reverend Sudderfeld asked.

'That would be most helpful.'

And so, for the remainder of the dinner, the Reverend outlined the various and momentous changes that had taken place in government over the last ten years, as well as the changes the reform parties were still working towards—including, Jocelyn added with a grin at him, expanding the vote to all able-bodied men and perhaps to women, too. Discussion continued as they adjourned to take tea back in the sitting room.

Once he'd drunk a cup, Reverend Sudderfeld stood. 'Like many an old man, I'm early to bed. But don't let my departure send you home, Mr Cheverton.'

'I'm not interested in brandy and cigars either, Papa,' Virgil said, standing as well, causing Alex and Jocelyn to rise in his wake. 'Would you mind, Alex, if I excused myself, too? With our departure to London looming, I'm determined to complete the next section of the translation before we leave, when I'll be forced to cease studying for a few days while we travel and settle in. Thereby completely losing my developing sense of where the passage is going! There's a reference I want to consult tonight before we get back to work tomorrow. That is,' he added, looking over at his sister, 'I'll excuse myself if Jocelyn will promise to behave and not drive you to deliver a very ducal set-down.'

After rolling her eyes at her brother, Jocelyn said, 'I think I can promise that. Goodnight, then, Papa!' After rising on tiptoe to give him a kiss on the cheek, she turned to her brother. 'I'll see you tomorrow early, Virgil.'

'Goodnight, Reverend Sudderfeld, Virgil,' Alex said. 'Thank you again for dinner. I very much enjoyed our chance to chat together.'

'Thank Jocelyn,' Virgil said as he walked his father out. 'She arranged it all. Goodnight, Alex.'

As soon as the two men left the sitting room, Alex turned to Jocelyn—and felt an immediate intensifying of the sensual tension simmering between them.

For a moment, both simply stood silently, gazing at each other.

Finally, turning her eyes away, Jocelyn motioned to Alex. 'Sit and I'll pour you one more cup of tea. Although my oblivious family didn't seem aware of the lapse, I'm sure my great-aunt would be indignant at them leaving us alone together.' She shook her head wryly. 'They still see us as an elder brother and the younger sister who harasses him, not as an unmarried gentleman and a young lady with a reputation to safeguard. But I'm afraid our casual country ways won't do once we reach London. We'd better make the most of our last opportunity tonight.'

Alex knew the opportunity he *wanted* to make the most of. As soon as the Sudderfeld gentlemen made their exit, proper conversational topics were swept from his brain by the memory of the kiss they'd shared on Trethfort Hill…followed by an eagerness to repeat it.

But it would be dishonourable to take advantage of her father's indulgence by tempting her into indiscretion—even if she had claimed to want his kisses. Beating back desire, he took the refilled cup she offered him with a sigh.

There were good reasons for society's rules requiring unmarried maidens to entertain virile young men only with a chaperon present. Although over the years he had ridden out, walked, taken tea with Jocelyn without any such guardian, after the intimacy they'd shared the day of their picnic, he now couldn't be near her without wanting to repeat that compromising gesture.

'With Papa and Virgil out of the earshot, I can admit to several more desires,' Jocelyn said.

Like when she'd admitted she wanted him to kiss

her? At the possible implications, a tingling flash of arousal raced through him.

Completely distracted, he took a gulp of tea before realising the liquid was still scalding. Gasping and coughing, he looked up to see Jocelyn looking abashed.

High colour in her cheeks, she said, 'Are you all right? You should have let the tea cool longer. And I misspoke. I should have said I have several more *intentions* about what I'd like to do in London.'

Had she misspoken? Or did being around him arouse in her the same sort of desire he was fighting to control?

'Neither Papa nor Virgil care much about riding,' she was saying, 'but I simply cannot do without it! One of my stipulations in accepting my aunt's invitation was that I must be able to ride. Which she agreed to permit, if I do so in the Park early, when there is no one of importance around to witness me galloping. Another attraction I must visit is Astley's Amphitheatre. I've read that the equestrian displays are wonderful! Though neither my family nor my great-aunt will likely be interested in accompanying me, so I shall have to drag a maid along.'

He gave an elaborate shudder. 'The London authorities should probably forbid it. Since afterwards, you will feel almost compelled to try to duplicate the stunts when you ride in the Park. Probably running down innocent bystanders in the process, if not injuring yourself by getting thrown on your head.'

'Certainly not,' she said primly. 'I shall practise the tricks very carefully.'

Alex turned his face to the ceiling. 'Heaven help us.'

After chuckling for a moment, she continued, 'Much as I am looking forward to exploring London, I am very much *not* looking forward to having to follow London society's rules. Aunt Elizabeth has already written, warning that I shall have to be much more careful about my behaviour. No walking or riding in the parks without a footman or groom accompanying me. No exploring galleries or shops or museums—or Astley's—without taking along Papa, Virgil, or some hapless maid,' she concluded with a sigh.

Before he could open his mouth, she held up a hand, 'And don't do the chivalrous thing and offer to escort me there yourself! For one, we would still have to bring a maid along, stifling conversation, and for two, you will probably be too busy learning how to be a duke to concern yourself with old friends from the country, whom Farisdeen will consider now to be socially beneath you.' Her tone now devoid of all teasing, she said quietly, 'I wouldn't want you to make a promise you might later feel guilty about not being able to keep.'

'I don't intend to let the Duke control my life completely—including choosing my friends!' he protested.

'I'm sure you are not *planning* on it. But at this point, you can't yet know what sort of demands will be placed upon you. All you can be sure of is that the change in your life will be drastic. Oh, I hope we will be able to meet in London! But I'm not counting on it—and I shall not take it as an act of faithlessness on your part if we do not see each other.'

'But I will *want* to see you,' he said, realising with a little shock just how strong that desire was.

'Will you? Then why have I had the impression, this last two weeks, that you've been deliberately avoiding me?'

Alex felt his face heat. 'I've been busy trying to accomplish everything that must be done before I can leave.'

She nodded. 'Conveniently busy.'

He blew out a sigh. 'If you must know, it's more that I've been…angry. Resenting that my life has been suddenly taken out of my control.' *And unsure, with that resentment coupled to his strong attraction to her, that he could conduct himself with suitable restraint.*

Though he certainly couldn't admit *that* to her.

She smiled sadly. 'It is hard to relinquish control. But you must move on to assume other responsibilities, as must I.'

The odd tone in her voice made alarm bells ring in his head. 'What new responsibilities? Has your aunt convinced you to find a husband during your sojourn after all?'

'She's certainly pressing for it in the letters she's written me,' Jocelyn admitted. 'Pointing out that if I delay marriage long enough to assist my brother to complete his work, by that time I might be too old for any man to find me desirable as a wife. And if that should happen, and my father were to pass and my brother marry, I would be left a dependent hanging about Virgil's household, useful only as a nursemaid to his children. Which, as you and I have discussed before, I do not want. She's strongly urging me to use this opportunity in London to find a convivial gentleman who could install me as mistress of *his* household and mother—or stepmother—to *his* children. Someone whose position in life would make taking a gentlewoman of modest dowry a more equal match.'

'And are you finding her arguments persuasive?' he asked, disturbed at the strength of his resistance to the idea of her finding someone she'd like to marry.

'Not particularly. I honestly don't think I would find it any more distasteful to marry a man for whom I feel only a tepid affection than to remain a dependent in my brother's house. In any event, I would never marry someone who would forbid me to complete Virgil's project and I really can't see any gentleman inviting my brother to join his household for however long it would take to complete the translations. And no gentleman with the means to support a wife would wish to abandon his property and come live with us at Edge Hall.'

Her face taking on a mischievous look, she leaned closer. 'Don't tell anyone,' she said in a conspiratorial whisper, 'but do you remember I told you about my plan to be become a companion? What I really hope to accomplish in London is to find some possible candidates for the role of wicked, learned older lady who could hire me. While Lady Bellingame is evaluating suitors, I shall be evaluating their widowed mothers, sisters and aunts.'

She reached out to take his teacup and set it on the tray. 'Now, I should start practising propriety and walk you out.'

'I would still wish a better fate for you than to end up an old lady's companion,' he said as he rose to follow her. Her fire, her passion, her wit devoted to some elderly curmudgeon? It would be a tragic waste!

But he didn't have anything to suggest as an alternative. The idea of her married to a man who didn't appreciate her wasn't appealing either.

'There are benefits to becoming a companion,' she was saying. 'Not only would it give me opportunities to continue my work with Virgil, I've a little money of my own, enough to keep myself in theatre tickets and fripperies, as long as I don't have to bear the whole expense of maintaining a household. I'd not have to dance to a husband's tune.' Upon reaching the entry door, she paused and turned to him. 'I might even take a lover.'

'What?' he gasped, not sure he'd heard her correctly.

'Well, probably not,' she conceded. 'Much as the idea of experiencing passion appeals, it would be too dangerous. Although I think it very unsporting that men may take lovers, with little risk. Why do they get to have all the excitement?'

'You really do say the most outrageous things,' he said, barely refraining from clapping a hand to his chest to still his galloping heart. 'A trait I'm sure your aunt will want to curb!'

'Perhaps. But what I say is also true.'

'Brutally honest,' he said wryly. 'Yes, I'm well aware of it.'

And how was he now going to pry his mind away from the image of her with a lover? A lover he could all too vividly imagine to be him?

She halted beside the entry door to hand him his hat and cane, then opened it and stepped out with him on to the flagstone steps, shivering a little in the night chill before turning to face him.

Something about the intensity of her look as she stared up at him set his desire aflame again. While he tried to rein it in, she said softly, 'I do hope we see each other in London. I wish you a safe trip and all the best. Goodbye...my dear friend.'

With another sad little smile, she turned to go back inside. But as he hesitated, his chest tight at the bittersweet image of her walking away from him, she whirled around.

Before he realised what she was about, she rose up on tiptoe, seized his neck to pull his face down to hers, and kissed him.

After a moment of shocked immobility, the burn-ingly sweet, soft brush of her lips sent a surge of sensation through him, making him dizzy and firing his need for more. Despite knowing they stood just outside the open doorway where any servant walking into the front hall might see them, his hands rose to her shoulders to hold her in place while he deepened the kiss, sliding his tongue against the seam of her lips until she opened for him.

He had one, thrilling taste of her mouth before she pushed him away and stumbled backward. 'G-Good-bye, Alex.'

With that, putting a hand to her lips, she ran through the doorway and closed the portal after her.

For a moment he stood numbly, staring at the oak panels while his heartbeat thundered and desire thrummed in his blood.

Jocelyn, taking a lover. Right now, he wanted that lover to be him.

But that couldn't happen. It must not happen.

If he saw her again in London, it could only be as her 'dear friend'.

Slamming his mind shut against anything more, he turned and walked into the darkness in the direction of Edge Hall.

Chapter Nine

In the afternoon three weeks later, Jocelyn entered the Statue Gallery at the British Museum. Her father and Virgil were still in the reading room, studying tracings of the Rosetta Stone the curator had allowed them to make, excitedly cataloguing the comparisons of the ancient Greek to the hieroglyphic symbols. She'd worked with them for several hours, until, her interest not matching their level of fascination, she decided to walk a bit and stretch her legs.

Fortunately, the museum would soon close for the afternoon, forcing them to abandon their study. Until then, she would wander again through Charles Townley's collection of classical sculptures.

One's eye could not help being immediately drawn to the life-size figure of Venus. The voluptuous, half-naked female figure, her braided hair pinned up to better display her nude breasts and torso, posed with one arm catching up the drapery at her waist, the other arm raised.

Beckoning to a lover? Jocelyn wondered. She certainly couldn't have been waving in dinner guests in that state of undress.

Jocelyn chuckled, thinking again how fortunate it was that Aunt Elizabeth had no interest in ancient art. She'd be scandalised if she realised the nude or semi-nude condition of many of the statues and would certainly consider them unfit to be viewed by a virginal maiden.

And perhaps they shouldn't be, Jocelyn admitted. One could not help being affected by the erotic appeal of woman's gesture, which reminded her of her attraction to Alex…and the delicious, forbidden delight of the farewell kiss she'd shocked them both by impulsively giving him.

The intimate caress of his tongue against hers had triggered such a powerful response, she'd almost forgotten where they were. Fortunately, before she completely lost her senses and urged him to even greater madness, a panicked caution had forced itself through her sensual haze, prompting her to break away from him and flee to safety.

Safety from her own desires, more than from his, she acknowledged with a rueful sigh.

Reckless as it had been, she wouldn't regret it. That kiss might well turn out to be her very last memory of their time together.

Turning away from the Venus, she wandered down the gallery, past the statue of the boys playing knuckle-bone, to pause by the bust of Clytie that had arrested her attention the first time she'd entered the gallery. What had caused the look of pensive sadness the sculptor had captured on the woman's face? Had she, too, longed for a man she could never have?

Much as she'd told herself not to count too much upon the promise Alex had given before they'd left Edge Hall that he would call on her aunt in London, she couldn't deny how disappointed she was that he had not. The possibility of extending their friendship for a while longer in London now looked remote.

As Jocelyn had hoped would not be the case but had feared would be, she had seen nothing of Alex since their arrival in the city. She'd read in the papers the Duke's announcement about his new heir, which had followed closely after the black-bordered notice of Penlowe's death. She knew when Alex had taken up residence in Grosvenor Square, had skimmed some accounts in the paper about private dinner parties and soirées at which he'd been present.

For the first two weeks after his arrival in town, she'd listened breathlessly each time Aunt Elizabeth's butler walked in to announce afternoon callers.

And there had been many. None of them was Alex Cheverton.

Each disappointment caused another dull pang in her heart. But perhaps not seeing him was for the best. Her affection for Alex Cheverton was the lingering remains of a youthful infatuation. Once she no longer saw him almost daily, her memories of their times together, and the feelings he aroused in her, would fade. As the things of childhood always do. She would leave those happy girlhood memories behind, and no longer distracted by the hold he seemed to have over her, she could devote all her energy to securing her future as a scholar.

Somehow, she couldn't quite convince herself of that heartening conclusion.

Frustrated and distracted, she'd just stopped herself before she ran her fingers along the sculpted lady's marble hair—a grave breach of museum rules—when a voice at her ear made her jump.

'Where else might I have thought to find you, except among classical statuary?'

She whirled around, her heartbeat accelerating so quickly she felt dizzy—while a foolish joy fizzed in her heart like champagne uncorked.

'Alex!' she gasped. 'Of—of course I'd be visiting here! But why are *you* here? And how are you?'

She could scarcely bear to look at him, smiling at her—his golden-brown hair swept back, laughter in those deep green eyes, his tall, muscular form in his fashionable tight jacket and trousers looking so handsome, it was all she could do not to throw her arms around him and kiss him again on the spot.

While she struggled to control herself and recover proper decorum, he was looking around the gallery, eyebrows raised. 'I assume your brother must have accompanied you, though I don't see him. I can hardly believe your great-aunt would have permitted you to view such shocking sculptures. Indeed, I blush to stand beside you in the same room with them.'

'I see just how embarrassed you appear,' she said drily. 'More likely, you're evaluating whether or not you can afford to purchase the Venus to decorate your new accommodations in the Duke's town house.'

He laughed. 'It would make a wonderful addition! Sadly, I won't have the funds to back a purchase of that magnitude until I truly inherit.'

'You are right, though,' Jocelyn granted, too effervescent with delight at being with him to continue their normal teasing. 'Neither Papa nor Virgil, both of whom are in the reading room comparing the Rosetta Stone's Greek inscription to the hieroglyphics, seem to have any notion of how scandalised my aunt would be if she knew what I was viewing. I only hope none of her friends is more informed about the contents of the Townley collection than she is! Should anyone enlighten her, she'd probably forbid my returning to the Museum, and it is such a fascinating place! But how are you? What have you been up to? And what brings you here today?'

'I'm about as well as can be expected. The Duke has set up a regimen of meetings, study and social gatherings, which, as you predicted with such accuracy, demand almost every moment of my time. Occasionally, though, I reach the point where I have had about all I can stand. So here you see me, escaping from an afternoon call on one of the Duke's oldest friends...who just happens to have a far too interested maiden daughter of suitable birth and dowry. A nice girl, but one who doesn't attract me in the slightest.'

While that predictable but none the less distasteful scenario momentarily robbed her of any suitable reply, Alex continued, 'Speaking of which, can we go into a different gallery? Should some society matron wander in here and see us alone together in such scandalous company—' he gestured to the half-naked statue '—she'd rush back to report to your aunt that you'd been compromised.'

'We can't have that!' Jocelyn replied with a shudder. 'Follow me.'

Not that the Duke would ever allow Alex to marry her, she thought as they walked out of the gallery, even if some beldame decided she'd been compromised. But she wouldn't want either of them to have to endure the unpleasantness that would undoubtedly ensue, should some hysterical matron bring an account of their meeting to her aunt. Nor would she want to stir up a scandal that would distress that lady, who had been nothing but kind to her.

'Unlikely as it is that any society matron would appear at the British Museum to discover us, we should be quite safe in the Bird Gallery. No shocking nakedness here—the displays are well covered with feathers.'

Alex halted in the middle of the gallery and gazed around with interest. 'Some of the specimens are fascinating!'

'Yes, and there's such a wide range of shapes and sizes. The Egyptian ibis and the bird of paradise and their nests are huge. But my favourite is over here—this tiny bird with the iridescent red throat. A hummingbird, from the Americas.'

Alex followed her over and peered at it. 'The nest is hardly bigger than the tip of my finger.'

'I've read that the bird beats its wings so fast, it can hover in one place without moving. That the rapid movements make the air around it vibrate until it hums—hence the name.'

'And I thought you interested only in antiquities.'

'Oh, no! I'm interested in everything...that's interesting. So, you escaped your afternoon call with the attentive, eminently suitable daughter. Will the Duke take you to task for your desertion?'

'No, because he escaped before I did.' Shaking his head, Alex gave a rueful laugh. 'I had expected that our being in mourning would restrict our society appearances sufficiently that I wouldn't be faced with many occasions at which I needed to avoid determined feminine pursuit.'

'And that has not been the case?' she asked...curious despite not really wanting to know the answer.

Alex shuddered. 'Alas, no! I would never have imagined that salons and music rooms contained so many secluded corners and dark alcoves one must be careful to avoid. To say nothing of leafy trails in the Park.'

'Ah, the terrible burden of being the most desirable bachelor in London.'

'It's not kind of you to make sport,' he said loftily. 'It *is* a burden.'

'I have no doubt.' She looked him up and down. 'Having to endure being dressed in the latest twig of fashion, too. Insupportable!'

He returned the favour, inspecting her as well. 'I wouldn't scorn too much. You're looking quite fashionable yourself. And quite lovely!'

The genuine admiration on his face forestalled the tart reply she'd intended. Bittersweet longing filling her—along with that insidious desire to kiss him again—she fumbled for words, finally managing a feeble, 'Thank you.'

To her indignation, Alex chuckled. 'Had I known a simple compliment would rob you of a sharp reply, I would have tried it years ago. Think how many scathing remarks I would have been spared!'

'Trust you to be charming only to disarm me!' she volleyed back. 'I'll not let myself be sidetracked again!'

'It wasn't all tactics. You do look lovely—rivalling the dashing hummingbird in your fine new feathers. So, tell me what you've been doing. Has Lady Bellingame had you out dazzling young men?'

Smiling, she shook her head. 'In spite of the fine feathers, I haven't the dowry to "dazzle" anyone. In addition to which, I'm already long enough in the tooth not to be a prime attraction.'

'Long in the tooth! What, at—twenty?'

'Two-and-twenty, if you must make me confess. Even my aunt expects I'm more likely to catch the eye of some older widower who needs a manager for his household and a supervisor for his children than a dashing younger gentleman just now ready to set up his nursery.'

'My, that sounds depressing! Surely she expects better than a doddering old man who needs you to help him don his slippers.'

'There have been a few younger than that. An Oxford scholar, although I think he was really more interested in meeting Virgil so he might talk with him about translation.' She laughed. 'One or two younger sons with little to live on have found my modest dowry attractive. Even to the point of expressing admiration for my "scholarship", although any attempt to discuss the subject soon shows they have no knowledge of ancient Greek dramatists whatsoever. Indeed, continuing to discuss it generally results in a lessening of their initial enthusiasm for my company. I suspect, even to obtain funds to live on, most needy gentlemen would prefer a wife who possesses greater competence at playing the pianoforte or embroidering seat cushions than at intellectual pursuits.'

'And have you had occasion to display your improved ability at piano?'

'Yes, we've attended several musical soirées. My aunt was quite proud of me, I'll have you know. I believe even you would have approved of my performance.'

Her teasing smile faded as his gaze once again captured hers—and held it.

'I wish I could have been present. And I do apologise for not having called on you.'

Fighting the attraction that drew her to him, she forced herself to look away. 'No need to apologise. I wasn't really expecting to see you. I knew you would be…occupied by the Duke.'

He gave a sigh. 'I am, that. Much as I would never have chosen to be placed where I am, I'm still conscious of the responsibility—and the duty. The Duke isn't by nature warm or outgoing, but he is making as much of an effort as someone of his disposition can to make me feel welcome. Naturally, he wants to train me to perform the role I must one day fulfil so that I can uphold the honour of the family. But he also, I think, wants to familiarise me with what I must do so that, when the time comes, I am comfortable performing those duties, rather than being completely out of my depth. Which is how I feel now more often than I'd like.'

'Not with ambitious mamas and designing daughters, I would imagine. But with politicians and statesmen?' she guessed.

'Yes. I'd hardly even read about Parliament before and now I'm included in meetings with the Cabinet and prominent Whig and Tory legislators from both the Lords and the House. It's…humbling.'

'And exciting, I would think. What a chance you will have to affect, not just the welfare of the residents on one great estate, but the citizens of the entire nation!'

'Exactly. So I'm working hard to learn what I must… even if most of it doesn't appeal to me.' He gave a wry laugh. 'I'm not sure which is worse—the long looks down aristocratic noses by some of the high-ranking who don't think I'm worthy of the place I will some day occupy, or the blatant toad-eating of some of the lower-ranking who want to ingratiate themselves with a future duke.'

'I can only imagine!'

He walked a few paces away, then turned back to her. 'Meeting you today, having this conversation—it's such a contrast to what I escaped in that fashionable Mayfair drawing room, to what I have to deal with every day! It makes me realise how long it's been since I've spent time with someone who knows and wants to be with, not the "future Duke", but *me*. How I've missed that! How I've missed *you*. I will call on your aunt, Jocelyn.'

Impulsively, before her brain could warn her such a gesture wasn't wise, she touched her finger to his lips. 'You shouldn't make promises you can't keep.'

He brought a hand up to hold her finger in place and kissed it before releasing it. 'I will keep this one. That is, you're not too angry at my neglect? You will permit me to call?'

She stood mutely, dazzled by sensations created by that simple kiss to her fingertip. Before his surprise appearance in the gallery, she'd almost convinced herself it was just as well that she hadn't seen him in London. That it would be better for each of them to continue separately along their divergent paths.

Allowing him to call would mean stretching out the delight and anguish of spending time in his company. Knowing full well the painful sense of loss she would suffer when, sooner or later, he was fully caught up in his new world and their association ended.

But she just couldn't bring herself to deny him.

'Of course you may call,' she replied at last.

'You took so long to answer, I was afraid you were going to refuse!' he said, unmistakable relief on his face. 'I see I *have* offended you. I shall do my best to make up for it! I can't predict how often I will be able to get away, but I assure you I will make every effort. That said, which days are you and your aunt at home?'

'Lady Bellingame receives on Tuesdays and Thursdays.'

'The museum is about to close, isn't it? I would invite

you and your father and brother to take tea right now, but I have this blasted meeting with the Duke and his solicitor. I'll already need to hurry, or I shall be late.'

'You must go straight away, then.'

'I'm afraid I must. But I will call!'

'I'll be happy to see you if you do. Papa and Virgil, too.'

This time, he grabbed her hand and kissed it. The brush of his lips against her gloved knuckles sent a tingle rippling all the way through her.

'I'm so glad I chanced upon you today! I will see you again soon. I promise.'

With that, he gave her a quick bow and paced out of the gallery.

Jocelyn stood where he'd left her, gazing down at her still-tingling fingers.

She truly was an idiot. It would be much better for her to turn her back on that girlhood attachment now, trust time and distance to make it fade and set her gaze firmly towards the future. While her family remained in London, she should use her aunt's extensive contacts to broaden her acquaintance and hopefully discover a genial old lady for whom she might one day become a companion.

She had no trouble envisaging herself accompanying some feisty octogenarian. But she couldn't see herself as a helpmate—or lover—to any man but Alex Cheverton. Even once she did wean herself of her *tendre* for him.

pecially when accompanied by a gentleman, who can make sure the pace is not too violent for her.'

His eyes widening in surprise, Alex raised an eyebrow at her, to which she responded with a little shrug.

Apparently her aunt had schooled her to be much more polite with her gentleman callers than she'd ever been to him. But—surely she wasn't looking to encourage men with whom, based on what he'd just observed, she could have little in common!

Hoping her aunt wasn't wearing down her resistance to the idea of marrying to secure her future, Alex subjected each man to a closer scrutiny.

Reverend Singleton was the younger of the two, a pleasant-looking man, though the way he spoke and carried himself seemed a bit self-important. Oglesby, with a touch of grey silvering his temples, seemed dignified and perfectly genteel—if a bit crassly concerned with replacing a wife who'd neglected her duty by dying and leaving him with a house and children that needed tending.

But both seemed entirely...ordinary. Alex decided that he didn't much like either of them, nor were they anywhere close to being Jocelyn's intellectual equals. Either of them would bore her in a week.

The mantel clock bonged as he reached that conclusion, prompting both gentlemen to rise. 'Delightful as it is to speak with you, I must be off,' Reverend Singleton said. 'I shall see you tonight at the Wendlefords' ball?'

Jocelyn nodded. 'I believe my aunt plans for us to be present.'

'I'm afraid I must take my leave as well,' Oglesby said. 'Would that it were polite to linger in such charming company, but the rules of an afternoon call must

Chapter Ten

Two days later, at the beginning of afternoon calling hours, Alex strode up to the door of Lady Bellingame's town house in Upper Brook Street. After being admitted by the butler, he was led to the first-floor reception room and his name announced.

As he lingered on the threshold, Jocelyn looked up. The warmth of the smile that sprang to her lips when she saw him made up for having to suffer the Duke's annoyance when Alex informed him he'd rearranged the schedule set out for him today so he might call on 'a friend of long standing'.

'Any "friend of long standing" worthy of being seen,' the Duke had replied frostily, 'should already be on the list my secretary has compiled of calls to be paid or entertainments to be attended.'

To which Alex had responded evenly, 'I am making every effort to accommodate your plans for me. But I do not intend to cut all my former friends, even if some are not of a rank to mingle in the same circles as a future duke.'

He'd then bowed—and left. Setting down the first marker, he hoped, to let the Duke know that though he was willing to be instructed, he was not prepared to abandon everything and everyone from his previous life which did not meet ducal standards.

Several other people were already present in Lady Bellingame's parlour, none of whom he knew. After he'd paid his respects to his hostess, who greeted him with a surprising lack of enthusiasm, Jocelyn presented him to the other guests, three older ladies who were friends of her aunt, and two gentlemen.

After an exchange of courtesies, the older ladies resumed their conversation with Lady Bellingame, while Jocelyn motioned Alex to a chair beside the other men.

'Reverend Singleton is just back to London after receiving the gift of a living in Bexton from Lord Manwaring, husband of Lady Bellingame's good friend, Lady Manwaring,' Jocelyn told Alex. 'He was acquainted with Virgil at Oxford, though a few years ahead of him. Mr Oglesby, the nephew of my aunt's friend Mrs Charles Robeson, is returning to town after a period of mourning following the loss of his wife.'

'Please to meet you, Reverend, and my condolences, Mr Oglesby. It must have been a very heavy blow.'

'Yes, and especially hard for my three dear children. But…one must go on living, eh? No matter how heavy one's heart.'

'Especially when one has a household to maintain and children to care for,' Jocelyn inserted, with a significant look at Alex.

Oglesby must be the widower Lady Bellingame was cultivating for Jocelyn, Alex thought.

'I was just asking these gentlemen if they like to ride. Since Lady Bellingame does not care for it, she keeps only carriage horses in town, but I've found an excellent livery stable where I've been able to hire a mount.'

'A docile, well-mannered mare to ride during the Promenade Hour, if you don't wish to accompany your aunt in her carriage, would be an excellent, genteel exercise,' Reverend Singleton said.

Mr Oglesby shook his head. 'I don't agree. It's much too crowded for a lady to be on horseback—there, or in any area of London, really. Miss Sudderfeld would do better to refrain from riding while she is in town.'

His lips twitching in amusement at the image of Jocelyn tamely walking her mount through a throng of slow-moving carriages, pedestrians and riders, Alex said, 'I very much doubt that Miss Sudderfeld wishes to ride during the Promenade Hour in any event.'

'Quite true,' she confirmed. 'I only ride early in the morning. One cannot gallop with all those people about and why ride unless one can have a good gallop?'

Mr Oglesby frowned. 'I am surprised your aunt permits such a thing, Miss Sudderfeld. Galloping about the Park? Even in the morning, there may be nursemaids with their charges, or other riders about. It's not at all safe.'

'I must agree, Miss Sudderfeld,' the Reverend said. 'Regardless of your location, I recommend confinin[g] yourself to nothing faster than a trot. One never kno[ws] what one might encounter around the next bend! Rid[ing] in a carriage driven by an experienced coachma[n] much better way for a lady to take the air.'

Hardly able to hide his smile at such nonsen[se] waited with anticipation for Jocelyn to take the[m] for their timidity.

Though she winced—and he was almos[t] nearly rolled her eyes—she replied instead pose for most ladies carriage rides are v

'Indeed,' the Reverend replied ap

be respected. I shan't be at the Wendlefords' ball, but I trust you will be attending Lady Southford's musicale.'

'If Lady Bellingame brings me.' After rising to curtsy to their bows, she walked them to the door. 'It was kind of both of you to stop by.'

'I shall look forward to having the pleasure of your company again soon,' Singleton said.

'As will I,' Oglesby echoed.

Then, as Alex had hoped, Jocelyn walked back to pause beside the ladies gathered around Lady Bellingame. 'Excuse me for interrupting your discussion, Aunt Bellingame. It's such a lovely afternoon, with your permission, I should like to show Mr Cheverton the garden, which is looking quite fine with the daffodils just coming on. Ladies, as my aunt may have told you, Mr Cheverton is a friend from childhood. I haven't yet had a chance to catch up on all his news since he came to town. Mary can walk with us, of course.'

Lady Bellingame frowned. Afraid her charge might miss seeing some other gentlemen callers if she went off with him? Alex wondered.

But apparently unable to come up with a valid reason to refuse the request, at length, she nodded. 'I suppose it will be all right, as long as Mary accompanies you.'

'Thank you, Aunt. We won't be long. I'm sure Mr Cheverton's time is limited, and he will want to stop by and see Papa and Virgil before he must set off. Mr Cheverton, if you'll have Phillips return your hat, cane and overcoat, I'll meet you by the door to the garden.'

'Thanks for arranging that,' Alex murmured as they walked out of the drawing room. 'I don't imagine we'd have managed much useful conversation around those sharp-eyed observers.'

Jocelyn chuckled. 'More like *they* wouldn't have

managed any—being far too interested in trying to overhear ours. I'll just be a minute. I must send Mary down and fetch my pelisse.'

A few minutes later, having reclaimed and donned his outer garments, as Alex waited by the garden door, a young maid scurried down the hall towards him and halted with a curtsy. 'I'm Mary, sir. Miss Sudderfeld said to tell you she'd be right down.'

Alex produced a coin from his pocket and flipped it to the girl. 'Do you think you can protect your mistress…while loitering far enough behind us that we can have a private chat?'

After tucking away the coin, the girl nodded. 'That I can, sir. Not kissing far, of course, but conversing far,' she assured him with a saucy look.

Alex was still chuckling when Jocelyn joined him. 'I'm so pleased you stopped by!' she said as he opened the door and led her out into the sunny, chilly March air. 'Afternoon calls are the dullest things! But I try to be dutiful and endure them, for my aunt's sake. She has been making quite an effort to introduce me to everyone of her acquaintance and see that we are invited to about as many balls, routs, musicales and soirées as I can stand.'

'As well as introducing you to eligible gentlemen?'

Jocelyn sighed. 'She does try.'

'I have to admit, I'm impressed by your restraint. I thought for sure you were going to lambast that sorry duo for suggesting you limit yourself to carriage rides and the tamest of trots.'

'But as you noticed, out of respect for Aunt Bellingame, I refrained. You see, I can behave with decorum.'

'When you want to.'

She chuckled. 'Very well, when I want to. Speaking of decorum, how did you manage to escape the traces today? Is the Duke out of town or closeted in Parliament?'

'No. But this afternoon's schedule didn't include anything that could not be done at some later time, so I told him I was going to call on a friend.'

'If you said on whom, he probably didn't like that.'

'I didn't identify the friend,' he admitted. 'But I did say I had no intention of giving up all the people from my former life who were not part of his, or his late heir's, social circle.'

'Oh, my! Throwing down the gauntlet? How did he take that declaration of independence?'

'I didn't stay to find out. I simply bowed and left.'

'To face retribution later? Perhaps I should have Phillips bring the port bottle in when you stop to see Papa and Virgil!'

'The port would be welcome, but I don't know that there will be retribution. After all, I'm doing everything he is asking of me. It wasn't a bad idea to take this opportunity to make it clear that, cognisant as I am of my responsibility to him and the family, I don't intend to blindly follow his views on everything. Without being contrary, I will remain true to myself and my friends. Besides, what can he do to me? When it comes right down to it, unless he marries again and breeds another heir, I will inherit whether he's happy with me or not.'

'Bold words!'

'Ones I intend to adhere to. But speaking of being happy with me—have I done something to offend your aunt? Her greeting was frosty enough I was wishing I'd worn my topcoat into the parlour and she was certainly not enthused about the idea of you walking with me—even with the attentive Mary trailing us.'

'That's because she believes my seeing you is a waste of valuable time. In fact, she scolded me when I told her you intended to call.'

'A duke's heir isn't good enough for the great-niece of a viscountess?' Alex asked incredulously.

'Quite the opposite, actually. Since the Duke would never consider the daughter of his librarian good enough for his heir, spending time with you takes me away from charming more attainable gentlemen who might actually consider marrying me. And attention from you might scare away gentlemen of lesser importance, who believe what they have to offer couldn't compete with the temptation of becoming a duchess.'

'Men like Singleton and Oglesby? "Riding in a carriage is a much better way for a lady to take the air,"' he quoted, his high-pitched version of Singleton's patronising tone making her smile. 'Surely you wouldn't consider either of them!'

'My aunt is very fond of Mr Oglesby. He's the nephew of her good friend, and I think she considers him my most promising prospect.'

'But are *you* fond of him?' he pressed.

'"Galloping about the Park? Why, Miss Sudderfeld, it's simply not safe!"' she mimicked and burst out laughing.

Relieved, Alex laughed, too. 'Thank goodness! If you'd confessed to developing feelings for either of them, I'd have to conclude that the London air had addled your brain.'

'It wasn't good of me to make fun of Mr Oglesby—although I can't like him at all. If it weren't almost sacrilegious, I'd suspect his late wife died just to get away from him, although I'm sure she wouldn't have wanted to leave her children. '

Laughing again, he shook a finger at her. 'You do say the most outrageous things. Utter a statement like that in your aunt's parlour and she'd probably send you back to Edge Hall.'

'Yes, which is why I refrain. I must force myself to endure at least a month or two of this, by which time she should feel she's done her duty by me and can with good conscience leave me to my single fate. If I'm truly lucky, before then I shall have made the acquaintance of several potential employers. Though I've not had much luck so far. The matrons I've met are all her good friends, which means they too are all much more interested in gossip and fashion than in intellectual pursuits.'

'So you still intend to end your London days single.'

She nodded. 'Unless I meet a gentleman a great deal more exceptional than the ones I've thus far encountered. Over the course of several meetings with those two gentlemen, I have been able to discern hardly a particle of humour in either of them and not much intellect. I couldn't live with a humourless soul, nor with one who was always asking me what I meant. It's bad of me, but I often speak with irony, which invariably goes right over their heads.'

'Like when you agreed with Oglesby that a man mustn't let a grieving heart hold him back when he has a household to maintain and children to tend?'

'Exactly.'

'I'm relieved to see you are standing firm about not being forced into marriage with just…anyone.'

She looked up at him, all teasing gone from her expression. 'I could never settle for just…anyone,' she murmured as she gazed into his eyes.

The sudden intensification of the pull between them had him wanting to step closer and take her in his arms—until he remembered the maid. Who wouldn't be trailing 'kissing far' enough behind them.

Still locked in his gaze, Jocelyn seemed about to say something more—but then looked away. 'We should probably go back to the house,' she said, her tone now impersonal. 'You can't have much time left and Papa and Virgil would be so disappointed if you left without seeing them. But I am pleased we had a chance to talk today.'

She turned to head back to the house, perforce requiring him to turn back, too. Ending their already limited private time together.

He wanted to linger in the garden with her. Well, he really wanted to kiss her again—but that wouldn't be honourable, even without the maid's inhibiting presence.

No gentleman repeatedly kissed a maiden unless he intended to wed her—and that was impossible. He needed to make a suitable match and Jocelyn didn't want to make a match at all.

No matter how hotly the physical spark burned between them.

Still, though she might not be suitable as a wife, he wasn't yet ready to give up their friendship.

'When do you return to the British Museum?'

She halted, looking over at him curiously. 'We usually go Monday mornings and Friday afternoons.'

Alex did a rapid mental review of his schedule. 'I'll look for you there Friday afternoon.'

She smiled. 'So as to avoid my aunt's frosty drawing room?'

He nodded. 'And meet in a place where we can have a conversation without the annoyance of a trailing maid.'

She nodded, that beautiful smile returning to light her face and buoy his spirits. 'We'll look at the Elgin Marbles. You haven't seen them yet, have you?'

'Not yet.'

'You must, then! They are magnificent.'

So are you, he thought. *And if you were a duke's daughter...*

Alarmed, he pushed that thought from his head. He could never marry Jocelyn! Even if she were of proper rank, he sensed she might be able to arouse emotions that could be as difficult to control as his response to her physical appeal.

They would remain friends, just friends. And he would follow his initial intention to choose a conventional bride who didn't possess the ability to arouse in him any turbulent, unsettling responses.

They reached the house, the maid scurrying up to open the door for them.

'You can go back upstairs, now, Mary,' Jocelyn told the maid as they walked into the hall.

'Very well, miss,' the maid said, bobbing them a curtsy—before throwing Alex a pert glance. 'And thank you, sir.'

Angling her head, Jocelyn looked up at him with curiosity. '"Thank you, sir"? What was that about?'

'You don't want to know. Let's just say your maid is...bribable.'

'How naughty of you!' Jocelyn said with a laugh. 'But useful information I shall keep in mind, in case I should need to use it. I'll show you to the back study, where Papa and Virgil work. Then I'm afraid I must

return to the drawing room and attend my aunt for another hour at least.'

'I hope you will have more interesting callers.'

'So do I. But I'm not counting on it. Well, here we
are. Goodbye, Alex. Thanks again for calling.'

'My pleasure. And I'll see you again—soon.'

Nodding as though she didn't quite believe him, she
rapped on a door, then opened it. 'Papa, Virgil, look
who's come to pay a visit!' Waving him in, she stepped
aside to allow him to enter, then turned and walked
away down the hallway.

Yes, entertain more interesting company, he thought
as he watched her walk away. But not too much more
interesting. Not interesting enough to change your mind
about wedding to secure your place in society.

As depressing as it was to imagine her wasting her
wit and warmth on some elderly widow, he found it even
more distasteful to envisage her married to one of her
aunt's 'suitable' gentlemen.

Chapter Eleven

The following Friday, Jocelyn once again accompanied her father and brother to the British Museum. After making sure they were comfortably settled in the reading room, their Rosetta Stone material retrieved from the museum official to whom they'd entrusted it, Jocelyn told them she wanted to stroll about and investigate more of the museum's fascinating displays.

Which was true. But her main reason for leaving them was a restlessness she simply couldn't contain—at least, not while studying the Rosetta Stone. The intricacies of Greek drama could still fully engage her, but the priestly praises of the pharaoh inscribed in the stone's trilingual passages were too stylised to hold her attention—especially when she was distracted by wondering whether Alex would in fact meet her.

Would he be able to get away? She was torn between hoping he would and hoping he wouldn't.

If he did, it would mean he felt continuing their friendship was important enough to risk annoying the Duke by juggling his obligations. Continuing their relationship would be a joy—but also a promise of future pain. For seeing him was as unfair to her realistic prospects as her aunt contended. Compared to him, men like Singleton and Oglesby forfeited whatever limited appeal they might possess—and she was afraid they were not the only London gentlemen who would suffer by comparison to Edge Hall's former estate manager. When Alex was in the room, it was hard for her to pay attention to anyone else, a struggle to continue politely conversing with anyone else, when all she wanted was to talk and walk with him.

All right, and kiss him, too. It was fortunate that her aunt insisted on her bringing along a maid, which was probably the only reason she'd been able to restrain herself in the garden—especially when he gazed into her eyes with an intensity that hinted he might want to kiss her again, too.

Since she'd been accompanied to the museum by her family, there would be no maid to watch over her today. She'd have to rely on these august surroundings to restrain her. August surroundings whose beautifully sculpted nude figures also made her long to explore the strong body hidden beneath Alex's clothing.

Just the thought of running her fingers down his bare torso made her breath catch.

But would he appear?

If he didn't, it would indicate either that it was too difficult for him to adjust his schedule—or that his interest in continuing their relationship wasn't great enough to offset the friction it was likely to cause in his dealings with the Duke. In which case, she should begin immediately her campaign to forget him.

She hoped she wouldn't have to.

Which just showed how truly foolish she was.

Sighing with exasperation, she halted. If he did come, she didn't want him to find her pining away in the Parthenon Marbles gallery, pathetic as the lovesick maid back at Edge Hall. Even though her dithering over him showed she *was* almost that pathetic.

She'd go somewhere else in the museum. Maybe to visit her hummingbird. That brilliant bit of flying magic would lift her spirits.

Decision made, she headed off for the gallery displaying the birds, passing all the larger and more imposing specimens to search out the tiny North American dweller. She smiled again as she saw it, angled her head this way and that to catch the way the light played over the brilliant, iridescent feathers at the creature's throat.

What a busy little thing it must have been to be able to hover and then dart away in any direction it liked. Would that women could control their movements so completely! So often, their direction in life and their ability to change it depended on the permission of some man—father, brother, husband. Like this small, now lifeless bird, they were trapped in conventional roles, pretty objects for a man to display.

Would that be one boon, once she weaned herself from her feelings for Alex? Regaining her tranquillity, as well a measure of independence in determining whether she remained at Edge Hall or ended up somewhere else as a companion, once the translation project was completed? Allowing her the freedom to pursue other projects on her own, if Virgil didn't wish to continue with her? Virgil had said to her how concerned he was for his reputation if her involvement was ever revealed.

Such a worthy end would be worth mastering once and for all her childish emotional links to the past, wouldn't it?

She heard footsteps and her breath caught. By the cadence of the walk, she knew it was Alex.

She turned around, her spirits rising in rush of excitement, a smile coming unbidden to her lips like the foolish maid she ought not to be. As he approached, she simply stood there, drinking in the sight of him.

'Communing with your hummingbird?' he asked as he halted beside her.

She nodded. 'It's such a delicate and fascinating creature.'

'I have to admit I'm drawn to delicate, fascinating creatures myself.'

Surely he didn't mean her, Jocelyn thought, flustered by the possibility. She was much more accustomed to insults than compliments from him.

Pulling herself together, she said, 'If you are drawn to beauty, prepare to be awed. Are you ready to view the Parthenon Marbles?'

'In your company, I'm ready for anything—since one never knows what you might do.'

That was more in the usual vein of their exchanges. Grinning, she said, 'You may be easy. I shall not alarm the staff or embarrass you by suddenly deciding to ride the statue of a satyr or scale one of the columns.'

'I am relieved.'

'After all, I'm not dressed for it. I should have to be in breeches.' A laughing Alex beside her, she led him towards the gallery housing the famous Greek marbles.

A few minutes later, they entered the darkened space where the sculpted figures were set up on a long pedestal. Above them along the walls, about six feet from the ground, were displayed the panels from the frieze that had been inside the temple, and above that, the metopes that had run above the architrave of the temple's exterior.

'So, what am I looking at?' Alex asked, gesturing towards the sculptures on the platform.

'Aside from some of the most magnificent figures ever created?'

'Well, you have to admit it is rather more difficult to appreciate when none of them have heads—save that one gentleman.'

'The figures were designed to fit the triangular space of the pediments of the temple's two exterior ends, which means the central figures were standing, with figures seated or reclining as the space narrowed to the edges. The scene portrayed here is the birth of Athena, who is your central figure,' she explained, pointing. 'Descriptions from the second century tell us a now missing Zeus would have been standing to her left, with a vanished statue of Hephaistos, the blacksmith, to her right. Do you remember your mythology?'

'Only vaguely,' he admitted.

'The blacksmith used his axe to split open Zeus's head and allow Athena to be born. Like men for time eternal, Zeus tried to prevent the emergence of an intelligent woman, fearing her wisdom might exceed his.'

'Since she *was* the goddess of wisdom, his prediction was correct.'

'Oh, that we had axes to use on the heads of recalcitrant men today!' Jocelyn retorted. 'We're not quite sure who the figures are, seated on the chests, but the lucky fellow reclining there, the only one to have retained his head, is Dionysus, god of wine.'

Lounging there, arrogantly confident in his nudity, making her even more conscious of the virile man be-

side her. Did Alex feel it too, this spark and crackle of attraction between them?

Not daring to look in his eyes, she forced her thoughts back to scholarship. 'Dionysus, perceptive individual that he is, appears to be happily celebrating the birth of the goddess of wisdom. Perhaps that is why he still has his head.'

'Perceptive, indeed. Or at least thirsty.'

Ignoring that, Jocelyn continued, 'On the other side, we have three female figures. Once again, we're not sure who they are, although some believe the lady coyly showing her bare shoulder is Aphrodite. The narrowest spaces at the two points of the triangle displayed the chariots of Helios on the far left, bringing in the sun, and Selene, goddess of the moon, on the far right. The "dawn" horses are somewhat damaged, but one of my favourite pieces,' she continued, walking over to it, 'is the head of Selene's horse—weary after having pulled the sun through the sky all day. Is he not magnificent?'

Alex stood, studying the piece. 'What incredible skill the sculptor possessed! One could almost imagine the beast snorting and trotting away.'

'Indeed! Although the building was completed in such an incredibly short time, they must have had many sculptors working simultaneously, I like to think that Phidias, the master himself, carved this horse.' Turning to look up at Alex, she smiled. 'I have to admit, were he a complete statue and not just a head, I *would* be tempted to ride him.'

Alex shook his head. 'Thank heaven he's a fragment! Now, what is going on in the large pieces along the wall?'

'The low-relief carvings are from the frieze that was inside the temple. It shows a procession that was made once every four years in which the ancient wooden figure of Athena housed in another acropolis temple, the Erechtheion, was given a new woven garment. I love these panels! Such an intimate view into the life of a long-disappeared people! From gods seated on stools, to officials, to musicians, to judges holding olive branches, boys carrying trays of refreshments, more wonderful horses and horsemen—and a most impressive bull!' she said, pointing out the animal. 'The hairstyles of the men and women, the beautiful folds of the draperies... one can almost hear the trumpets and cymbals, smell the roasted meats.'

He smiled at her enthusiasm. 'A glimpse into an ancient past. I begin to understand your family's enthusiasm for translation, trying to reveal to the modern world some of the secrets of one long vanished. Now, what about the larger panels above?'

'The metopes. They would have been placed above the architrave on the temple's exterior. The best-preserved ones show Greeks fighting centaurs. The story goes that the centaurs were invited to a wedding feast, imbibed a bit too much wine, and decided to try to carry off the Greek women. Which did not sit well with their hosts.'

'I would certainly object to someone trying to carry off my lady.'

Jocelyn shot her gaze up to his, trying to decide if he were merely making a general comment—or whether his words carried a deeper meaning. 'Would you?'

'Indeed. Once I decided to claim her, I would defend her against every attack.'

He looked serious...but he surely couldn't mean what she was reading into his words. That if he decided he'd fallen in love with her...he would even defy the Duke?

No, she was being ridiculous. He must be referring to the stand he'd taken by insisting on continuing to visit his old friends despite the Duke's disapproval. Besides, when it came right down to it, she couldn't marry him anyway. She would be nothing if she gave up her work and she couldn't risk her family by revealing her secret.

She should just be glad he *had* taken a stand and enjoy his friendship for the limited time they had left before she left London—or he succumbed to the pressure to marry.

Looking away from his too-captivating gaze, she said, 'Shall we wander and admire a bit more? Then I shall need to check on Virgil and Papa.'

'I'd like that.'

For nearly an hour, they strolled through the gallery, Jocelyn pointing out details she found particularly informative or enchanting, Alex asking questions and seeming genuinely interested in the setting and period she found so fascinating.

'I think I've pointed out all the best bits,' she said at last. 'I could go on for hours, but you would probably expire from boredom, even if you had the time, which I assume you do not.'

'I haven't been bored at all. I've always wondered what could be so interesting about a time so long ago that your father and brother would choose to make a life's work of delving into its mysteries. You share their enthusiasm and do a masterful job of bringing that society to life.'

Jocelyn chuckled. 'My aunt doesn't wonder, she despairs. At least once a day, she mutters something about how she'd feel much better about my future if I displayed a tad more enthusiasm about the society of the present day and a lot less about a culture that disappeared over a thousand years ago. So thank you for indulging my interest with such kind restraint.'

'I wasn't merely indulging you. I enjoyed it, too. It provided an intriguing glimpse into how you think.'

'Oh, dear, that must have been alarming! I wonder that you didn't run away screaming.'

He chuckled. 'Not a bit. I knew you were intelligent, but the hoyden has grown up to have quite a superior mind.'

'Why, thank you! And I didn't even have to split your head open with an axe to get that admission. Now, I expect you must get back to your usual duties.'

'Actually, I don't—yet. I made sure on this visit I would have sufficient time to offer all of you that tea at Gunter's I mentioned when I encountered you here the first time.'

'Let's re-join Papa and Virgil, then. Though your offer is very kind, don't be offended if they turn it down. I'm afraid they are likely to be far more interested in mastering the Rosetta Stone than in taking tea at a fashionable establishment!'

As they walked into the reading room, Jocelyn called softly to her father and brother, prompting both men to look up. 'Alex!' her father exclaimed. 'Are you here studying too?'

'Not studying, sir. But I did want to view the Parthenon Marbles, which I'd never seen before. Jocelyn proved herself a wonderful guide.'

Reverend Sudderfeld nodded. 'Marvellous, are they not?'

'Absolutely breathtaking. As a thank-you for her tour,

I thought to offer you all some tea at Gunter's. It's said to be the best in the city.'

Reverend Sudderfeld looked at his son, who gave a negative shake of the head.

'That's very kind of you, Alex, but I fear we will be discourteous and refuse,' her brother said. 'We have just two more hours until the museum closes and our opportunities to study here are limited. Since we don't want to fall too far behind on our own work, we shall not be able to return again for another two weeks.'

'It's partly my fault,' Jocelyn admitted. 'Fulfilling my promise to my aunt to attend her visiting hours several afternoons a week has cut into our work time more than we anticipated.'

'Since you are also out almost every evening,' Virgil pointed out.

'We mustn't begrudge your sister this chance to enjoy the frivolities of London,' the Reverend said, patting his son's hand. 'It will only be for a few more weeks. You two will be able to resume your normal schedule once we return to Edge Hall.'

'Yes, hopefully by then Aunt Bellingame will have turned up another suitor who appreciates the value of our work enough that he is willing to wait for Jocelyn until we've finished it,' Virgil said.

'Someone with a greater sense of loyalty than Charles Finley,' her father said with asperity.

'I was shocked and so disappointed in his character,' Virgil admitted. 'But Aunt Bellingame is determined to find Jocelyn a husband and she knows everyone. If anyone can find the right man who will allow us to both finish our work and secure Jocelyn's future, it's her.'

'I'm sure Mr Cheverton isn't interested in Aunt Bellingame's matrimonial schemes,' Jocelyn said, vaguely uncomfortable at having Alex hear this discussion. She really didn't like discussing the matter even among the family. She trusted her father and brother, but the idea of having to turn over to a husband control of her freedom and the small inheritance her mother had left her made the whole idea of marriage distasteful.

A distaste none of the prospective suitors she'd met thus far had dissipated. And no one—save Alex—attracted her enough that she was even a little tempted to give up her intention to pursue an independent life.

'Another time, then,' Alex was saying.

'I can't say that I'm not disappointed, but perhaps I can visit Gunter's later with my aunt,' Jocelyn said.

'It is disappointing that the Reverend and Virgil can't accompany us, but I'm sure your father would allow you to go there under my escort, as long as I promise to return you by the time the museum closes—wouldn't you, sir?'

'Of course,' her father said. 'I wouldn't like to see Jocelyn denied her treat, when Alex is kind enough to offer one.'

'That would be delightful,' she said, enthused at the prospect of spending additional time with him—until the social constraints occurred to her. 'But not possible, I'm afraid. I didn't bring my maid with me and I couldn't ride with Alex alone, in a closed hackney. Not in London.'

'But it is permissible for a lady to ride with a gentleman in an *open* carriage. Expecting a larger group, I brought the Duke's landau today, not my curricle. And I've been assured that it is perfectly acceptable for a respectable lady to accompany a gentleman to Gunter's without her maid, since refreshment can be taken out in the square, under the plane trees, with all the world passing by to chaperon.'

Virgil laughed. 'A "respectable" lady? That may leave out Jocelyn, unless she promises to be on her best behaviour.'

'Thank you, dear Brother,' she said drily. 'I do promise to behave myself, Papa. No climbing the plane trees in Berkeley Square or seizing the reins to race the landau through the streets.'

'In that case, you have my permission,' her father said, smiling at her.

'Don't be late getting back!' Virgil warned. 'You promised to go over the passage we worked on yesterday before you accompany our aunt to your entertainments tonight.'

'Yes, I remember and I promise to return promptly,' Jocelyn said.

'In that case, we should leave at once,' Alex said. 'Good to see you again, Reverend, Virgil. I'll get her back in plenty of time.'

'I'd still keep a close watch on the reins,' Virgil advised. 'You know Jocelyn. The temptation to try her hand at driving a new vehicle on city streets might be almost impossible to resist.'

'I'll keep a firm grip,' Alex said.

'Brothers can be so impossible,' Jocelyn grumbled as they walked out. 'The way he talks, you'd think I were still a hoyden of sixteen.'

'Wasn't it just last year that you talked the guard into letting you drive the Royal Mail coach around the village square while the coachman was collecting the mail from the posting inn?'

'Well, yes—but I didn't attempt to race it! And the chance to drive a team of four—how could anyone resist? And you may cease laughing at me!' she finished indignantly.

'True,' he said, controlling his mirth. 'For anyone fascinated by horses and carriages, such an opportunity was too tempting to forgo. I can only hope a landau holds less fascination.'

'I would only drive it—as I did the mail coach—with permission. Since that is unlikely and I wouldn't want to do something that might embarrass my aunt, I can promise to ride with you to the museum and back without attempting to steal the reins.'

'I am reassured.'

'Speaking of respectable behaviour, how did you learn that it was permissible for a lady to visit Gunter's without her maid? Hints by eager maidens seeking your escort—or by mamas eager for you to escort their daughters?'

'True enough,' he admitted with a grimace. 'But the Duke, who overheard the suggestion, confirmed the propriety of it. He later informed me that if I wished to take up any of the subtle hints being offered, I could do so safely without it being thought I'd compromised the lady.'

'Important knowledge for a single gentleman. And even more important for the heir to a dukedom who wants to avoid being trapped into marriage.'

'For once, I will not dispute your assessment. I know my duty, but regardless of pressure from the Duke, I shall not marry unless I am convinced the union will be not just suitable, but have a reasonable chance of success.'

'I do hope you will hold to that resolve! Navigating the hazards of life in a position you'd never anticipated or desired will be difficult enough, without the mill-stone of an unhelpful partner hung about your neck.'

'A fate I firmly intend to avoid. No matter how beau-tiful, rich, or well born the lady trying to charm me, if I do not sense that we might be compatible, I will, politely, of course, resist her lures. Now, if you will wait here at the entrance for a short while, I'll fetch the carriage.'

Jocelyn nodded and sent him off with a wave. It was silly for her to find a frank discussion of his even-tual marriage painful, she thought as she watched him walk off. She'd known since hearing the news of his inheritance that his marriage with a rich and high-born woman was now inevitable and would probably happen sooner rather than later.

Rather than feeling downcast, she should be reas-sured that he was determined to resist a match based solely on the bride's wealth and social prestige and hold out for a woman of character. Jocelyn wanted the friend she'd cared about for so many years to be happy—as happy as he could be, trapped in a role he didn't re-ally want.

And now she should stop wasting the precious little time she had left to share with him feeling sad about the future and concentrate on enjoying the present. Espe-cially the titillating prospect of snuggling beside her—sadly, clothed—personal Greek hero for the duration of their visit to Gunter's.

Fortunately, travelling in an open carriage would forestall any possibility of another kiss. *Un*fortunately, much as she knew she shouldn't even consider such a thing, as she spent more time with him, she found it harder and harder to stop longing for one.

Chapter Twelve

He shouldn't be so pleased that he'd managed to sneak some time alone with Jocelyn, Alex thought as he guided the landau through the busy streets, but he was. How fetching she looked in the carriage gown of a burnished brown hue that brought out the chestnut highlights in her hair and emphasised the velvet depth of her dark eyes! With her completely absorbed in telling him stories about the sculptures while they toured the gallery, he'd been able to indulge himself just looking at her—while listening to a fascinating and impressive bit of scholarly explanation.

She was just as intriguing and even lovelier than the ancient Greek sculpture she'd described. Generally, they spent much of their time together trading quips and barbs. He truly had appreciated the opportunity to listen while she talked at length about the era that engaged her whole family. She was not only thoroughly versed in the subject, she had a real aptitude for explaining it, an ability to compare facets of ancient Greek life to contemporary equivalents in a way that made the long-ago past both approachable and interesting.

He couldn't wait to draw her out further.

As the carriage approached Berkeley Square, Alex slowed the horses. 'Gunter's establishment occupies numbers six and eight,' he said, nodding with his chin in that direction. 'Once I've pulled up the horses in the centre of the square, I'll signal a waiter to come and take our order.'

'The plane trees are handsome, but I'm glad they haven't fully got their leaves yet,' Jocelyn said as he guided the carriage to a halt. 'With the buildings to block the breeze, it will be pleasant to sit in the warmth of the filtered sun. Now, as you'll note, I was on my best behaviour on the drive here. Not a single attempt to steal the reins. Although...'

He looked over to see a half-smile on her lips as she angled her head up at him, her eyes dancing—an expression that experience told him promised mischief.

'"Although" what?' he asked warily.

'Since I have been so polite and ladylike, I thought it might be only fair, if you should drive the landau to Hyde Park some morning, that you allow me to try the ribbons then.'

He shook his head. 'I should have known you'd want to exact some concession for your exemplary behaviour. On the few occasions when I can get away in the early morning, I usually ride, or drive my curricle.'

She made a little moue of disappointment that instantly made him want to grant her what she'd asked. Fighting to resist it, he said, 'Do you ride there every morning?'

'Yes, unless the weather is very bad. As you know, riding is one of my chief joys, important enough to me that I didn't accept my aunt's invitation until I made sure she would allow me to ride here. Not that the job horses one can hire have the spirit or the speed of the

Duke's hunters, but the hack I've found gives me an acceptable ride.'

Alex signalled to a waiter. 'Will you have tea?' he asked as the man approached.

'Actually, even though it's a bit chilly out, I'd really like to sample some of their famous ices—if they have any available.'

'They supply them for parties all the year round, so I imagine they will.'

'That would be splendid!'

Her enthusiasm making him smile, Alex turned to the waiter and enquired about the availability of ices. Upon confirming that the establishment had an assortment of fruit ones, including pineapple from a supply of the fruit grown in their own greenhouses, they ordered tea, sweetmeats and pineapple sorbet.

'I think you will really enjoy the pineapple,' Alex said, delighted to be able to offer her that treat. 'It's sweet, but also tangy.'

'You've had it before?'

'Yes. The Duke enjoys ices and has a standing order for them. Particularly the pineapple, which is his favourite.'

'How fine to have the resources of a duke! Aunt Bellingame has promised to order ices for the *soirée dansante* she is giving for me, but they are so dear, she will do it only for that one occasion.'

'A small compensation for having your life thrown in disarray,' Alex said wryly.

'There is that. I suppose I'd rather remain as I am and not have ices.'

'Will you remain as you are?' he asked, keenly interested in her answer. 'Virgil seems to think your aunt is determined to have you end your London stay, if not engaged, at least with a serious suitor or two.'

'That may be her intention. But as you well know, I have little inclination to marry. I enjoy my work with Virgil and Papa and have no desire to exchange a scholarship for arranging dinners and ordering ices for a husband.'

'What if a husband supported your scholarship? And tasked his housekeeper to tend to the routine matters?'

Jocelyn laughed shortly. 'He would have to be a most exceptional gentleman indeed!'

'You don't think such a person exists?'

'I don't deny it—in theory. But in my admittedly limited observations, regardless of a woman's favoured pursuits before marriage, most gentlemen believe a wife's purpose is to run his household and please him, not engage in activities unconnected to his comfort and well-being.'

'Ah, but you are not "most women".'

That drew a laugh. 'True. Most women are happy, indeed eager, to find a husband whose household they can run and whose desires they can please.'

'And you wouldn't wish to…please a husband's desires?'

She looked up at him, her eyes darkening. 'That might be the only aspect of marriage I could anticipate with eagerness…if I had the right husband.'

As could he, Alex thought, his mouth drying and his body hardening at the prospect. Dragging his thoughts from that titillating vision, Alex said, 'Surely marriage offers other pleasures. What of children? Will you not miss having offspring of your own, if you settle for becoming a companion to your naughty old lady?'

She shrugged, not answering, though the look of

sadness that briefly crossed her countenance seemed to indicate she would. 'I doubt I'll need to go to the extreme of marriage to have children to tend. Virgil will surely wed eventually and I'll have his children to spoil on visits from the home of my naughty old lady. I'm hopeful that if the project we are working on is very well received, Virgil might earn enough from its publication to be able to lead a scholarly life of leisure, without having to seek a clerical position.'

'He doesn't have another project in mind for after he finishes the Euripides?'

'Not at present. For one, the Duke has said he is not interested in sponsoring additional work. And there are other translators already delving into the other ancients—Socrates, Homer, Aeschylus. If this project does as well or better than Papa's have, Virgil could, like Papa, devote himself to reading and study, without the pressure of having to prepare something new for publication.'

'While you amuse your naughty old lady?'

'While I amuse my naughty old lady.'

'Won't *you* miss scholarship? After all, as you informed me, you are not merely a scribe recording your brother's words, but a participant who offers suggestions.' He smiled. 'Before today, I suppose I thought you exaggerated your importance to tease me, but that tour of the gallery was a masterful demonstration of the depth and scope of your knowledge and insight. I'm now completely convinced of your active participation.'

For a moment, she looked almost…alarmed. Then her face cleared and she laughed. 'Well, thank you for that vote of confidence! I'm relieved to learn that you don't consider all women to be lack-witted.'

'Many are intelligent. But you, like Athena, are

exceptional. Any man who failed to appreciate that uniqueness isn't worthy of you.'

She looked up at him at that. 'You truly believe that?'

'I do.'

For a moment, he simply gazed at her. He'd always known she was intelligent, but he'd truly been struck today by the keenness of her intellect—and found it attracted him almost as much as her beauty.

He'd never thought finding a woman who was intellectually gifted to be that important. And though he still felt a conventional bride would be best, he was beginning to think he'd prefer one with a lively intellect—like Jocelyn.

'Th-thank you,' she said. 'Though I hardly know what to say. I'm not much accustomed to receiving compliments from you.'

'Nor I from you,' he agreed, smiling. 'But we don't have to be adversaries, do we? We could be allies.'

'I've always considered you my friend and ally, no matter how much we might bicker.'

'As I have considered you...from the time I met you as a scrubby brat. But already a well-informed scrubby brat! Your father instructed you, didn't he?'

'Yes. Mama thought it silly to hire a governess when Papa was willing to teach me, for which I'm so grateful. I received an education that was much more varied and interesting than any I could have obtained from a mere governess.'

'Not many governesses can claim to be masters of ancient Greek! It's fortunate for the projects of your father and brother that you were both interested and gifted. Did you always have an aptitude for languages?'

'Mama tells me that I talked very early—disdaining single words, I began with simple sentences. Some of my earliest memories are of drawing symbols on my slate, mimicking those I saw on Papa's papers. He started teaching me French and Italian as soon as I could write in English. The idea of expressing thoughts in different languages captivated me from the start. I soon begged him to teach me Latin and Greek as well.'

'What led your father to choose to devote his efforts to Greek theatre? I read various translations—painfully—of Homer and Aristotle while at university. Most scholars have chosen to study the philosophers, the mathematicians, or the historians.'

'Papa studied those too. But much of the translation of their works had already been done and he wanted to try something different. Then he almost stumbled upon Euripides and found him fascinating. The dramatist began gaining recognition for his work only ten years or so after the Parthenon and the Acropolis had been finished. Can you imagine, living in Athens when those sculptures we viewed at the museum were whole, intact, the temples pristine! Euripides lived in a city that Pericles had established as the foremost in the world for art, culture and philosophy. And yet what he wrote was quite different from the other classical writers.'

'How different?'

'We can trace our modern concept of drama to him. Shakespeare certainly used his techniques! While the other Greek dramatists used the myths and legends simply to tell a story, Euripides was the first to probe the inner thoughts and feelings of his characters, to show the struggle between reason and passion for control over one's life. There's a feel for common people, not just heroes. And he shows the pressure of ordinary people having to react to extraordinary events. Although many of the myths tell stories that are shockingly violent, there is still nobility of character. Heracles, who insists on taking individual responsibility, even though the madness that caused him to murder was brought on by the gods. Alcestis, who was willing to sacrifice herself for her husband and children, and Iphigenia, who agreed to sacrifice herself for the good of Greece.'

At that moment, the waiter trotted over with a tray bearing their drinks and sweetmeats. Jocelyn fell silent while Alex busied himself with settling the tray between them and paying the waiter.

As the man walked off, Jocelyn said ruefully, 'A timely interruption! One innocent question, and off I went on a lengthy discourse on my favourite subject. I am sorry! I promise now I shall make more appropriate conversation.'

'No need to be sorry. I enjoy seeing you enthusiastic. And your project does sound fascinating. I'm afraid I knew very little about Euripides.'

'No more ancient Greek,' she said, waving a finger at him. 'I shall concentrate on enjoying this lovely treat.' After sipping the hot tea, she took a spoonful of the pineapple sorbet and sighed.

'That is wonderful! I may have to revise my opinion. It might be worth having your life thrown into disarray to be able to serve this after dinner every night.'

'Says she whose life will continue to proceed according to her own wishes! But proceed to what, once your project is complete? Will you seek out your naughty old lady immediately? Or will you remain with your father and brother until Virgil marries?'

'Probably the latter. I'll almost certainly remain with Papa until he passes, by which time I assume Virgil will be married.'

'Will you continue your studies?'

She opened her lips to reply, then hesitated, an odd look on her face. Before he could ask her if there were something wrong, she continued with a smile, 'I'll read to Papa, certainly—his eyesight does not allow him to indulge that pastime as much as he'd like. For myself, I think I should like to explore other writers. Much as I've enjoyed the Greeks, I would like to read the Roman dramatists. The philosophers of the Enlightenment. Compare the classical theatre of Greece with the classics plays of Racine and Molière.'

'No scandalous novels?'

'But of course! Those, I shall be reading aloud to my naughty old lady.'

'Along with doing needlework by the fireside?'

'Definitely not that!' she said with a shudder. 'Mending if I must, but no embroidering pillows or fire screens. I should like to become a better pianist, though.'

'I'm sure your companion would enjoy listening to you play.'

'I enjoy playing, even if no one is listening. And speaking of enjoyment, I cannot thank you enough! The sweetmeats are delicious, the tea is excellent and the sorbet is beyond wonderful. I'm so grateful, I might even not pester you about driving the landau.'

'Now that is restraint indeed! Much as I'd like to order us another dish of sorbet, I had better get you back. I don't want to inconvenience your father and brother by being late.'

While he signalled to a waiter to come and retrieve the tray, Jocelyn arranged their cups, glasses and saucers. 'They would not appreciate being left standing on the museum porch after the building closed. Virgil will be keen to get back to Aunt Bellingame's so we can do a bit of work before I have to get ready for dinner. After viewing the sculptures at the museum, I'm even more inspired to continue!'

Though the sculpted horses had been magnificent, it was the Athena who reappeared in his mind's eye. A goddess of wisdom...like the tempting lady beside him. He couldn't help thinking how marvellous Jocelyn would look, clad only in a few wispy classical draperies.

The waiter returned, jolting him out of his amorous thoughts. Their tray handed over, Alex took up the reins and gave the horses the office to start. Though Jocelyn looked longingly at his hands, she pressed her lips together firmly—forestalling asking for a chance to drive, Alex thought, smiling at her forbearance.

'In any event,' she said after he'd navigated out of the square and directed the landau back towards the museum, 'I won't have to tease you for an equestrian event. I've arranged to get tickets to attend the early afternoon show at Astley's next Monday. Unfortunately, they only perform the grand events, like "The Battle of Waterloo", at the evening performances. But I shall be very excited to see some of the trick riding I've heard so much about!'

He would love to watch her watching them, Alex thought, mentally reviewing his schedule. 'Next Monday, you said?'

'Yes.' Eyes brightening, she said, 'You wouldn't happen to be free then, would you? But, no, I won't even ask! It was good enough of you to get away today. With your success at it to inspire me, I intend to bribe my maid to attend with me.'

'I would like to see the show myself, but I don't know whether I'll be free. You must promise me, though, not to attempt any of the tricks you see.' When she said nothing for a long moment, he said, 'Promise me!'

'I'm considering it!' she replied. 'I don't like making promises I can't—or don't intend—to keep.'

'Heaven help us,' he exclaimed. 'If you can't promise to refrain completely, at least promise me you'll not attempt anything until you return to the country, where you might practise in broad, wide meadows empty of pedestrians, vehicles and other riders.'

'I probably would have difficulty trying anything here in my new riding dress,' she admitted. 'It's terribly fashionable, which means it boasts ridiculous ballooning sleeves, wide skirts and a long trailing hem.' She shook her head. 'Fashion designed to demonstrate one is a person of leisure, since the style makes it practically impossible for one to do anything useful.'

'If it prevents you from attempting tricks, I'd call it a blessing,' he declared.

'Have you been to Astley's before?'

'Several times. As a boy, I saw the show when John Astley, the founder's son, was running the business. Then again after John's death, while I was at Oxford, Ducrow, the current owner, took over. He's quite a performer! Not just as a rider, but as a tumbler and a master of rope tricks. He's also originated a number of spectacular horsemanship acts. I think you will be thoroughly entertained.'

'I'm sure I will be. Although I do regret not being able to see the grand spectacles.'

'Perhaps you'll be able to attend an evening performance at another time.'

'That would be wonderful, but I doubt it. I couldn't go in the evening attended only by a maid and my aunt has no taste for equestrian spectacles. She much prefers dinners, parties and balls, although she will settle for the theatre if we have no invitation to a more favoured event. And Heaven forbid we spend a quiet evening at home, reading by the fire!'

'I can sympathise! The Duke isn't enamoured of his own hearth, either. Fortunately, he approves of gentlemen's clubs, so I'm not forced to make pleasant social chatter every evening.'

'Ah, the clubs! Where the elite of England gather. Has he made you a member?'

'I'm proposed for membership at White's, but the voting hasn't taken place yet. He's brought me several times as his guest.'

'The voting? I doubt there's much question about whether or not White's will admit the Duke of Farisdeen's anointed heir.'

'Probably not,' he agreed and smiled wryly. 'Each time he ushers me in, to be bowed to by the doorman and catered to by waiters and greeted by the great peers of the land, I imagine what the reception would be like if I were to enter those august halls as merely Alex Cheverton, owner of the modest estate of Wynborne.'

Jocelyn laughed. 'Oh, you are well born enough to be welcomed, if not with as much fanfare as the Duke! As long as you have the blunt to stand the fees.'

By now, they were nearing the museum in Russell Square. Jocelyn spotted her father and Virgil walking out of Montagu House and waved.

As Alex slowed the horses, Jocelyn turned back to him. 'Thank you again for the most marvellous afternoon! An hour communing with the Parthenon marbles, then indulging me to run on about my favourite subject, then gifting me with the most delicious treat ever! Being able to share all of that with you made it so much better.'

'I'm glad I was able to share it with you, too.' He must work out how to see her again, and soon, he silently promised himself.

As the carriage rolled to a stop, Jocelyn said, 'I do hope we shall meet again. I feel quite awful, having monopolised the conversation. I hardly allowed you to tell me anything of what you've been doing!'

'If you're interested, I can tell you about it next time I see you.'

'Of course I'm interested!' As her brother walked over to open the carriage door for her, she pressed his hand. 'Goodbye, Alex. Thank you again, and I do hope to see you—soon, I hope.'

'Our appreciation for returning her right on time,' Virgil said as he helped Jocelyn to alight. 'Good to see you, Alex. And thanks for watching out for our hoyden.'

'Hoyden!' Jocelyn repeated indignantly. 'I'll have you know I was perfectly well behaved. Was I not, Alex?'

'Impeccably,' he affirmed, grinning at them. He enjoyed that sort of teasing, good-humoured repartee as much as Jocelyn and her brother obviously did. A lively sense of humour and sensibilities not easily offended were definitely qualities he'd want in a wife—both attributes Jocelyn possessed. 'And it was my pleasure.'

Virgil nodded, then offered Jocelyn his arm to walk her over to the portico where their father waited. After exchanging a little wave with the Reverend, Alex picked up the reins.

There was no reason to linger until her party summoned a hackney. She had her father and brother to safeguard her.

Still, he felt strangely reluctant to leave her.

Their time together today had been delightful—and further strengthened his resolve to see more of her.

As he drove back to Grosvenor Square, a series of images flickered through his head. Jocelyn, pointing out the head of Selene's horse. The avid enthusiasm on her face as she related the myths and stories about their creation and the dramatist who created them. The surprising breadth of her interests, from French theatre to Renaissance philosophy. Her delight in riding, in the sweet, tangy taste of pineapple sorbet.

Her distaste for needlework, he recalled with a grin.

Probably because it was so...passive. While she was so vibrantly alive, he thought, wondering why he'd never quite realised that before. Energy, enthusiasm, enjoyment radiated from her to stimulate anyone around her.

One way or another, he *would* make time to see her. He couldn't wait to be near her and drink in that energy and enthusiasm again.

Chapter Thirteen

The following Monday afternoon, a hackney deposited Jocelyn and her maid in front of Astley's Amphitheatre. Though Jocelyn could hardly contain her excitement, Mary was much less enthused. A look of genuine alarm passed over the girl's face when, after paying for their seats, Jocelyn led her into the Amphitheatre itself and down to the front row of a box right on the floor over-looking the performance arena.

'We're not going to sit here, are we, miss?'

'It's the best place from which to see exactly how the performers do their tricks.'

'That's as may be, but what if one of them horses runs away, or a carriage turns over? It could smash smack into us!'

Jocelyn was trying to soothe the girl's fears when a voice at her ear made her jump. 'I thought I'd find you in a seat right on the ring.'

'Alex—Mr Cheverton!' Jocelyn exclaimed. Though she'd sternly warned herself there was little likelihood of seeing him today, she hadn't been able to completely squash that hope—and was beyond delighted that he'd turned up after all. 'You are able to join us?'

'I hope so. I haven't bought my ticket yet—I wanted to see where you were sitting.'

'You can have my seat, Mr Cheverton,' the maid said.

'That's kind of you, Mary, but I wouldn't want to deprive you of your treat.'

'I wouldn't mind a bit! I… I'm a little afraid of horses, you see.'

'How courageous of you to accompany your mistress here today, then. Such bravery deserves a reward.' Reaching into his waistcoat pocket, Alex drew out a gold coin. 'Why don't you have a meat pie and some cider at the posting inn around the corner, The Dancing Mare? Miss Sudderfeld and I will meet you there after the performance.'

Her eyes growing wide as she spied the coin, Mary bobbed a quick curtsy and snatched it from Alex's fingers—as if afraid he might change his mind if she didn't seize it immediately. 'That's ever so nice of you, sir. That is, if it's all right with you, miss.'

'Go ahead. Given your opinion of horses, I'm sure you'll enjoy the meat pie and cider a good deal more than the equestrian show.'

'Thank you, miss, sir. I'll meet you there after the performance, then.'

After slipping the coin into her sleeve, the maid bobbed them another curtsy and practically ran out of the box.

'That was kind of you,' Jocelyn said as Alex waved her to a seat. 'And generous! That coin could keep her in cider and meat pies for a month!'

'Always best to stay on good terms with the servants. They can be uncommonly helpful if they wish to be.'

'Especially bribable ones,' Jocelyn said drily.

'Exactly,' Alex said with a grin. 'I'm surprised, though, that she didn't want to see the show.'

'She was uneasy about sitting this close to the arena. As you arrived, she was predicting our imminent demise at the hoofs of rampaging stallions and overturning carriages.'

'The Cassandra of Astley's?' he suggested.

'No mention of Greek classics today,' she said, waving a finger at him. 'I'm still embarrassed about monopolising the conversation at our last meeting. We shall simply enjoy being able to watch this display—together. What a handsome arena! I'd read that it was well done, but I wasn't expecting chandeliers, opulent curtains and a full stage.'

'They probably won't use the stage this afternoon. It's reserved for the tumbling acts and tricks done by two-legged performers.'

'Before the show begins, you must tell me how you are faring. Does the Duke continue to be helpful? Have you met many interesting people?'

'The Duke continues to be...the Duke. Honestly, sometimes I can't figure out if he approves of my efforts or not. I can't begin to keep in my head all the people I've met. Perhaps the most interesting has been sitting in on meetings with some of his associates in the Lords. You must convey my thanks again to your father for the primer he gave me on recent legislation during our dinner at the Dower House! Else I should have appeared even more ignorant than I am.'

'You may not have mastery of all the details, but you learn quickly. Just as you did when you were handed Edge Hall to manage, with no prior experience in running so vast an estate. Is there important legislation pending?'

'The Reform Act that eliminated rotten boroughs and redistributed representation in Parliament is probably as far as the Tories will allow voting reform to go, at least for the present.'

'So women will not be voting in the next Parliamentary election? What a disappointment!'

'I'm afraid there is still a great deal of opposition to that.'

'Zeus and Athena again,' she said with a sigh. 'So what reforms will get passed?'

'Lord Grey and many of the Whigs don't feel the Factory Act went far enough in protecting child workers. There's still discussion ongoing about that.'

'And how does the Duke stand on that?'

'With the conservatives, of course.'

'But you do not?' she guessed.

'I agree with Lord Grey on that. But if Grey wants to press for universal suffrage, the voters need to be educated. Even those who work in the mills and factories. Ah, here comes the master of ceremonies! They're about to start.'

Jocelyn settled back in her seat, eager to watch—and supremely happy to have Alex beside her, his shoulder almost touching her own. For a moment, she simply drank in the sensual awareness of being so near him.

Kissing close. Although once again, the crowd around them would protect her from succumbing to the temptation she couldn't quite seem to master.

Better to just enjoy his company. She'd been looking forward to this performance, but being able to experience it alone with Alex—no maid or chaperon looking on to overhear their conversation—made it even more precious. How many more such meetings would they manage?

But she didn't intend to spoil this wonderful experience by worrying over how soon the Duke would sweep him out of her sphere for good. Cabinet ministers and legislative leaders and reform bills! They were as foreign to her everyday life as ancient Greek was to his.

Determined to suck every bit of enjoyment out of this afternoon, as a man driving a chariot entered the arena, she leaned forward, smiling.

For the next hour, Jocelyn watched with delight as men and ladies drove vehicles in tandem and in opposite, used their whips to guide horses who danced or walked on their hind legs, and performed theatrical tableaux on horseback. To set the seal on her pleasure, she was able to keep up a running commentary with Alex on the acts they were viewing.

Finally, the ringmaster announced the final spectacle, to be performed by owner himself. '"The Courier of St Petersburg" is Ducrow's most famous trick,' Alex said.

'I've read about it,' Jocelyn said. 'I can't wait to see how he does it.'

As the music swelled, the horse master came into the arena—riding two horses while standing up, one foot on the back of each as they cantered side by side.

'Spectacular!' Jocelyn breathed. 'I thought the ladies balanced on the back of a single horse were fabulous, but standing up on *two*!'

'He's just getting started,' Alex said, pointing as more horses entered the arena, each bedecked with flags.

'They carry the flags of all the countries one would ride through if one were carrying a message from St Petersburg to London,' Alex explained. As they watched, captivated, the horses galloped towards the maestro—and ran between his two horses, beneath his parted legs.

Jocelyn joined in the roar of approval from the crowd as each flag-decorated horse successfully passed beneath the rider. After making several circuits, the horses exited, with Ducrow, after a victory lap bowing to the cheering crowd, following them out.

'That was marvellous!' Jocelyn declared, taking the arm Alex offered to walk her out with the throng. 'Such poise! Such balance!'

'Such courage—or maybe foolhardiness,' Alex said. 'One slip, one small loss of balance, and Ducrow could be killed or crippled.'

'Now you sound like Mary. She probably would have had her apron over her eyes, expecting the worst, through the entire ride.'

'I assume that "The Courier of St. Petersburg" was your favourite spectacle?' Alex asked as he led her out of the Amphitheatre.

'Nothing could surpass that,' Jocelyn said. 'Although I thought the theatre pieces quite fine, too. "The Tyrolean Shepherd and the Swiss Maid", with Ducrow and his wife miming meeting, wooing, quarrelling and making up, all while standing on horseback, and then the intricate pas de deux riding in patterns together after their reconciliation was very fine, too.'

'Would you like some cider and a meat pie before I summon your hackney home?'

'I would...but I'd better not. I promised Virgil I would be back in time to work for several hours. We are to attend a dinner and a musical soirée at the home of one of Aunt Bellingame's good friends tonight, so there will be no time later in the day.'

'Your brother is quite the taskmaster.'

'No, he's right. The more often one takes a break from the story, and the longer the break, the harder it is to pick up the threads and re-establish the correct mood and tone. I don't like to be away from it too long, either. Besides, I'm sure the Duke has plans for you, too.'

Alex grimaced. 'Yes. Dinner with some friends—one with a marriageable daughter, the butler warned me.'

'The *Duke's* butler warned you? Wasn't that rather... insubordinate of him?'

Alex grinned. 'Mary isn't the only servant amenable to a gold coin in the hand. And I think Thurgood likes me. He's very loyal to the family, served the previous Duke before this one, and was very upset at Penlowe's death. I think he wants the new heir to marry soon, but to a wife of his *own* choice, not merely a suitable one. The better to breed numerous sons to secure the succession, you see.'

Alex—his body and his kisses given to someone else.

Resolutely Jocelyn pushed away the dispiriting thought of Alex married and producing sons with some unnamed lady of high birth. 'Good that you have someone in the household watching out for you.'

'I'm glad of it.' With a wry smile, he added, 'Much as I understand that duty requires me to marry, I have to confess, it's hard to resign myself to it.'

She angled a glance at him. 'Are you so opposed to marriage?'

He sighed. 'I suffered a...rather painful disappointment when I was very young—just before I went to university.'

Alex—with his heart broken? 'I'm so sorry!' she exclaimed. 'How could anyone—but pardon me, I don't mean to pry.'

'Maybe I should tell you, and you can mock me. Gaining a bit more perspective could help me face the inevitable with better grace.'

'Surely you know I would never "mock" you on a matter close to your heart!' she protested.

Nodding, he held up a hand. 'I do. You may be "brutally honest", but there's a great deal of kindness in you, Jocelyn Sudderfeld.'

'So…what did happen?' she couldn't help asking, concerned to know about something that had affected him so deeply. 'If you don't mind revealing it.'

'Eliza was the daughter of a baronet in the next county. We met at a cotillion ball and soon fancied ourselves desperately in love. I proposed, she accepted. Then I asked her father for her hand. After telling me he'd never consider giving his daughter to a callow youth who had absolutely no means to support her, he called me an irresponsible, thoughtless rogue for toying with his daughter's heart and almost literally threw me out of his library. I was all of seventeen.' He blew out a breath. 'It was and remains the most shameful, humiliating episode of my life.'

'I can understand humiliating, but why shameful?'

'Because he was right. Had we married, I would have been dependent on the very limited income of my estate for support—an added expense the family didn't need and a difficult situation for any bride, forced to live under the nose of her mother-in-law. And though I didn't intend to be a rogue, I was thoughtless and irresponsible for encouraging Eliza to love me when I could offer her nothing. I…let my emotions blind me to reason and responsibility. There was nothing I could do to make it up to her for breaking her heart, but it's a mistake I vowed never to make again.'

He gave her a smile, which looked a little forced. Jocelyn had to blink back tears at the idea of her dear friend enduring such a searing experience. 'So that's why you don't believe in love at first sight. Because yours...ended so badly.'

'Right,' he said briskly, seeming to shake off his melancholy. 'Fortunately, the marriage of a duke is more about suitability and family connections than emotion. I should be able to handle that.'

'What of friendship? Or affection?' It pained her to think of Alex wed to someone who wouldn't appreciate and support him.

'I would require a mutual respect and a modicum of affection wouldn't come amiss.'

She shuddered. 'It sounds dreadful. I will hope for much better for you!' *Even if it must be with someone else.*

He laughed. 'Since you yourself are so opposed to wedlock, I imagine you would consider such an arrangement dreadful. Ah, I think we've reached our destination.'

He clearly didn't wish to discuss the matter further. Still, Jocelyn's heart ached for his pain. *I'll say no more...but I will pray you end up as happy as I want you to be. As happy as I would hope to make you.*

They paused for a moment to admire the hanging sign of a horse prancing around an arena, then walked inside. Her eyes adjusting to the dimness, Jocelyn spotted Mary at the bar, chatting with the young man behind it. Mary looked up as they entered and nodded, and waved a goodbye to the barman. Who, Jocelyn noted with a smile, followed her progress across the room with admiring interest.

'Did you enjoy the show, miss?' she asked as she reached them.

'It was wonderful! I really think you would have liked it.'

'I think Mary enjoyed her time at the inn just as much. And certainly the company,' Alex said, winking at the girl.

'Ned were right conversable,' Mary said, her cheeks growing rosy. 'Thank you again, sir, for the cider and meat pie.'

'You are very welcome, Mary. Why don't you ladies wait inside in the warmth while I summon you a hackney?'

'That would be kind of you, Alex.'

'At my ladies' service,' he said with a wink. 'I'll have your carriage waiting for you shortly.'

'Ned says lots of people see the shows over and over,' Mary said as Alex walked out. 'If you want to come back to Astley's again, miss, I'd be happy to return with you and wait for you here at the inn.'

'With the conversable Ned?' Jocelyn suggested with a smile. Though she didn't mean to tease the maid too much. She was too ruefully aware just how much more enjoyable an event could be when shared with an agreeable gentleman.

How glad she was to have shared this special performance with Alex!

How much she was going to miss him when he went on to his great destiny...and his high-born bride.

And she absolutely refused to think of him making love to someone else.

Pushing away a wave of sadness, she turned her mind instead to reviewing the various equestrian tricks that had been performed. And evaluating whether it might be possible for her to duplicate any of them.

A few minutes later, Alex returned. 'Your chariot awaits.'

'Would that it were a chariot!' Jocelyn said with a smile. 'Perhaps with your ill-gotten ducal gains, you could one day order a few chariots for Edge Hall. On your visits back, we could race them.'

'Tearing up the roads and terrorising the livestock?' he said with a laugh. 'The farmers would be up in arms.'

'You're just afraid I would beat you.'

Waving a reproving finger, he opened the hackney door for her. 'It might be worth the risk to watch you drive a chariot.'

'Consider it, then.'

'Oh, I'll be considering a lot of things.'

'Thank you again for coming to share the event with me. This afternoon will be one of my favourite memories of my visit to London.'

'As it will mine.'

With that, he closed the door behind her and signalled to the jarvey, who set the horses in motion.

Jocelyn watched him until the carriage bore them out of sight. She would love to race Alex in a chariot. He made doing almost anything they did together more enjoyable.

But racing chariots, like most any other event she might foresee in future—like lying entangled with her lover in the sheets of a marriage bed—was unlikely to be shared with him.

Still, as she'd told him, she would have the fond memories of this afternoon to cherish for ever. And her work to fulfil her.

Somehow, those reflections didn't comfort her as much as she'd like.

* * *

Several hours later, dressed in one of her new evening gowns, Jocelyn followed her aunt into the drawing room of Lady Sterling's home in Mount Street. She was actually looking forward to the entertainment this evening—a piano performance by a leading London musician of works by Beethoven, Bach and Handel. It would set the seal on what had been an almost perfect day—beginning with the wonderful performance at Astley's with Alex, followed by a very productive work session with Virgil, and now an interlude enjoying her favourite music.

It would have been truly perfect, were she able to end the day with Alex.

Or if he'd surprised her with one of those kisses she must not yearn for.

But one must count one's blessings and not be so greedy as to wish for everything, she told herself. She should concentrate on the performance, observe the maestro closely and perhaps pick up some finger-work techniques that could improve her own playing.

Along with the guests who had come to dinner, they mingled now with the additional people who had been invited for the performance. While her aunt chatted with some friends, Jocelyn stood beside her, trying to politely discourage the attentions of Mr Oglesby. Irritated again by his persistence when she'd given him not the slightest encouragement beyond mere politeness, she was struggling to refrain from responding with some truly rude remark when a tap at her elbow diverted her attention.

Jocelyn turned to see her hostess and a tall, dark-haired gentleman with traces of silver at his brow standing beside her.

'Excuse me for interrupting you, ladies and gentle-men,' Lady Sterling said. 'The performance will begin shortly, and I've a friend just arrived who very much desired to be made known to you ladies—I believe he and Mr Oglesby are already acquainted. Lady Bellin-game, Miss Sudderfeld, may I present Lord Darnsby? A neighbour of my son's, he's just come up to London from Waverly Park, his estate in Kent.'

'Very pleased to meet you, ladies,' the newcomer said as bows and curtsies were exchanged. 'Might I pro-cure you some refreshment before the concert begins?'

Though Darnsby addressed both her and her aunt, his keen, dark-eyed gaze was fixed on Jocelyn. Appar-ently noting the intensity of the gentleman's interest, after exchanging a significant look with Jocelyn, Lady Bellingame said, 'Not for me, thank you. I'd like to have another word with Lady Sterling before we take our seats. But I'm sure Miss Sudderfeld would appre-ciate a glass.'

'Miss Sudderfeld?' he asked, holding out his arm.

'I could have taken her to fetch one,' Mr Oglesby protested.

'Ah, but apparently you didn't offer. An opportu-nity missed. If you would be pleased to accompany me, Miss Sudderfeld?'

'If you wish, Lord Darnbsy.'

'I would indeed. Lady Bellingame, I will restore her to you in a moment.'

As she laid her hand on his arm, Jocelyn wondered why, if Darnsby were newly arrived in London, he'd asked to be presented to her, rather than to any of the other dozen unmarried ladies present tonight, almost all of them younger and better dowered than she was. As he led her into the adjoining salon, where light refreshments had been set out, she said, 'That was neatly done, my lord.'

'The gentleman obviously wanted to monopolise you. And you were resisting his efforts.'

'I was resisting—' Jocelyn echoed, looking up at him in surprise. 'What could possibly make you conclude that?'

'I watched your little group for some minutes. While Oglesby talked and talked, you said nothing, only nodding occasionally, your eyes looking about the room rather than fixed on his face. With a rather desperately polite smile on your lips, as if you prayed for rescue. How could I not answer that plea?' he asked as he took a cup of punch for each of them from the servant manning the refreshment table. 'Shall we?' he asked, indicating a less occupied section of the room.

'Indeed, sir, I hope I did not appear to be so discourteous to poor Mr Oglesby!' she protested as he escorted her to the quiet corner. 'I should be ashamed of such behaviour and my aunt would be horrified. He's a particular favourite of hers.'

'Were you enjoying his attentions?'

'Well, no, but—'

'I rest my case. And you may be easy. You appeared polite enough to the casual eye. Only I was studying you more closely.'

'I can't imagine why. And I certainly wasn't "praying to be rescued",' she objected.

'You are certain?'

'I may have been anxious for the performance to begin,' Jocelyn said, trying to walk a tightrope between truth and courtesy, 'but I enjoy music very much. Is that why you singled me out, rather than any of the other ladies present? Because you thought I needed "rescuing"?'

'Only partly. I know Oglesby, you see. I also know your brother and admire very much the translations your father has published. With which, Virgil told me, you were of much assistance to Reverend Sudderfeld as you are to Virgil's project now. A woman intelligent enough to help with work of that sort would have a hard time enduring the attentions of Ernest Oglesby. I don't mean to disparage him—he's a very correct and courteous gentleman. But not a scholar and hardly an intellectual.'

'And you are, sir? I'm sorry, but if my brother has mentioned you, I don't remember it.'

'That's probably because he would have referred to me as "James Ramsey", which was how I was known when we were at Oxford together. Before I inherited the barony.'

'James Ramsey? Yes, he has spoken of you! As I recall, you preferred the later Roman period writers— Plutarch, Plotinus and the Neo-Platonists.'

'Exactly. See, you do remember me.'

'Now that I know who you are—or were. Did you continue your scholarship after leaving university?'

'No, sadly, my father passed away about the time I left Oxford. Since his death, except for some reading in the evenings, I have been fully occupied running the estate. But I have kept up with all your father's works, purchasing each as soon as it was published, and am very much looking forward to acquiring the Euripides collection as soon as Virgil—and you—are finished with it.'

'He will be delighted to hear that.'

'Sip your punch, now. We shall have to take our seats

in a moment. I do hope you will permit me to sit with you and Lady Bellingame.'

'If you wish,' Jocelyn said, both intrigued and a little uncomfortable at the Baron's marked attentions. On the one hand, it was flattering to be singled out by a well-dressed, well-spoken, handsome gentleman—who also happened to be a classics scholar. On the other, at her rather advanced age and after gossip had sped through the *ton* that she was a hopeless bluestocking, she wasn't accustomed to receiving much attention from eligible bachelors.

That is—if Lord Darnsby were one.

'Your wife did not accompany you to London?'

He chuckled. 'No. Let me quickly reassure you, I am not married.'

Jocelyn felt her face redden. 'Not that it matters,' she hastened to assert.

'Of course it matters. It would have been most dishonourable of me to seek you out if I were a married man.'

Not much used to teasing repartee, Jocelyn tried to figure out Darnsby's intent. Upon hearing that he'd been a university colleague of Virgil's, she assumed he'd wanted to meet her because he knew she was involved in the translation work. But his words seemed to indicate a more…personal interest. Or did they?

She wished she were more versed in the arts of flirtation!

'Ladies, gentlemen, if you would take your seats, please?' Lady Sterling called to the gathering from the doorway of the refreshment room.

Jocelyn gulped down the rest of her punch and handed the glass to Darnsby, relieved that it was time for the music to begin. Fortunately, she would have the span of the performance to try to determine the reason behind the Baron's marked attentions—if he in fact continued them after the music ended.

After returning their glasses, he offered her his arm again. 'You *will* allow me to sit with you?'

'Of course, if Lady Bellingame has no objections.'

Which, upon Darnsby's cordial request of the honour, her aunt did not. Jocelyn found herself seated near the front of the room, the Baron at her elbow. His presence was distracting enough that she found herself unable to fully concentrate on the performance—so much so, that when the first segment ended, she only belatedly began to clap with the other guests.

As they rose and moved towards the refreshment room, Darnsby bent close to her ear. 'Am I making you uncomfortable?' he murmured. 'That was certainly not my intention.'

Jocelyn hesitated. But unable to come up with a convincing denial, she said, 'Well…somewhat.'

'Would you prefer me to leave?'

'No, of course not! The music is marvellous; I wouldn't have you miss that. It's just… I—I can't quite discern the purpose behind your very flattering attentions. Whether you sought me out simply as a fellow scholar, or whether your interest is more…particular. Although I can't imagine how it could be, when I know we've never actually met before this evening.'

'Your intuition is as keen as your intelligence. I *have* approached you with more than a scholarly interest. Though it's true that we hadn't formally met before tonight, I have seen you. Every morning this week, riding early in the park. You ride with such joyous, energetic abandon—as if being where you are, doing what you are doing, were the most sublime experience in the universe! I adore riding myself and was so intrigued, I confess I followed you home and tipped the groom to reveal your identity. Imagine my surprise and delight to discover you were not just a beautiful Iris, travelling with the speed of the wind, but also a scholar and the sister of my old friend. So I started asking about until I found an acquaintance—Lady Sterling—who might present me to you.'

'Forgive me for being so blunt and please accept my apology if I am wildly misinterpreting your interest— I'm afraid I'm not skilled at all at dalliance. But are you...seeking a wife?'

'I intend to marry at some point, yes.'

'I only ask because if you are looking at me as a possible candidate for that role in the near future, I must tell you that I cannot consider wedding anyone until after Virgil and I finish the Euripides. Not that I am irreplaceable, but it would be inconvenient and time-consuming for him to have to find someone else to help him who possesses a sufficient knowledge of Greek and the ability to take down his words quickly in legible script.'

'You don't intend to marry until the Euripides translations are complete?'

'No. Odd and singular of me, I know, but there you have it.'

Smiling, the Baron shook his head. 'Now I know I was right to seek you out.'

Puzzled, Jocelyn shook her own head. 'Though you have lauded my intelligence, I don't understand your meaning at all.'

The Baron chuckled. 'I'm in no great hurry to wed, either. But to be equally blunt, I have two interfering sisters who have been trying to marry me off since the day I became Lord Darnsby. Over the few weeks each year I could spare to leave Waverly for London, I've been dragged to balls, musicales, soirées and parties, introduced to shy maidens, bold maidens, young maidens, older maidens and desperate maidens. Who all share one thing in common: an overwhelming desire to marry and to marry as quickly as possible. To discover a lady who does not share that ambition is… singular. To discover one who is also a scholar is exceptional. And to discover an independent-minded young woman who is both a scholar and a beauty is almost miraculous. Providential, I would say.'

Surprised, amused—but still uncomfortable—Jocelyn said, 'I don't quite know what to say.'

'You needn't say anything. I realise I have been rather…forward, but although I have no desire to marry immediately, I also, as I just mentioned, can only afford to spend a few weeks in London. I'd like you to permit me to call on you. Over the years of having my sisters trying to foist pretty, polite, well-brought-up young ladies on me, I gradually formed a picture of the woman I hoped some day to marry. Someone lovely to look upon, yes. But even more important, I longed to find someone to whom I could talk about more than just the everyday matters of running a house and an estate, squabbles among the staff or problems with the children. Someone of intelligence, someone who loves the classics and philosophy that have always intrigued me, who could read and discuss them with me of an evening. One who loved horses and riding would be an added bonus. Frankly, I didn't believe such a woman existed. Now I'm not so sure.'

'I'm hardly a paragon!'

'What mortal is? I don't seek perfection—only a compatible companion with similar interests, someone I'd frankly given up hope of finding—until I saw you galloping in the Park that first day. Will you give us the chance to become better acquainted? That is, you are not opposed to marriage on principle, are you? You do envisage some day finding a partner who could appreciate your intelligence and share your interests?'

'No, I'm not opposed to wedlock,' she said, giving her standard answer. 'Although frankly, I have held even less hope than you of finding a "compatible companion" who would appreciate my intelligence and interests. I rather expect I shall end up as a companion to an elderly bluestocking who wants me to read to her and take care of her pug.'

'Heaven forfend! I would hope for better than that for you. So you will allow me to call?'

His frank interest still made her vaguely uneasy... but then, she'd never really spent much time around any man save her brother and Alex, not even with her erstwhile former fiancé. Of course she felt comfortable with Alex, who had been a friend for a long, long time.

But even friendship with him would probably be impossible in future. Her long infatuation was a relic of childhood she was going to have to overcome.

Might Lord Darnsby represent the future?

Of course she didn't feel as easy with him as she did with Alex—they had only just met. But if they proved to have the same interests and outlook, he might become a friend with whom she felt as comfortable as she did with Alex.

Not that she'd truly consider marriage with him either. Much as he seemed to admire her scholarship, she could no more risk revealing her secret authorship to him than she could to Alex. If she could persuade Virgil to continue translating after the Euripides project ended—if the volumes earned enough so he could live comfortably without the Duke's sponsorship—she would need to still be independent in order to continue the work that meant so much to her.

She smiled wryly. Before catching herself to modify her statement into a remark about 'studying', she'd almost blurted out to Alex that going on to do other projects was her true goal. It would be easier to continue with Virgil, although that was looking less and less likely. Unlike Papa, who seemed unconcerned by the possibility that her true contribution might be discovered, Virgil was much more worried about the consequences to his work and reputation should their secret ever be revealed. Living independently with her naughty old lady would allow her the freedom to discreetly look into publishing her work anonymously.

She sighed. Although she hadn't yet figured out how she would manage that. For one, she'd not yet discovered any lady of her aunt's acquaintance who showed promise of becoming a future employer. Then, with very few exceptions like Miss Austen, women did not publish books. Certainly not scholarly works. She would need to establish contacts with publishers, probably by way of a solicitor or some other go-between, and as yet wasn't sure how to go about that.

But, as she'd assured Alex, finishing the Euripides would take years. She'd have time to work it all out.

As long as she wasn't impeded by having to deceive a husband.

Still, if she were to develop a fondness for Lord Darnsby, and he for her, it might make weathering the inevitable end of her friendship with Alex easier. A friend to replace a friend, even if they never progressed to the more intimate relationship he seemed to want.

She ought not to summarily reject such a chance.

'Yes. Lord Darnsby. I would be happy to have you call on me.'

'Excellent!' he said, blowing out a breath. 'I must say, you hesitated so long before giving permission, I was afraid I'd been too bold and given you a distaste of me. I'm afraid I have to leave now—another reason for my pressing you, so I must return you to your aunt and say my goodbyes to our hostess. But expect to see me soon.'

He walked her over to her aunt and bowed. 'Lady Bellingame, thank you for lending me your niece. It was a pleasure to make both your acquaintances. I look forward to calling on you.'

'We would be very happy to see you again, Lord Darnsby,' her aunt said.

Fortunately, her aunt was worldly enough to preserve a dispassionate expression for the rest of the evening and to refrain from questioning Jocelyn about the Baron while there were so many curious ears listening in. But as soon as they were alone in the carriage on their way home, Lady Bellingame turned to her.

'You seem to have acquired quite an admirer! A highly eligible one, too. Lady Sterling tells me his estate in Kent is extensive and his income is handsome. You did encourage him to call, did you not?'

'Yes. It turns out that he's a college friend of Virgil's. I didn't recognise his title, but when he told me his given name, I recalled Virgil talking about him. He admires Father and owns all his translations.'

'A fellow scholar, then. Excellent! I'm so pleased for you, my dear. Quite frankly, I'd begun to despair of your showing enthusiasm about any gentleman—save the out-of-reach Mr Cheverton. Landed, titled, handsome and a scholar—Lord Darnsby might just be the one for you. How relieved I would be to have you so well settled!'

'Heavens, Aunt, don't be ordering the wedding trousseau yet!' Jocelyn exclaimed. 'I've only just met the man. An acquaintance with your brother and a knowledge of the classics do not necessarily a marriage make.'

'They make a promising beginning, though. I shall remain optimistic that, in Lord Darnsby, my efforts on your behalf will finally come to fruition!'

Her aunt had just given her a perfect opportunity to confess that she didn't really intend to wed anyone, something she'd several times considered doing. On the one hand, it seemed…dishonest to enjoy Lady Bellingame's hospitality when she had no intention of seeking the outcome her aunt wanted for her. But on the other, to confess her true feelings would only spark a disagreement that could not be resolved. Her aunt, like all of society, would not be able to understand that she truly didn't wish to marry.

Nor could she tell her why. Lady Bellingame would probably be more horrified to discover her true role in the translation project than the Duke.

It was easier, and perhaps kinder to her aunt as well, to simply continue playing the expected role and end her visit by claiming, quite honestly, that she had found no man who could tempt her to marry.

She pushed away the image of Alex's face. Well, *he* might tempt her. Fortunately, the Duke would never find her acceptable as future Duchess, so she didn't have to worry about being torn between her affection for him and her driving need to be true to herself.

The distance between their hostess's town house and her aunt's being short, by this time the carriage was pulling up in front of their destination. Patting her hand, Lady Bellingame prepared to alight.

Accepting the help of the footman to hand her down after her aunt, Jocelyn followed Lady Bellingame up the front steps.

She shouldn't feel unsettled at the prospect of the Baron calling, but rather...encouraged, Jocelyn told herself. She'd already told him she wouldn't consider marriage for years. His potential friendship wouldn't threaten anything she held dear—her ability to finish the project, or the reputations of her father and brother. Though she would have to confess early on that she couldn't really consider marriage. It wouldn't be fair to let him continue in that false hope and perhaps pass up opportunities to pursue more conventional women.

Although... If, by the time the Euripides concluded, she had not found a way to continue her work, he might offer her an unexpected second option for her future. Since by then, Alex would be long wed and hopefully a father.

She should just relax and see what developed between them. It would be pleasant to have another intelligent gentleman to talk with about the subjects that engaged her, wouldn't it?

After all, she wouldn't be able to command the exclusive attention of Virgil—or Alex—for ever.

Chapter Fourteen

In the morning two days later, Alex sprinted his gelding towards the Park. He'd hoped to get away much earlier, but the Duke, who generally didn't rise until noon, had surprised him by unexpectedly arriving in the breakfast room just as Alex was preparing to leave. Simple courtesy had demanded Alex remain long enough to drink another cup of coffee and make light conversation.

The weather this morning was fair and warmer, which meant that if Jocelyn held to what she'd told him that afternoon at Astley's, she should have gone riding. He only hoped she hadn't already left the Park.

He had intended to call on her the day after their Astley's excursion, but an unexpected meeting with one of the Duke's Parliamentary colleagues had pulled him into a long afternoon of consultations at White's. His schedule for the rest of today and all of tomorrow was fully booked, and after that, he was to accompany the Duke to the country home just outside London of another colleague for several more days of talks.

Alex didn't want to miss seeing Jocelyn for that long without first letting her know why he hadn't called again. He didn't want to hurt or offend her by having her think he was intentionally neglecting her.

Not when having her lively and intelligent companionship had often become, he was forced to admit, the highlight of his days.

He pushed his mind away from considering the implications of that fact. For now, he would just look forward to the pleasure of riding with her.

He'd set his horse to trotting down Rotten Row when he spotted a woman riding side saddle on a cross path that intersected at an angle with the Row. Even at a distance, by the posture of the figure and the ease with which she was controlling her mount, he knew it must be Jocelyn.

Adjusting his pace so he would arrive to intercept her, Alex had to smile. The rider was slowing her mare to a walk. Jocelyn must have just finished a rousing gallop and was letting her mount cool down, which was the only reason she ever rode at a walk.

As he watched, she eased herself up on the side saddle. His smile faded as she straightened her left leg in the stirrup and rose over the saddle, manoeuvring her right leg out from the leaping pommel and attempting to place her right knee on top of the saddle. Puzzlement giving way to alarm, he realised with her left leg fully straightened and her heel jammed down on the stirrup, she was trying to *stand*—as much as one could stand—in the side saddle.

Damn and blast! He thought he'd dissuaded her from trying any tricks inspired by the show at Astley's. He wanted to shout at her to stop at once and resume the proper side-saddle position. But he dared not call out, lest he distract her, perhaps causing her to lose her concentration and fall.

But when she urged her horse faster, from walk to

trot, he increased his own pace, even more eager to intercept her, but knowing he must do so carefully, so as not to divert her attention or startle her mount.

As he got closer, he could hear her murmuring—probably trying to settle the skittish mare, whose pricked ears and uneasy whickers indicated her unhappiness about the unusual shift in balance of the weight on her back. But while he approached cautiously, he suddenly realised another rider was cantering towards him—and the intersection of the two trails towards which Jocelyn's horse was headed.

Reaching the intersection seconds before the mare, the man shouted, 'Hey, there, look what you're about!' before thundering by, swerving around Alex as he passed.

Jocelyn looked up quickly, scowling at the intercepting rider and following his progress with her gaze. Until she saw him and her eyes widened.

At that moment, the mare shied. Alex heard her call his name just as her right knee slipped, she lost her grip on the pommel and with it her balance. With a cry, she pitched sideways off the horse, which reared and took off running.

Fear scouring him as the mare flashed by him, Alex raced his mount to the intersection and leapt from the saddle. Running to Jocelyn, who was lying prone on the ground, he cried, 'Are you all right?'

He reached her, realised she was struggling to sit and gave her a hand up. 'Are you injured? Does anything hurt? Shouldn't you lie back down?'

She'd lost her hat and half her glorious chestnut locks had come unpinned. But she wasn't grimacing in pain and he couldn't see any immediate injuries. He wanted to run his hands over her legs and arms, to check for breaks, but he didn't dare. Instead, he repeated, 'Are you all right? You didn't strike your head, did you?'

'I'm fine. The only thing injured is my pride. I thought I'd quite mastered the position—I've been practising it with good success for half an hour. But all it required to overset me was one shouting stranger—and the unexpected appearance of a friend.'

'If I'm in any way responsible, I'm sincerely sorry. But honestly, I ought to thrash you! I thought you promised not to practise any tricks while still in London!'

'If you will recall correctly, you *asked* me to promise. I never gave you my word. Besides, with a leaping head, that trick is really very simple. If I'd had one of my regular mounts from Edge Hall, who are more trusting of my commands, I'd be able to do it at a canter by now. Would you help me up, please? I seem to have landed in a tangle of skirts.'

'You are impossible!' he declared, not sure whether he was more relieved or angry with her. But he gave her his hand and helped her to stand.

'If you would be useful, could you ride after my mare and retrieve her? The naughty girl will be halfway to Hyde Park Corner by now. Left on her own, I suspect she will head straight back to the livery stable, causing consternation among the grooms should she show up without me.'

'Speaking of grooms, where is yours? Surely your aunt wouldn't permit you to ride in London without one.'

'Catch my horse first, please, and I'll tell you all about it.'

She had a point there. Not only would the livery stable staff be alarmed should the horse return without a rider, the mare could well be injured by the busy traffic on the London streets without a rider to guide her. 'Very well, I'll find her and be back in a trice. If you are sure you are unharmed?'

'The only thing damaged is my wonderfully intricate coiffure. Mary will weep when she sees what I've done to it.'

'I'll be right back. You stay here and don't move!'

'Nonsense, I'll walk down the trail after you. I'm not an invalid! This is certainly not the first time I've taken a tumble and it wasn't nearly as hard a fall as some.'

'Honestly, Jocelyn Sudderfeld, you are—!'

'Yes, yes, I know,' she interrupted. 'An irresponsible, reckless brat. I've had the lecture before,' she added unrepentantly.

'You're about to get the latest version when I return,' he retorted as he caught up his gelding and threw himself back in the saddle.

But she merely laughed. 'On your way,' she said with a wave.

Swearing under his breath, Alex set off and soon overtook the riderless mare, who was indeed headed in the direction of the livery stable at an uncertain trot. She seemed relieved to have her reins caught up and be led by a rider again.

A few minutes later, he reached Jocelyn, who had fetched her lost hat and was attempting to pin up her fallen locks.

'Thank you for retrieving her! She doesn't seem the worse for her runaway gallop.'

'She's fine. Still skittish, so I'd be careful on your ride back. Can I do anything to help?' He gestured towards her hat.

'My hair is hopeless, I'm afraid. I've lost too many pins to secure it properly. I'm going to have to just jam it under my hat. I'll probably still look like an escapee from Bedlam, but that's the best I can do. Could you could lower the hat back on my head while I hold up my hair?'

'Of course.' Jumping down, Alex took the reins from both horses and looped them over a nearby branch, then came over to take the hat she held out.

He would have preferred to lift that fall of dark curling tresses, he thought, envisaging the silk of it slipping through his bare fingers. But obediently he grasped the hat, and at her nod, fitted it over the hair she pushed up and held the whole in place while she withdrew her fingers.

'Thank you. Now, if you would brush the dirt and twigs off the back of my jacket, I'll have done all I can to look presentable enough not to send Aunt Bellingame off in a fit of hysterics if she should happen to see me before I can change.'

She offered him her back. Starting at the velvet collar, which seemed to have attracted the majority of the twigs and bits of grass, Alex brushed downward… resisting the impulse to let his fingers slow and caress the round of her shoulder, the points of her shoulder blades, and back up to the curve of her neck. Desire built in him again, that familiar tightening in his body and dryness in his mouth as he contained himself to a brisk brushing-off.

How he wished he could let his fingers linger on her body, even barricaded as it was under layers of jacket, gown and undergarments. Ah, to slowly remove them layer by layer until he reached the soft skin beneath…

And he must not be having these thoughts about Jocelyn.

All debris from her jacket removed, he drew his hands back reluctantly,

'Thank you, kind sir.' Jocelyn turned back to face him. 'Now,' she added with a wry grin, 'you may abuse me as you like. I can see you are dying to ring a peal over me.'

Desire vanished as he remembered that moment of terror as he watched her fall. Anger came roaring back.

'True, you didn't promise not to try any tricks, but I thought I could count on you being sensible! That gown, as you noted, is completely unsuitable for attempting any tricks, even this "modest" one as you called it.'

'Yes, I'm sure you noticed that the ladies at Astley's who stood on horseback were much more sensibly dressed.'

If she'd been trying to divert him, she'd succeeded. Envisaging Jocelyn in one of the low-necked, sleeveless, ballerina-length gowns that exposed the rider's lower legs and bare feet momentarily drove all other thoughts from his head.

Dragging himself away from that mental image, he tried to recapture his indignation. 'Dress is a minor point. It isn't safe to attempt tricks in the Park—as that near-collision should have proven. That rider almost ran you over! Only imagine how your aunt and father and brother would feel if something should have happened to you!'

How *he* felt. He'd never truly considered the prospect of losing her—not even while acknowledging that sooner or later, he must wed a high-born woman approved by the Duke.

A world without Jocelyn in it? How diminished it would be of light and laughter and joy!

The idea shook him.

'Well, he didn't collide with me and there was never any chance of my getting seriously injured,' she was saying. 'I may have been concentrating on my balance, but I was aware of what was going on around me and would have adjusted. Besides, as I said, I've been bringing the mare along and I've almost perfected the move. Once I can transfer balance to my straightened left leg long enough to move my right knee on to the centre of the saddle, maintaining that stance is easier. And would be even easier, if I were able to wear more reasonable garments.'

'Like breeches?'

'Exactly. It's so unfair that gentlemen get to wear garments that are so much more practical than a female's dress.'

Alex sighed. 'By the way, where is your groom? Still nowhere in sight! You promised to explain his disappearance, you may remember.'

She gave him a guilty look. 'Well, yes. I knew he would not be any more...enthusiastic about my practising the trick than you are. So the last few days, towards the end of the ride, when it is late enough that there are nursemaids and their charges about and other riders I could call on if I ran into difficulties—and when we've been here long enough that he's thoroughly bored with trotting along in my wake—I've persuaded him to ride to Hyde Park Corner and have an ale at the inn across the street, with me meeting him after half an hour.'

'Did you happen to slip him a coin to help persuade him?'

'I have it on good authority that it's always useful to stay on good terms with the servants.'

'Who can be uncommonly useful,' he added with a grimace. 'Especially when it comes to allowing you to do something he would feel compelled to prevent. I suppose your near-accident is my fault for recommending that sly trick.'

Jocelyn chuckled. 'I suspect he thought I've been secretly meeting a gentleman. By the look on his face, his conscience struggled with his desire for the coin. I'm guessing he concluded that nothing too dire could occur to me in the Park in broad daylight. That said, you'd better help me mount so I can go meet him before it gets any later—and he begins to fear I've had a mishap.'

'He ought to worry. Taking a coin in exchange for information is one thing. But he was risking your safety, letting you ride alone.'

'Oh, dear, you're not going to take him to task, are you? He'll stick to me like ink on a printer's fingers after this if you do.'

'I will refrain, but only if you promise—really *promise* this time—not to attempt any more tricks while in London, and to ride conventionally in the side saddle at all times.'

'If I do that, there will be no need to send him off for an ale!'

Alex shrugged. 'Those are my terms.'

She tried to stare him down, but he returned her gaze without flinching. 'Despot,' she accused with a sigh. 'Very well, I promise not to attempt any more tricks while in London.'

'And to ride side saddle conventionally from now on.'

'And to ride conventionally,' she added with a resentful look.

'I'm only looking out for your best interests. Only think what would happen if you did take a fall that injured you. How would Virgil manage? You keep insisting you couldn't possibly marry until his project is completed. If you broke a hand, it would create just as many difficulties for him as if you married.'

'Perhaps. But one can recover from an injury. There's no recovery from marriage.'

He chuckled. 'That may be true. But you do need to be more careful. Please.'

She sighed. 'I hadn't considered how it might impact our work if I hurt myself. I suppose I must be more circumspect—at least until the project is completed.'

'When the image of Astley tricks simmering in your head could be resurrected? I may regret having encouraged you to go!'

She laughed. 'Give me a leg up, please?'

He laced his fingers together for her, focusing on the delight of her hand momentarily clutching his shoulder. He was almost tempted to shift his weight and make her slip, so he would be able to catch her, hold her, just a bit longer.

Bend his head down and steal the kiss he longed for.

But that wouldn't be honourable, so he refrained.

'By the way, before you go, let me tell you what I came looking for you to say.'

Remounted, she looked back over at him. 'You came here to find me?'

'Yes. I haven't been able to get away and tomorrow the Duke is taking me out of town for a few days. So I probably won't see you again until next week. But I didn't want you to think I had...forgotten you.'

For a moment, they stared at each other, that ever-strengthening sensual energy pulsing between them. As he gazed at her, a swell of those pesky emotions he must suppress rose in him, a longing for her that went well beyond desire. Biting his tongue before he could impulsively give them voice, he said instead, 'I'll look to see you again soon after our return.'

'I'd like that. And I do thank you for helping me today. I would have been hard-pressed to catch up to my horse—or get my hair back under my hat.'

'My pleasure—if I've convinced you to be more careful in future.'

'I'll not do tricks, as I promised, but I'm always careful. Sometimes I think you believe I'm still that sixteen-year-old hoyden my brother calls me!'

She was that...and so much more. So much that was desired and dear—and more precious to him than he'd realised.

The sound of pounding hoofs caught his ear. He looked up, as Jocelyn did, to see the groom galloping towards them.

'Be ye all right, miss?' he asked, pulling up his mount. 'When ye didn't meet me as ye always do, I was right worried!'

'I'm fine, Jeffers, and I do apologise. I... I met Mr Cheverton unexpectedly. We started talking and I forgot the time. I am sorry for worrying you.'

Alex raised an eyebrow, but at the pleading look on Jocelyn's face did not dispute her explanation.

'Just thankful to find you unhurt, miss,' the groom said. 'Best get you home now.'

The groom must not be much acquainted with the feminine fashion, Alex thought. He hadn't blinked an eye over her loosened hair and dusty garment—else he might have suspected she *had* just returned from an assignation.

Would that she had—with him. He would much rather have pulled her into the shrubbery and kissed her senseless than been frightened out of his wits by watching her fall.

'I'm so glad we chanced to meet, Mr Cheverton. Enjoy the rest of your ride.'

'It was good to see you, too, Miss Sudderfeld,' he said. 'Have a safe ride home.'

'Oh, I will. And every ride after that, apparently.' Giving him a nod, she set off with the groom.

Grinning, he watched her ride off. It would take more than a little tumble to dampen that irrepressible spirit.

Turning his own horse towards home, he thought again how dear she was. How much he would miss her when their lives careened off in different directions. But the very turmoil of emotions he was struggling to suppress should convince him that going their separate ways was wiser.

He would need to marry soon. And he didn't dare marry her.

A polite, conventional marriage with a woman he admired would be...safe. Would never threaten the devastation that might happen if he married someone who could inspire him to heights of passion and emotion he feared Jocelyn might.

But after a moment of entertaining the unthinkable, he had to chuckle.

She'd very likely turn him down if he were rash enough to throw caution, and the Duke's good will, to the winds and admit he had serious intentions towards her. She'd stated on numerous occasions that she didn't wish to marry.

But he would never try to restrain that restless spirit. He...valued her, he inserted, needing to come up with a word less frightening and all-encompassing than "love". Yes, *valued* her too much to ever put stumbling blocks in the way of what she most desired. He'd be proud to have a wife of her intelligence and ability.

And if his thoughts were straying more and more often into this forbidden territory, he'd better limit his meetings with Jocelyn and make more of an effort to find a woman who could be that suitable, *safe* wife. One who, if he should ever lose her, did not possess the power to bring his world crashing down around his ears.

Back in Grosvenor Square a short while later, Alex mounted the stairs, intending to head to his chamber and change out of his dusty riding clothes before the Duke bore him off to White's for dinner and cards. But as he reached the top of the stairs, the Duke appeared at the door of his library.

'You had a good ride, I trust?'

'Yes, sir. It was…most entertaining.'

The Duke nodded. 'I've just received a dispatch from Edge Hall about a problem on one of the farms. Would you stop a moment and give me your opinion on which course of action Larson should pursue? I should like to send back instructions at once.'

'Of course. If you will forgive my intruding in the library in all my dirt.'

'Fortunately it's dry today. I don't think you'll track in enough to cause the maids to revolt.'

Alex followed Farisdeen back in and, declining a seat, stood by the desk while the Duke described the difficulty the interim estate manager was having with repairs on one of the farms. Having approved Larson's suggested course of action, Alex bowed and turned to go. 'It will only take me a few minutes to make myself presentable, and then I'll be ready to accompany you to White's.'

'Good. I received an invitation from a friend for us to attend a *soirée dansante* tonight. I should like to proceed there directly after dinner at White's.'

Alex nodded, wondering if he should find the butler and try to ferret out who would be attending that particular party. 'As you wish.'

'One other thing,' the Duke added a moment later, halting Alex as he headed towards the door. 'I understand that you escorted Miss Sudderfeld to Gunter's the other day.'

Alex felt himself tense. 'Yes. You may remember I mentioned wanting to take time to see old friends who happened to be in town. Miss Sudderfeld, the Reverend and her brother are presently visiting her aunt, Lady Bellingame. I encountered them at the British Museum and invited them all for tea. As you can probably predict, her father and brother declined, preferring to spend a bit more time studying—the Rosetta Stone, in this instance. So only Miss Sudderfeld accompanied me.'

Saying nothing, the Duke studied him. Not wanting to volunteer any information beyond that which was requested, Alex waited to see how the Duke would react.

'They have always been exemplary employees,' he said at last. 'I have been justly proud of sponsoring the work of the Sudderfeld scholars.'

'I'm not expert enough to be a judge, but I understand their translations are highly regarded.'

The Duke nodded. 'I shall see you presently, then,' he said and looked back down to the papers on his desk.

Torn between being unsettled and relieved, Alex walked out. Perhaps he should have indicated that he was more interested in seeing Jocelyn than in visiting the rest of the family. But that might have resulted in the Duke vehemently protesting that course of action.

On a happier note, the Duke hadn't attempted to dissuade him from visiting the family—even if he had pointedly referred to them as 'employees,' rather than social equals one would invite to dine.

Perhaps the Duke wouldn't be as opposed to Jocelyn as he'd feared. After all, though she wasn't the daughter of one of the highest in the land, her aunt was a viscountess, she was gently born and every inch a lady.

Then he recalled her appearance earlier today in the park, half her hair coming down, dirt and grass on her collar. Well, maybe not *every* inch, he thought with a grin.

No, better to stick to his original resolve and inspect the current crop on the Marriage Mart with an eye to finding a conventionally-brought-up maiden of suitable breeding to become the next Duchess.

Though wedding such a lady now inspired in him even less enthusiasm than when he'd first realised Penlowe's death had passed on to him the responsibility of continuing the ducal line.

Chapter Fifteen

Late that evening, Alex followed the Duke into the Countess of Richland's chandelier-bedecked ballroom. After greeting their hostess by the door, the Duke led Alex further into the room, stopping at times to greet friends and acquaintances, most of whom Alex had already met.

Curious about the Duke's purposeful progress across the room, he was not surprised when Farisdeen halted at last before an older couple—with a young, dark-haired lady in tow whose resemblance to the woman indicated she must be their daughter.

The girl was quite lovely, her dark hair arranged in curls, her face pretty and her figure graceful and, of course, gorgeously gowned in the latest fashion. As she was not as tall as Jocelyn, he had to look down at her, noting as he did that her dark hair lacked any burnished chestnut highlights and her eyes were fine rather than fiery.

'Herringford, well met,' the Duke said as he halted before them.

'Good evening, Duke,' Herringford replied, as the

whole group exchanged bows and curtsies. 'Allow us to express again our very great sympathy over your loss.'

'Your loss as well,' Farisdeen said, his voice as usual devoid of emotion. 'Lady Herringford, Lady Anne, Herringford, may I present my new heir, Mr Cheverton. Cheverton, the Earl of Herringford, his wife, Lady Herringford and their daughter.'

'Pleased to make your acquaintance, Mr Cheverton,' Lady Herringford said, while the Earl nodded and the daughter smiled.

And smile they might. Alex suspected he'd just been introduced to the Duke's preferred candidate for the role of his future wife.

'You managed Edge Hall for the Duke?' Herringford was saying.

Alex nodded. 'I had that honour.'

'A handsome property! It's been some years now since we last visited,' Lady Herringford said. 'I'm still hoping we may do so again in future.'

'You must all come down for the hunt next season,' the Duke said.

'Anne and I don't ride to the hunt, but I'm sure Herringford would enjoy that,' the Countess said.

Just then, the master of ceremonies announced the next set. 'Are you dancing tonight, Lady Anne?' the Duke asked.

'I have been, but I left this set free. I'm a bit fatigued and rather thirsty!'

'Cheverton, why don't you escort Lady Anne for some refreshments, while I catch up with Lord and Lady Herringford?'

Alex thought ruefully that the Duke was wasting no time throwing them together. But, as civility required,

Alex bowed to the lady. 'If you would permit, Lady Anne, I should be delighted.'

Giving him a nod, Lady Anne placed a hand on his arm. Once they were out of earshot, she laughed. 'Oh, dear! I'm afraid the Duke isn't very subtle, Mr Cheverton.'

'It doesn't require any prompting for a gentleman to ask a lovely lady to take some refreshment,' Alex said.

'Gallantly spoken, sir.'

They walked into the refreshment room, conversation ceasing for a few minutes while Alex procured them each a glass of punch and led her away so they might drink them. After both had taken a few sips, Lady Anne said, 'Speaking of speaking, has the Duke…said anything to you about me? I rather think not, since you didn't seem to react at all when he introduced us.'

'No, I'm sorry, but he has not. Is there something I should know?'

She smiled. 'Probably he is giving you a chance to adjust to your…unexpected position before trying to place any demands on you.'

'And you expect there will be…demands placed upon me?'

'Only the most important duty required of any gentleman of high rank. That he marry and produce heirs. But I'm sure you are already well aware of that one.'

Alex nodded. 'I am. The Duke has not yet made any recommendations on that score. He is…reserved by nature. Although he has not expressed a great deal of emotion about it, I'm sure the sudden death of his son has been difficult for him. Bringing up the need to marry and produce heirs might still be too painful a reminder of his loss.'

'I imagine it is, but men of rank must shoulder their

burdens and do what is required, regardless of personal feeling. My family has only just arrived in London. When my father sent word to the Duke that we were in residence, Farisdeen asked that we come to this affair tonight, rather than to the ball we'd initially planned on attending. As you know, the Duke believes it possible to visit small gatherings, but thinks it inappropriate in his mourning status to attend a large entertainment. Farisdeen wanted us to become acquainted as soon as possible.'

'You are hinting that he sees you as a possible daughter-in-law?' Alex guessed. 'Have our families been long acquainted?'

'Not particularly. But the Duke was certain that, before his unfortunate demise, Penlowe had been about to ask for my hand. It would have been a suitable match for both families, one which my father would have approved and I would have accepted.'

Something about the matter-of-fact way Lady Anne spoke about the potential engagement made Alex feel chilled. 'You and Lord Penlowe were sweethearts?' he asked, hoping his impression was wrong. 'I am most sorry for your loss.'

Frowning a little, Lady Anne shook her head. 'We did not know each other all that well. Penlowe was... not very social. At least, he didn't attend many *ton* functions. He preferred gaming and...other pursuits. None the less, it was my understanding as well that, had he not been prematurely taken from us, he would have made me an offer.'

Suspecting he knew what was coming, Alex tried to keep his tone neutral as he replied, 'It must still have been a sore loss, despite a lack of more...personal feeling.'

Lady Anne nodded. 'It was. Mother was quite distraught, but fortunately Father was more level-headed. He contacted Farisdeen at once. The Duke immediately informed him that there was another heir whom he intended to take under his wing. So all was not lost... necessarily.'

'The Duke and your parents hoped you would be able to transfer your affections—' Alex had a hard time keeping the sarcasm out of his tone when he pronounced that word '—to the new heir?'

Lady Anne nodded. 'After a suitable interval, of course. This time, he told Papa, he wanted his heir to spend more time in my company from the very beginning. Which is why we hastened back to town, once Farisdeen wrote to tell Papa you had arrived and were beginning your training.'

He might be seeking just such a bride, but he did not appreciate being boxed in. Reining in the anger that was beginning to fray his façade of cordiality, he asked, 'And did Farisdeen anticipate his heir having any say in this matter?'

Lady Anne smiled faintly. 'Part of the heir's training would be for him to understand his duty to marry well.'

'And you have no objection to this arrangement?'

'Of course, I wanted to have a closer look at you before I agreed. Even to become a duchess, I'd not align myself with a boor, or a country dolt or a dull-witted man whose only qualification for my hand was chancing to possess the correct ancestor. But you may pride yourself on having created an excellent first impression. Your dress, speech and manner confirm you as a gentleman of intelligence and refinement.'

Gritting his teeth at her condescension, Alex inclined his head. 'I am flattered.'

'As you realise, persons of rank do not have the luxury of allowing…emotion to sway a decision as important as marriage. Should I pass muster with you, let me assure you I should be an understanding and undemanding wife. Respect me and my position, take care of me and our children and I am prepared to turn a blind eye to any…side pursuits.'

'You would not find turning a blind eye difficult?'

'If you are asking whether I would throw tantrums or demand retribution for any…neglect, I assure you I would not. It has been the duty of high-born wives from time immemorial to look the other way at their husbands'…little interests. Though I would not be unappreciative of a trinket now and then to reward my discretion.'

Although he'd accepted the vague idea of 'wedding someone of suitable rank and position', Alex hadn't thought much about what else that might imply. The you-go-your-way-I-go-mine after the requisite heirs had been bred struck in him an unexpected repulsion. Surely there would be more than that, even in a convenient marriage!

Needing to be sure, he pressed, 'A union of high rank is the only thing in marriage that matters to you? What of compatibility? What of passion?'

She shrugged. 'Passion between male and female is a fact of nature. And a union based on mutual respect and shared expectations, sadly, has a better chance of lasting success than one based on strong emotion.'

Though he shared that opinion, somehow her coldly rational approach to wedlock still disturbed him. 'Was there a particular time period envisaged for my training, before wedlock should be commenced?'

'Nothing formal. Farisdeen wanted to give you time

to become acquainted with your fellow peers and your duties, until you felt you'd found your feet and better understood your future role. Of course, Penlowe's unfortunate death has underscored the urgency the Duke feels to settle the matter of the succession.'

'I'm beginning to understand a number of things more clearly and thank you for pointing them out.'

She shook her head. 'Now you sound…angry. I didn't mean to offend you! Since you were not raised at the elevated rank to which fate has brought you, I wasn't sure you understood how we look upon marriage, especially once you informed me the Duke has as yet said nothing to you about it. I think that honesty between us is more useful than flattery or empty courtesy.'

'I do appreciate honesty, at least,' he acknowledged. 'So where do you see us proceeding from here?'

'I'm quite encouraged, actually. I must confess, when I first learned how distant your connection to Duke was, and that you'd formerly been a simple estate manager, I was quite uneasy. But now I am sure, with such promising material to start with, the Duke will soon have you completely prepared to fill your role.'

'And fully cognisant of my duty?'

'Exactly. I'm so pleased that we understand each other,' she said, seeming totally unaware of the irony of his last few replies—something Jocelyn would have sniffed out immediately.

'We do indeed. If you have finished your punch, I should return you to your parents. I'm not sure how long the Duke intends to remain. To respect his mourning status, he doesn't usually stay long at social gatherings.'

'Of course. One wishes to observe the proprieties.'

'Naturally. For the same reason, you will understand

why I would not wish to pay you particular attention just now.'

He thanked his lucky stars for that respite. Despite intending to contract exactly the sort of marriage she'd just described, now that he was faced with the imminent prospect of embarking upon one, he was suddenly filled with doubt that he could actually make himself do it.

Not unless he could convince himself this was truly all he should look for in a marriage. All the companionship and compatibility he needed to last him for the rest of his life.

Unless he chose to take Lady Anne up on her offer, and pursue 'little interests' elsewhere. Such as taking Jocelyn as his lover?

But he could never ask something so dishonourable of her. Jocelyn deserved everything—an all-out commitment, pledged before the whole world. A passionate declaration of love and complete devotion, not the tepid arrangement spelling out dowry, property and pin money Lady Anne looked for.

Was he capable of giving one?

'I understand,' she agreed, patting his arm. 'I shall be ready when the time is right.'

Would the time ever be right? Could he 'train' himself to accept a convenient, cold-blooded arrangement with the bride chosen for his predecessor?

His mind roiling with doubts—and more than a touch of anger—Alex walked Lady Anne back to where the Duke stood with her parents, all of them watching the couple closely as they approached. Did Farisdeen expect him to be grinning at the prospect of gaining a lovely, well-born earl's daughter for bride? Or were they checking to see whether the lowly former estate manager had managed to avoid giving the Earl's daughter a disgust of him?

But as much as he resented Lady Anne's condescension, he was a gentleman—just as he'd been when he was only the owner of the modest estate of Wynborne. So he nodded and smiled and bowed, thanked Lady Anne for her company and her parents for lending her to him. Turning to the Duke, proud he was able to keep his tone still perfectly cordial, he said, 'Did you intend to remain any longer, sir?'

'No, I think we accomplished what we came for.'

'I'll call for our carriage, then. Again, it was most... illuminating to meet you, Lady Anne, Lady Herringford, Lord Herringford.'

His ability to make polite conversation extinguished, Alex gave them a bow and walked away.

Since the Duke seldom indulged in idle chat, the silence that reigned between them on the drive back to Grosvenor Square was not unusual. But determined to broach the matter immediately, as they walked up the entry stairs, Alex said, 'I would like to have a word with you before you retire, Duke.'

Farisdeen gave him assessing look. 'Very well. We shall have some brandy in the library.'

Alex nodded, then followed the Duke up the stairs and into the room, where he poured a brandy for each of them. Once they were seated before the fire, Alex said, 'I don't know how far along in negotiations you and Lord Herringford have progressed on this matter, but please do not assume I will marry Lady Anne.'

The Duke held up a warning hand. 'Don't immediately kick over the traces, just because it was not your idea from the outset. Lady Anne has been brought up from birth to fill a high position and could be a real asset to you. With you not possessing the background or training for much you will have to do, her experience and knowledge of all the foremost people of rank could help fill the gap. Thus far, our mourning status has limited the number of society engagements we've been required to attend, but once that ends, the social demands on your time will markedly increase. Having a wife from a well-known family who already knows how to conduct herself in society will ease the transition for you. Not to mention, being already engaged will protect you from the many—and there are many— scheming females who would resort to practically any trick to become a duchess.'

'As opposed to Lady Anne, who states quite frankly she is prepared to take on the role?' he couldn't resist inserting.

The Duke didn't even smile, much less protest that assertion. 'You could do a lot worse than marry someone who knows the game and how it is played. I suggest you rein in that indignation, get to know Lady Anne better and see if your opinion of her improves upon further acquaintance. Just don't wait too long. I made that mistake with Penlowe and I don't mean to repeat it. I'm not pressing you to decide tomorrow, but within the year I would like to see you properly wed and setting up your nursery. The Herringfords have always been a fertile lot. Lady Anne would be a perfect person to fill it.'

'I will not marry just for title and position. As both you and she have pointed out,' he added, his voice dripping sarcasm, 'I wasn't *brought up* to it. I will consider my happiness and comfort, too, not just the cold calculation of position and privilege.'

Somewhat to Alex's surprise, the Duke didn't immediately respond with the wrath he'd been expecting. 'There's no reason you can't have both,' he said in mild tones. 'Especially if you marry someone like Lady Anne. Should hanging about the familial hearth become...tiresome, you could seek diversion elsewhere without having to suffer any tawdry little scenes.'

'The prospect of embarking upon wedlock with no intention from the outset of honouring my vows doesn't appeal to me either,' he said icily. 'Since I seem to be so resistant to fulfilling my "duty", why not marry Lady Anne or another suitable lady yourself and breed another heir? As you said, there are any number of females whose only qualification in a husband is that he be a cultured man of high rank. A description you fit better than I.'

'You think I didn't seriously consider that option before I informed you of our relationship? I've had a number of mistresses over the years since my wife's early death and especially after learning of Penlowe's condition, I've...tried for a child. None of the women ever quickened, though after our relationship ended, most went on to have children by other men. If I'd remained silent and wed again and my wife failed to conceive, by the time I concluded the matter was hopeless and announced you as my heir, I would have even less time to train you. Nor, frankly, at my age do I wish to bother with the attentions required by a wife. No, Cheverton, I have decided you must be the next Duke and ensuring the succession is now your responsibility. If you can't stomach Lady Anne, choose some other lady, as long as she is suitable.'

'It wouldn't cause you problems with Lady Anne or her family for me to look elsewhere?'

'If Lady Anne is unable to win the favour of the future Duke of Farisdeen, that is her fault.'

'Because a duke's desires are always more important than anyone else's, no matter whom he might hurt?' he retorted, promising himself he would never become such a man. 'So much for any loyalty to your late son's fiancée.'

The Duke sighed. 'You yourself said you wanted an amicable union. If you don't think you could have that with Lady Anne, you would of course want to look elsewhere.'

Alex was beginning to think he knew exactly where else to look. 'When it comes to choosing a bride, I will make you no promises.'

'And as you do not need to remind me, there is no way I can force you to do anything.' Exhaling a deep breath, the Duke took another drink of the brandy, his hand trembling.

For the first time, Alex noticed that the Duke's face looked tired and strained. Maybe the loss of his son *had* affected him deeply and his need to maintain an impassive veneer was wearing him down even further.

'Some days, I'm ready to hand over all the duties of the dukedom right now,' Farisdeen said quietly. 'They can be…wearying. I've been watching you for years now, ever since you first entered Oxford. You are intelligent, principled and responsible. You may resent me and my demands, but you know your duty. In the end, I trust you will do it. And now I'm tired and wanting my bed. Goodnight, Cheverton.'

Still angry and more than a little frustrated, Alex stood and bowed as the Duke rose and walked out of the room. After downing the rest of his brandy in one swallow, Alex walked out after him.

He had stood his ground, he thought as he took the stairs to his chamber. He really had no desire to get to know Lady Anne any better. But would another woman of suitable birth feel much different than she did? *Persons of rank do not have the luxury of allowing emotion to sway a decision as important as marriage*, she'd told him.

Unfortunately, her calm, *unemotional* acceptance of entering a marriage with someone she'd only just met, based solely on his possessing suitable rank, made him feel as though he was bartering himself like a commodity on the Corn Exchange, while her condescension to the 'simple estate manager' still annoyed him.

What a contrast to the passion, fire and blazing intelligence of Jocelyn Sudderfeld! Both were well bred and physically attractive, but one was a lady of light and laughter and sparkling personality, the other, only the cold pasteboard silhouette of a woman.

The Duke wanted him to become engaged as soon as possible.

Maybe it was time to do just that. Maybe it was time to get past the anguish of his first unhappy brush with love and allow himself to risk it all.

The vision of Jocelyn, balancing on her side saddle in defiance of safety and convention, flashed into his head.

Time to embrace, rather than deny, his emotions. To embrace life as passionately and fearlessly as she did.

Letting his feelings run free could mean a devastation vastly deeper than he'd felt when he'd lost Eliza should a marriage between them go wrong. But the possibility of having Jocelyn at his side, in his bed, for the rest of his life, was surely worth the risk.

Excitement swept through him, while euphoria made his heart race. Yes, he would risk it. And finally acknowledge the emotions he'd been struggling to suppress, he now realised, almost since the day he suddenly awoke to find the beguiling child had become an arresting woman.

But would pursuing her be a mistake and not just for the risk it posed to his heart?

The Duke might eventually accept her, but he wouldn't be happy about a marriage that didn't match his heir to a family of similar wealth and stature. He might make her life difficult.

Jocelyn herself wasn't interested in marriage, as she had affirmed on numerous occasions. Though he thought her major reason for resisting the conventional role was her desire to continue working with her brother, something he would never oppose.

But if he were to court her and begin what would probably be the lengthy process of convincing her to trust him with her life, her talent and her love, he would have to be able to promise his unfailing devotion in return.

Uneasily, he remembered how his impetuous love for Eliza had faded.

Could he be certain that what he felt for Jocelyn would last a lifetime?

Then he recalled that he would be leaving London tomorrow with the Duke. There would be no possibility of seeing her or beginning anything until his return.

Maybe by then, he would have decided for sure whether to court her or not.

But when the thought of marrying anyone else now seemed so bleak and unappealing, how could he do anything else?

Chapter Sixteen

In the evening four days later, Alex mounted the stairs to Lady Almondsly's drawing room, where a small soirée with cards and dancing was being held. Upon arriving back in London this afternoon, he'd gone straight to Upper Brook Street, slipped Mary another coin and found out which entertainment her mistress was promised to attend that night. He'd had no trouble stopping by her ladyship's town house and procuring an invitation for himself.

He then returned to Grosvenor Square, tracked down the Duke in his library and informed him he had plans for the evening and would not be accompanying Farisdeen to dinner with Lord and Lady Herringford. He'd bowed and walked out, leaving the Duke no time to reply.

Now that he stood on the threshold of the drawing room, about to see her again for the first time in almost a week, his spirits rose in anticipation. This very night, he would get to dance with her for the first time. And during that dance, he'd make sure that she and Virgil would be working in the afternoon tomorrow, so he would find her at home when he called.

When he did, he intended to ask for her hand. Something which, after a week's worth of contemplation, he felt he must do—mistake or not.

He anticipated she would probably turn him down, initially. Because unlike Lady Anne, she was entirely unimpressed by the fact that he would some day be a duke. He would have to court her, cajole her, persuade her.

There would probably be kissing involved with the persuading part. He certainly hoped so. He couldn't wait to kiss her again.

Though, naughty minx, he was reasonably sure she'd let him kiss her, but would she let him marry her?

If she would, there would still be the problem of the Duke's approval. But as the man had admitted that night in his library, when Alex faced him down about marrying Lady Anne, there really wasn't much he could do about it.

They were both of age, so the Duke had no power to prevent him wedding her.

So much for persuading the Duke—how best to convince Jocelyn? He knew she liked him, had proof positive that she desired him and he was prepared to let her work with Virgil for as long as it took for them to complete their project, and any others they might undertake afterwards. He could live with her at Edge Hall, leaving the Duke in London to tend to his ducal business.

Ah, if only he could win her! And then claim her as his bride. With the right, finally, to worship every inch of that lithe, lovely body.

Warmth, desire and a quiet joy flooded him at the idea.

He intended to be very, very persuasive.

He was smiling at his mental images of sharing Edge

Hall with Jocelyn while he greeted his hostess and proceeded into the ballroom. He spotted her at once, dancing with a tall, dark-haired gentleman with silver at his temples.

But as he watched them, his smile faded. The man held her a bit too closely and the look he bent on her was a little too caressing for Alex's liking. And unlike the air of patient endurance he'd sensed in her the day he'd called and she'd been entertaining her other two suitors, Jocelyn appeared quite willing to receive *this* man's attentions.

Alex felt a wave of alarm flash through him. He had an immediate, instinctive feeling that this man, whoever he was, might be an impediment to the progress of what was already likely to be a tempestuous courtship.

Barely conscious of anyone else in the room, Alex manoeuvred his way through the dancing couples and the onlookers, following the progress of Jocelyn and her partner, intent upon positioning himself near her when the dance ended.

'So you will ride with me in the morning?' Alex heard the man ask her when he got close enough to make out their conversation.

'If you appear while I am riding, of course. But as you've observed, I ride early, when I can still get in a good gallop.'

He'd *observed*? Had the man been watching her? Alex wondered.

'Riding with you is well worth getting up early. Perhaps we could have tea after the ride?'

'Probably not. I shall go straight in to Virgil after I've changed. We're a bit behind and I promised him a few extra hours of work tomorrow.'

'I would never wish to be an impediment to your

completing Virgil's project,' the man replied. 'As you know, I'm not in any hurry. Some things are worth waiting for.'

By now, Alex had heard enough to be certain he didn't like the man, whoever he was. Fortunately, since he wasn't sure how much longer he could resist cutting in, the dance ended. The gentleman offered Jocelyn his arm and, smiling, she accepted it.

He'd stationed himself just off the dance floor, right in their path. As her escort began to swerve her around him, Jocelyn looked away from her partner—and saw him.

'Alex, what a surprise!' she cried, stopping short. 'I didn't know you were back in town!'

'I just returned today. As you recall, I promised to seek you out directly after I arrived.'

'Um, yes.' Was that a…guilty look that flashed across her face? Before he could decide, the look vanished, replaced by a smile. 'But I'm forgetting my manners. I don't imagine that you two are acquainted. Deferring to future rank, Alex, may I present Lord Darnsby? He's a friend of Virgil's from university who's just come to town from his estate in Kent. A most intelligent and discerning individual, he owns all the volumes of Papa's translations and has already promised to order a full set of the Euripides. Darnsby, Mr Cheverton.'

Alex returned the man's bow—noting Darnsby seemed to be appraising him as critically as he was inspecting the Baron. 'Cheverton,' the man repeated. 'You're Farisdeen's heir, aren't you? I'm sorry for the loss of your cousin, but congratulations on your eventual elevation.'

Alex nodded. 'I suppose congratulations are in order.

Though I often wish I had remained simply the estate manager for Edge Hall.'

'Ah, so that is where you became acquainted with Jo—Miss Sudderfeld.'

That the man had almost used her given name further alarmed Alex. An instinctive hostility raised the hairs at the back of his neck.

'Yes, Alex has known me since I was a scrubby brat,' Jocelyn was saying. 'If he's particularly annoyed with me, he's apt to proclaim that I am still one.'

'Only when you persist in trying to do things that might have you breaking your neck.'

'I envy you your long acquaintance with Miss Sudderfeld,' Darnsby said. 'I hope our own relationship will end up lasting even longer. Although I refuse to believe you were ever a "scrubby brat", Miss Sudderfeld.'

The man was well dressed, well groomed and carried himself with quiet authority. Attractive, Alex supposed, if one were inclined to prefer older men. If he had been a friend of Virgil's at university and owned a set of the Reverend's classic Greek translation, he must have some claims to be intelligent.

Alex decided he didn't like him at all.

The more important question, though, was—did Jocelyn?

'Oh, you may believe it!' she assured Darnsby with a laugh. 'Just ask Virgil.'

'Well, if you ever were, you have certainly grown out of it to become a most beautiful and accomplished lady.'

Barely refraining from rolling his eyes, Alex cast a quick glance to see how Jocelyn reacted to this gallantry. To his relief, the slightly uneasy smile she returned told him she wasn't entirely comfortable with it.

Praise Heaven, he thought, breathing a sigh of relief.

At least the Baron hadn't thoroughly charmed her yet. Even if he was a friend of her brother's and a scholar.

Though the Baron had better qualifications to tempt her into marriage than the cleric who had abandoned her, he realised, unease filling him again.

He'd better begin his campaign quickly.

'I don't suppose your father or Virgil accompanied you tonight,' Alex said.

'Lord, no!' Jocelyn said with a laugh. 'Papa would probably prefer to be surrounded by a ring of Egyptian scorpions than a ballroom full of ladies wanting to dance and Virgil would have already hidden himself away in the library had he been prevailed upon to accept her ladyship's invitation.'

'Then you must convey me to your aunt, so I can at least pay my respects to one member of your family.'

'She will be happy to see you.'

If so, it would be the first time, Alex thought. True to his suspicions, Lady Bellingame's fond smile at watching her niece return on Darnsby's arm faded when she noticed who was following them.

'See who I found, Aunt,' Jocelyn said as they reached her side.

'Lady Bellingame, how nice to see you again. And how lovely you look tonight,' Alex said, bowing as she curtsied. 'That deep ruby gown is so becoming to your dark hair and eyes!'

'Thank you,' the Viscountess said, inclining her head. 'Jocelyn gets her colouring from her mother's side of the family.'

'So I can see. Are you enjoying the evening?'

'It's been quite enjoyable—up until now,' Lady Bellingame said with enough asperity to warn him her resistance wasn't about to be overcome by a few gallant compliments. 'Did you enjoy your dance, Jocelyn? I must say, you two make a handsome couple.'

Alex gritted his teeth. Jocelyn's aunt obviously favoured Darnsby's pursuit.

'It was quite pleasant, Aunt.'

'Are you acquainted with Lord Darnsby, Mr Cheverton?' Lady Bellingame asked.

'Jocelyn just introduced us.'

'We are so pleased that he was able to come to town! Although, sadly, he will not remain with us long. Waverly Park, his estate in Kent, is large and so demanding! Almost as complex and time-consuming as Edge Hall. With him soon to leave London, Jocelyn, you must see that he gets his full quota of dances.'

'I see I shall have to pull my some-day-to-be-elevated rank, then, to claim the next one,' Alex said. 'After all, Darnsby has already danced with the lady and I've not yet had the privilege.'

'It's kind of you to pay attention to a girl who's accounted you a friend since her childhood, Mr Cheverton,' Lady Bellingame said. 'But surely old friends can wait. You've only just arrived and I know there are many other ladies here anxious to claim the honour of dancing with a future duke.'

'One should never neglect friends, Lady Bellingame,' Alex returned. 'New acquaintances may fade away, but a friendship dating back years has proven its worth and should be treasured.'

At that moment in the verbal sparring, the orchestra struck up for the next dance. 'Much as I appreciate Mr Cheverton's eagerness, I would humbly ask that you accord me the next dance, Miss Sudderfeld,' Darnsby said. 'I shall have to leave directly afterwards. You see, although I had already accepted Lady Sterling's invitation for tonight, when Lady Bellingame informed me you ladies would be here, I could not deny myself the pleasure of dancing with you. But Lady Sterling is counting on me and it would be most discourteous to disappoint her.'

Her expression wry, Jocelyn looked between Alex and the Baron. 'I suppose I must grant you your dance first, Lord Darnsby,' she said. 'Alex, could you claim yours later? After you've honoured a few of those other *eager* ladies,' she added, giving him a teasing look.

That teasing glance, much warmer than anything he'd seen her give the Baron, reassured him a little. 'I'll be here,' he confirmed. 'After all, some things are worth waiting for.'

With that parting shot, he saw them off to the next dance.

While he waited, he might as well see if he could soften Lady Bellingame's resistance. 'It was so kind of you to invite Jocelyn and her family to visit you in London. She works very hard for her brother and I was delighted to know she would have such a treat.'

Lady Bellingame nodded. 'Her mother was my favourite niece. I hated to think of Jocelyn sacrificing her life, buried in the country watching over a pair of self-absorbed scholars, like her mother did. But fortunately, my hopes of finding her a better future appear to be working out,' she said, smiling at Jocelyn and the Baron.

'You mean with Lord Darnsby?' Alex said, determined to assess just how much ground the Baron had gained.

'Yes. A gentleman and a scholar, he appreciates both her beauty and intelligence. And admires her brother's work enough to be willing to wait for her until the translation project is completed, something not many ardent suitors would be willing to do.'

An icy panic tightened his chest. 'Darnsby has declared himself, then?'

'Well…not formally. But his admiration is clear enough for anyone to see. I don't think it will be long before he makes her a formal offer.'

'And she's prepared to accept him?'

Lady Bellingame turned from following her niece's progress around the dance floor to look Alex squarely in the face. 'If you truly care about her, Mr Cheverton, you will encourage this match. I would think it most ungentlemanly of you to string her along, dangling a continuation of your friendship to encourage her to delay a decision and perhaps letting this opportunity slip away. Oh, I realise there may be a…fondness on your part, too, but it will never do and you know it. Farisdeen is not going to allow his heir to marry a mere Miss Sudderfeld and her dowry of a thousand pounds.'

'His heir, Lady Bellingame, is not a puppet who dances to the strings he pulls.'

'Perhaps not. But don't forget—he also pulls the strings that control his heir's income. And were his heir to displease him, he would make sure the man did not have sufficient funds to support a wife. Nor would he be likely to allow the man to resume his job as estate manager. And then where would he be?'

Alex had to admit, he'd never considered how he would support himself if the Duke were to object so strongly to Jocelyn that Farisdeen cut him off. He'd only barely arrived at the decision to court her.

But he wouldn't let a paltry thing like a threat to his income hold him back.

'Shouldn't Jocelyn be the one who makes that decision?'

'You would play upon the fondness you know she has for you to prevent her from making a more sensible choice?'

'I would have her make the choice that will truly make her happy.'

'Whereas I think you possess only the power to make her truly *un*happy.'

With that, Lady Bellingame turned away and stalked off to speak with another chaperon whose charge, like hers, was currently on the dance floor.

Grimly Alex stood and waited for Jocelyn's return, mulling over what he'd just learned.

That Darnsby was a serious contender for her hand. One her aunt, and no doubt the rest of her family, would encourage her to accept.

But she had not yet committed herself to him—yet.

Surely he hadn't lost her before he'd even begun to court her in earnest!

Horrified by the thought, he took a deep, calming breath. No need to panic. He had their years of friendship, their long affection—and that simmering passion—to build on. Far more tools in his arsenal of persuasion than Darnsby currently possessed.

But he'd need to put them to use and quickly.

Impatiently he tapped his toe to the music, until finally the dance ended. Darnsby walked back with Jocelyn on his arm. 'Lady Bellingame left you?' Jocelyn asked in surprise.

'Her attention was called away by a friend,' he said drily.

'I see. It appears you will have to leave without bid-

ding her goodnight, Lord Darnsby. Thank you for the
dances and the conversation.'

'The pleasure was mine. You will give my regards
to Lady Bellingame, I trust?'

'Of course.'

'Very good. Then I will see you again—soon. Goodnight, Miss Sudderfeld. Cheverton.' With a smile to Jocelyn and a stiff bow to Alex, the Baron walked away.

Jocelyn turned to Alex, the brilliant smile she gave
him melting his heart and defrosting some of his icy
dread. There was no question that she was glad to see
him.

Now he needed to set about winning her. The idea
of her with Darnsby—or any other man—made him
want to hit something.

Like himself. Why had he been stupid enough to
deny his feelings for so long?

'Were the talks the Duke took you to interesting?'
she asked.

'Long. I couldn't wait to get back to London.'

'Oh, dear,' she said with a chuckle. 'That doesn't
bode well for your future as a brilliant leader in the
Lords.'

'One hopes the need for that is many years away. In
the meantime, the Duke is welcome to the role.'

The orchestra was beginning to play again. 'Our
dance, I believe?' he said, offering her his arm. After
all that had just transpired, he couldn't wait to get close
to her.

'Fortunately, as you can hear, it will be a waltz.
Sometimes,' she said with a mischievous smile, 'there
is good reason to delay dancing with old friends.'

'Minx,' he accused with a chuckle. 'But I love you
for it.' Enormously encouraged he was that she'd saved

the waltz, the dance that would allow him to hold her the closest, just for him, he pulled her into his arms.

'Do you love me?'

'You must let me tell you how much.'

'Oh, don't start!' she said with a groan. 'I've had enough gallantry tonight from Lord Darnsby.'

'You don't appreciate his "gallantry"?'

Jocelyn sighed. 'I like him. I appreciate his interest and he is quite a scholar. But his blatant pursuit makes me uncomfortable. I've already told him several times I do not intend to marry—soon, at any rate. Yet he persists in being…gallant.'

Alex felt a surge of relief—even as he wondered a bit at her rebuffing a man who seemed so eminently suitable. Though he could only be happy that she was. 'But surely with me, you are…comfortable.'

She looked directly into his eyes, thrilling him with the smoky heat in her gaze. 'I wouldn't say…comfortable, exactly. I look at you—and I burn. But you already know that.'

Alex felt an answering conflagration firing within him and wished he could spirit her off to somewhere more private this very minute.

'Maybe we need to take another walk in Lady Bellingame's garden.'

'Maybe we do.'

'You will be at home tomorrow?'

'I'll be working with Virgil.'

'Every hard worker needs to take a break.'

While Alex felt desire pulsing in his blood, she appeared to consider the suggestion. 'Aunt Bellingame will be out making calls, since I told her I had to stay home and work with Virgil.'

'Sounds like the perfect time to call.'

She nodded, her heated gaze still fixed on his face. 'Sounds like the perfect time for a walk in the garden. You won't even have to bribe Mary.'

'I'll look forward to it.'

'So will I. But now you must twirl me faster. We are dancing so slowly, we're attracting attention.'

'Whatever my lady desires.'

'Is that a promise?'

'Oh, yes,' he murmured and pulled her more tightly against him.

Tomorrow, he thought giddily, drinking in the rose scent of her hair under his chin. Tomorrow he would begin his campaign to woo her. And if he were truly lucky, maybe even win both kisses—and her hand.

Relishing the feel of her in his arms, he relaxed—and realised he'd been clenching his jaw so long, it hurt. Darnsby's attentions, and Lady Bellingame's approval of them, had thoroughly alarmed him. But Jocelyn's response—the waltz, the invitation to the garden—encouraged him to believe that it wasn't too late to win her—yet.

For lovely long minutes he swirled her through the movements of the dance, the tantalising closeness of her in his arms just a foretaste of the deeper intimacy he hoped with all his heart they would soon share. When at last the music ended, they both remained in place, his arms around her, for one sweet moment before stepping apart.

He could feel her heart beating as rapidly as his own.

He could hardly wait to begin his campaign tomorrow.

As he looked up, smiling, to escort her back to her aunt—who was glowering at them from the edge of the ballroom—he caught a quick glimpse of a silver-haired gentleman near the door, his gaze also fixed on them. In the second it took Alex to recognise the man, he turned and vanished.

Alex clenched his jaw. The Duke of Farisdeen. Who must now be in no doubt of Alex's romantic preferences. If Alex could secure Jocelyn's acceptance and battle lines were drawn, so be it.

Winning her was worth whatever it cost.

Chapter Seventeen

Jocelyn had just returned from her ride the next morning—at which, alas, she had not encountered Alex, which made her even more eager to see him this afternoon—when the butler knocked on the door to her chamber, where Mary was helping her out of her riding habit.

'I have a note for you, miss,' Phillips called through the door. 'The messenger said it was urgent.'

'I'll get it,' Mary said, skipping over to open the door a crack, take the folded sheet from the butler and bring it back to Jocelyn.

'Thank you, Phillips,' she called absently, wondering as she broke the seal who in London would need to send her an urgent message.

A frisson of alarm shocked her as she opened the note—and found the paper embossed with Farisdeen's ducal seal.

Miss Sudderfeld,
I must speak with you about a matter of great urgency. Would you kindly call at Grosvenor Square at your earliest convenience?
Farisdeen

Her chest tight with dread, Jocelyn dropped the note and turned to Mary. 'My green morning gown, as quickly as possible!'

'What's wrong, miss?' Mary cried, her face paling.

'The Duke of Farisdeen has summoned me. I fear something must have happened to Mr Cheverton.'

'Oh, no! Not to that nice gentleman!' Making sounds of distress, Mary hurriedly pulled the requested garment out of the wardrobe and helped Jocelyn into it. Once all the laces were tied and the pieces pinned, Jocelyn grabbed a bonnet, jammed it over her head and gathered up her pelisse.

'Should I have Phillips summon a hackney, miss?' Mary asked, trailing in her wake as she headed for the stairs.

'No, it isn't far. It will be faster to walk than to wait for a carriage.'

'Shall I go with you?'

Jocelyn reached out to pat her hand. 'Not at the pace I'll be walking. It's only a short distance. I doubt any thieves or highwaymen will attack me between our doorstep and his.'

'I'll follow and wait for you, miss. Wouldn't want His Grace to think you wasn't proper, going about London without a maid.'

'Yes, if you like. Now I must run!'

'I do hope you find all is well, miss!'

With Mary's words echoing behind her, Jocelyn hurried down the stairs and out the door before a surprised Phillips could walk over to open it for her.

By the time she reached the Duke's residence, her heart was hammering so hard she felt faint. Halting a moment to compose herself, she walked up the stairs and knocked.

A wooden-faced butler admitted her. Before she could get a word out, the man said, 'Miss Sudderfeld, isn't it?'

'Yes.'

'His Grace is expecting you. If you'll follow me to the library.'

'My maid is coming after me and will arrive shortly,' Jocelyn said as they climbed the stairs. 'If you would please show her somewhere she could wait for me?'

'Of course.' Halting on the landing in front of an elaborately carved doorway, the butler knocked, then opened the door. 'Miss Sudderfeld to see you, Your Grace,' he announced, and waved her in.

'Your Grace,' Jocelyn said, walking towards the desk behind which the Duke sat and dropping a curtsy. 'I came as soon as I got your note. You must tell me at once what is so urgent. Is it about Alex—Mr Cheverton? He isn't injured, is he?'

The Duke looked at her steadily. 'You express a great deal of concern for Alex Cheverton, I see.'

'Of course. We've been friends for many years.'

'And is that all you are? Friends?'

'Friends with a great deal of mutual respect and affection, yes,' she answered warily.

The Duke sighed. 'I must tell you, Miss Sudderfeld, after watching you waltz with my heir last night, "just friends" is not how I—or any of the other onlookers— would have described your relationship.'

'So this summons wasn't about Mr Cheverton being hurt.'

'He has not been injured—yet. Whether that continues to be true depends on you.'

'Thank heaven!' she murmured, relief, for a moment, robbing her of any other thought. Then, recalling the Duke's words, she added, 'But I hardly see how his continued good health depends on me.'

'Don't be coy with me, Miss Sudderfeld. I know only too well how intelligent you are. No one witnessing the two of you dancing last night could fail to notice that neither of you had eyes for anyone else. The rumour that the Duke of Farisdeen's heir was paying you particular attention was flying around the room even during the short time I stood watching. And that simply will not do. You must know that I could never allow him to marry you—no matter how much you entice him. I don't mean to insult you; I am well aware that you are gently born and respectably raised. But the future Duke of Farisdeen must marry a woman of a rank commensurate with his own, from a family of suitable wealth and influence. A fact of which you must surely be aware.'

Jocelyn started to protest that she'd never enticed Alex, but the Duke held up a hand, silencing her.

'I would finish, if you please. Let me state the case with regrettable bluntness. Alex Cheverton will never marry you. Even if you managed to get yourself with child, he would not marry you. But since you present such a...temptation to him, you must promise not to see him again. Giving up your hopes of a duchess's coronet will be difficult, I know. I'm prepared to...compensate you for your co-operation.'

Jocelyn had been about to agree with the Duke and assure him that once Alex had learned of his place in the succession, she'd known there could be no relation between them closer than friendship. But after he continued on to imply she would try to trap Alex into marrying her by getting herself with child—and then offered to *pay* her to give up her supposed pretensions, she was so angry she couldn't speak.

It took a moment for the red haze of fury to recede enough for her to summon words.

Jerking her chin up, she marched to the edge of Farisdeen's desk. 'There's no need for something as vulgar as that, Your Grace. Though you may find it impossible to believe, I have no desire whatsoever to become Duchess of Farisdeen——I feel only sorrow for Alex that he will have to become Duke. As for getting myself with child to try to force someone to marry me, I would never shame my family or besmirch my own honour by doing something so reprehensible. I think you have insulted me quite enough. Good day, sir.'

Dropping him the briefest of curtsies, ignoring whatever response he was trying to make to her, she stalked out of the room, slamming the door behind her.

Still in a fury, she whirled around to stomp down the stairs—and almost collided with Alex. He caught her by the elbows, steadying her.

'Jocelyn?' he said, his eyes widening in surprise. 'What are you doing here?'

'You must ask your precious Duke. By the way, you needn't call today—lest afterwards you find yourself locked away by your guard dog.'

Wrenching her arm free, needing to escape the house before her anger faded and anguish set in, she ran down the stairs and out the door.

Surprise, irritation and an angry suspicion filling him, after running halfway down the stairs after Jocelyn, Alex halted. She was clearly furious, so it would probably be more productive if he delayed talking with her until her anger cooled. He'd confront the Duke instead.

Walking back up to the library, he knocked and entered without waiting to be bid. As he advanced towards the desk, he said 'What were you discussing with Miss Sudderfeld? You must have summoned her. She wouldn't have come here of her own accord.'

'It might have had something to do with her brother and his project.'

'It might have. But it didn't, did it?'

The Duke sighed. 'You saw me at Lady Almondsly's last night, didn't you?'

Alex nodded.

'Than it should not come as a surprise that I intervened. What were you thinking? You cannot pay such particular attention to just any marriageable woman! Remember, you are no longer a mere estate manager who can move about society more or less invisibly. Everything you do will be watched and commented upon. I find no fault with Miss Sudderfeld personally, but neither her birth nor her family connections make her suitable to become a duchess. Singling her out in such a public way will only lead to her being hurt and disappointed. Pain which, since you obviously care about her, surely you wouldn't want to cause her.'

'So you summoned her to warn her she was about to experience that hurt and disappointment.'

'If she had any notion of attaching your interest, yes. Your behaviour inspired a good deal of gossip last night. I thought it best to be blunt with her and nip any expectations she might be developing in the bud.'

'I thought we settled a week ago the fact that I will not be dictated to on the subject of marriage. I will choose a woman whom I think gives me a reasonable expectation of happiness. Not purchase one merely for her pedigree, as if I were bartering to buy a promising racehorse at Newmarket.'

'There is no need for insulting analogies. You have a duty to your name and position.'

'I won't be held hostage to a duty I never sought or wanted. I have a more important duty to myself first. Just as I had no choice about becoming your heir, you will have no hand in choosing my wife.'

'I advise you to think very carefully before you take a step that could irrevocably alter your entire future,' the Duke warned.

'I assure you, I have considered very carefully. Carefully enough that I have taken time and thought hard about what I mean to do. And that is to marry Jocelyn Sudderfeld, if she'll have me.'

Rising from his chair, the Duke leaned forward to shake a finger in Alex's face. 'Disregard my wishes in this important matter and there will be consequences!'

'So be it. Good day, Your Grace.' Turning on his heel, Alex walked out.

After closing the door, he stood in the hallway, apprehensive and uncertain. Whatever the Duke had said to Jocelyn—and he could just imagine the litany recited about her lack of qualifications to become a duchess— he'd put her in a rage.

Could the Duke have turned her against him?

Surely she knew him well enough to know he'd had no idea the Duke was going to send for her.

Surely she understood he wouldn't let the Duke dictate to him on a matter as vital to his happiness as marriage.

Then an even more dismaying thought occurred.

Surely she couldn't believe he would lead her on,

waltz with her, steal kisses from her in the garden, all while intending to marry someone more 'suitable'. Not when she herself had engineered the waltz and responded with such enthusiasm to those kisses.

Even the possibility that she might think that made him feel ill.

An urgent need filled him to seek her out immediately and begin repairing whatever damage Farisdeen might have caused. But difficult as it was to delay, it would be wiser to wait and call this afternoon, as they'd planned. By which time, her initial anger should have cooled and Lady Bellingame would be out visiting.

He needed to talk with her unhampered by the presence of a chaperon and free of the danger of being overheard.

Chapter Eighteen

After pacing in his room for hours—he'd had no desire to encounter the Duke, with whom he would have to have it out after his conversation with Jocelyn—Alex presented himself at Lady Bellingame's town house. To his relief, after his polite enquiry about the ladies of the house, the butler confirmed that Lady Bellingame was out, but Miss Sudderfeld was at home, working with her brother.

Aware that if Jocelyn were still angry and Phillips announced him, she might refuse to see him, Alex turned down the butler's offer to escort him.

'No need to trouble yourself,' he told the man. 'I know the way.'

After the butler bowed and left, Alex paced down the hall to the small library at the back of Lady Bellingame's town house that the Sudderfeld men had taken over as their retreat and office. After giving the door a brisk knock, he walked in, hoping he could charm Jocelyn into walking with him so he could begin to convince her of the depth of his affection and his urgent desire to be allowed to court her, despite what the Duke might have said.

Alex halted inside the doorway. Neither Jocelyn, who was bent over the desk, writing, nor Virgil, who was pacing about, frowning over the book in his hands, appeared to have heard his knock. Both completely absorbed in their work, he thought, his anxiety momentarily tempered by a smile.

Then something, a stir of air from the open door maybe, disturbed Jocelyn. As she looked up from her paper and saw him, her eyes brightened and her face lit in a smile.

For one brief moment.

Then the smile vanished. Her face now expressionless, she rose and walked towards him. 'I thought I told you there was no need to call.'

'You did. But there is something urgent we need to discuss.'

'Virgil and I are working. It will have to wait until later.'

'Oh, take him into the garden, Jocelyn, won't you?' Virgil said irritably. 'You know I'm not happy with the interpretation of this last passage. We're missing something, I'm sure of it, but I can't think with the two of you wrangling.'

The damage must be more extensive even than he'd feared. Alarmed, Alex tried to hold on to a reassuring tone. 'Won't you walk with me for a few minutes? Please, Jocelyn.'

For a moment she stood irresolute. Then, with her brother waving her towards the door, she caught up her shawl with an exasperated sigh. 'I suppose I can spare a few moments,' she conceded. Ignoring the arm he offered, she stalked out of the room.

He caught up with her, striding beside her as she approached the door to the garden. Driven as he was to begin pleading his case immediately, he held his tongue until they'd left the house and proceeded halfway down the garden path, well out of earshot of any servants.

'You can slow your pace now, Jocelyn. We're not in a footrace.'

She halted, wariness evident in the rigid set of her body and expressionless face, and turned to him. 'Why did you come after I'd told you not to, Alex?'

'As I recall, you said not to come if I feared being "locked away by my guard dog". I have no such fear. I do fear, though, that whatever the Duke said to you—and you must know I had no idea he intended to speak to you, else I would have prevented it!—has made you angry not just with him, but also with me.'

She sighed, some of the tenseness going out of her stance. 'Yes, I am—or was—angry with him. But I'm not really angry with you.'

A measure of relief filled him. 'I'm glad to hear that. But are you sure you're not angry? You still look quite upset.'

She grimaced. 'It is upsetting to be accused of something you never intended. And to be reminded of something you've never forgotten.'

'I thought I'd already assured you I would not permit Farisdeen to dictate to me in the matter of my marriage. That I would marry someone I believed gives me the best chance of enduring happiness. I apologise for taking so long to acknowledge to myself emotions that have grown ever more intense with the years, but surely you know that lady is you, Jocelyn.'

Catching up her hand, he went down on one knee. 'Will you make my life complete, Jocelyn, and agree to become my wife?'

She froze, simply staring down at him. A rapid succession of expressions crossed her face, a mingling of surprise, distress, uncertainty—and, he was almost certain, delight.

Then she pulled her hand free, tucking it behind her back as if afraid he might try to take it again—and she would be tempted to let him. 'Get up, Alex, and no more pretty speeches, please. No, I will not marry you. You know as well as I do that a marriage between us is impossible.'

'Why impossible? I am single, in possession of all my faculties and of an age to marry without anyone's consent. As are you.'

'If you are really in possession of all your faculties, you know why it is impossible!' she tossed back, a trace of anger colouring the distress in her voice. 'I've already told you I will not wed until Virgil and I finish our project. And I can't imagine any position in life more tiresome than that of a duchess. Endless obligations, offering no chance for one to do what one wants with one's life. Forced into a succession of boring events duty requires one to attend with no possibility of escape. I couldn't bear it! I know you are trying to make amends for the insults the Duke handed me and I thank you for that. But I need to get back to work. And given the…unpleasant way things ended between the Duke and I, it would be better if we did not see each other again. Goodbye, Alex.'

Avoiding his gaze, she stepped around him and hurried down the path towards the door.

Well, he'd suspected she might not accept him immediately—but he hadn't expected to be summarily dismissed. Dismayed and angry, he rushed after her.

'Wait, Jocelyn!' Catching up with her, he placed a hand on her elbow to prevent her escape and turned her to face him. 'You can't tell me you don't care for me at all! I won't believe it.'

After swallowing hard, she said, her voice a little rough, 'I don't deny I care for you. But one outgrows a girlhood infatuation. And regrettably, the paths of even good friends can diverge. We are moving on to different destinies, Alex. We've both known that would happen since the moment you announced you'd been named Farisdeen's heir. We've tried to hang on to our old friendship a little longer, but it had to end some time. No, it's not easy to bid you goodbye, which means it's best that the farewell be quick. Here and now. I'll always wish you well...my dear fr-friend,' she said, her voice breaking a little.

Then she shook off his hand and walked back towards the house.

Shocked, hurt, disbelieving, this time he let her go.

Unwilling to leave things between them on such a raw note, Alex paced in circles around the garden. Well, Jocelyn had refused him all right and on terms much more wounding than he could have imagined.

He'd expected that she would protest the difference in station and the difficulties a union between them would create for him with the Duke. Maybe plead her lack of training for the duties demanded of a duchess. Maybe even be shocked at hearing him declare himself, although surely she must have suspected how he felt about her.

He never expected she'd return a categorical refusal and terminate their long friendship all in one blow.

How did he recover from this? Did he even want to?

One outgrows a girlhood infatuation.

That statement cut and cut deeply. How foolish and

arrogant he'd been, worrying only about whether *he* was sure of his feelings for *her*. Quite hopeful of winning her, not once considering the fondness he knew she had for him might be so shallow, it could be easily uprooted by worldly considerations.

If an infatuation was all she'd felt for him, then perhaps there was nothing for him to build on. No solid base that persuasion could lead into recognition of how good they were for each other, how easily their long, ever-deepening friendship could turn into a lifetime of love.

An empty desolation filled him. Hadn't he just done exactly the thing he'd promised himself never to do again? Thrown his whole heart into a relationship that ended in disaster?

His *whole* heart, he thought with a mirthless laugh. Fine time now to discover with crystalline clarity that he had in fact given Jocelyn his heart. That he didn't just admire and desire her, didn't just have a 'fondness' for her.

At the prospect of losing her completely, he now realised that he *loved* her. Completely, passionately, far beyond the possibility of holding anything back and most certainly for ever.

Perhaps pursuing the pragmatic Lady Anne would have been better after all. A match based on bloodlines and family influence would never make him feel as broken and bereft as he did now.

But as he reviewed the times he'd shared with Jocelyn, that desolation eased. He recalled the years of teasing camaraderie, a steady friendship that had recently become deeper and more complex. The delight he *knew* she felt at their repartee, the tender affection and warmth of that picnic on Trethfort Hill, the tour through the British Museum...the heat in her eyes as she'd gazed at him last night. With such clear evidence to contradict what she'd just told him, he simply couldn't believe all she felt for him was a fading girlhood infatuation.

And the way she had clung to him, melted into him when he kissed her...as if she couldn't get close enough to him, even as he felt he wanted to consume all of her...

No, he would *not* believe she felt no more than tepid friendship.

He wasn't going to give up on winning her love in return, not unless and until he had as convincing a demonstration of her indifference as she'd given last night of her attraction.

Renewed determination filling him, he headed back to the house. It was probably better strategy to let Jocelyn recover—and think about the ramifications—of their last interview before he renewed his efforts. But before he gave her the space and time for reflection, he was going to let her know she had not succeeded in getting rid of him for good.

And that *he* would always consider *her* a friend, regardless of what she ultimately chose to do. And that he intended to try with every fibre of his being to convince her to let them be more.

He entered the house, paced down the hallway and halted outside the library door. Before venturing in, he needed to carefully consider what he intended to say to Jocelyn—since he would probably only be allowed enough time for a single brief announcement.

As he stood there beside the slightly opened door, going over the possibilities, he could hear Jocelyn and Virgil discussing their work.

'I already gave you my opinion on the tone of the passage, Virgil,' she was saying, an unaccustomed impatience in her voice. 'It is bittersweet. I think we should write it that way.'

'All right, I'll agree. I've gone over the lines several times, and can't come up with anything better.'

'Then I propose 'She walked the world in grace, her gold the darkness lighting…'

'Very well. Continue.'

Alex didn't pay much attention at first, trying to concentrate instead on perfecting his own wording. But the lyrical cadence of Jocelyn's voice kept distracting him, until he found himself listening to the developing lines.

The verses were lovely and bittersweet, and filled with longing, he thought, those emotions finding an echo in his own heart. He was grimacing at the irony when suddenly, the significance of what he was hearing struck him with the force of a boxer's roundhouse punch.

The vague clues—her intellect, her passion, her impressive scholarship, her resistance to being courted even by the eminently qualified Darnsby—suddenly coalesced into a realisation that had been there all along, teasing at the edge of consciousness. Jocelyn wasn't writing down what Virgil dictated—*Jocelyn* was composing verses that *Virgil* approved.

Almost certain he knew now what was really occurring, he listened more closely and for a good deal longer. Until a maid appeared, stopping short at the sight of him, and asking if he needed her to announce him to the family.

Assuring her in a quiet undertone that he didn't wish to disturb them, and was just leaving, Alex backed around her and headed for the door.

He wandered back towards Grosvenor Square, reviewing again what he'd overheard in order to reinforce his initial conclusion.

Virgil and Jocelyn discussing and agreeing on the accurate meaning of a section of the play. Then Jocelyn turning the raw translation into lyrical verse that captured both essence and mood. Verses to which Virgil occasionally proposed an alternate wording, which Jocelyn accepted or rejected.

Despite what she'd told him, Jocelyn Sudderfeld was in fact the true author of the Euripides translations.

Had she authored the works attributed to her father, too?

She couldn't have done all of them—her father had published a number of translations when she was still a child. But at some point, the gifted classics scholar her father had educated and encouraged had become not just proficient, but as fine a translator and a better poet that either her father or her brother.

She'd always insisted she would never marry until Virgil's project was completed, maybe not even then. Only for some years now, it had actually been *her* project.

How would the Duke react, were he to find out the translations he was sponsoring were being penned by a woman?

Most likely with shock, followed by the furious conviction that he had been deceived. Probably succeeded by a disavowal of the books already completed and immediate termination of the project.

Dismay chilled his blood at the thought of what would happen afterwards to the work, to the professors—and to Jocelyn.

He recalled again her refusal of his impetuous proposal and her abrupt, unexpected rejection of him and any future between them.

Did her authorship explain nothing...or everything?

Focus on the work, Jocelyn kept telling herself. Immerse yourself in the subtleties of case and verb tense, the intensity of adjectives and adverbs, in order to sift out the clearest and purest meaning to put into English verse of the highest lyrical quality.

Once she'd recognised in her teens that she possessed a unique gift for making a vanished world come alive for a different era in a different language, she'd felt a responsibility to develop and use that talent. The intellectual and creative process of doing so had always delighted and totally absorbed her.

Until today.

Now, the combined force of the challenge and obligation were barely enough to hold at bay the emotions threatening to overcome her.

When at last she and Virgil finished the section they'd intended to complete, she had a pounding headache and a pressing need to escape to her chamber and lock the door. Where she could in privacy finally release the flood of anguish, doubt, uncertainty and pain.

Barely taking the time to properly store her paper, ink, quills and the manuscript, she bid her brother a distracted goodbye and fled up the stairs, to lock herself into her room with shaking fingers.

She'd intended to lie down, but found she was too agitated to remain in one place, even to ease the aching in her head. Pacing the room, beginning to regret she'd chosen an indoor refuge rather than an escape to the broader expanse of the garden, she ran through her mind again the scene of Alex's shocking proposal.

She'd long known he had affection for her. She'd recently learned he desired her. And she'd always been certain he valued their friendship.

But she'd never believed he might truly *love* her... with anything approaching the depth and intensity of the emotion she'd always felt for him.

Once the shock of his proposal faded, for a single joyous instant, she'd almost accepted it. But she'd spoken the truth when she said she had no desire to become a duchess—whose elevated position in society meant nothing to her and whose duties and obligations would be a burden for which she was unprepared. To keep Alex in her life, as friend and lover and ally for the rest of their days...would it not be a bargain well worth accepting?

But though she wouldn't mind thumbing her nose in the face of the Duke's disapproval, incurring his wrath would have immediate and disagreeable consequences for Alex. The Duke could cut off his income, refuse to allow him to return as manager of Edge Hall and break off training him—leaving Alex pressed for funds and, when he did eventually inherit, ill prepared to handle the myriad duties of running a dukedom.

If the Duke believed her to be an impediment to achieving the plans he had for his new heir, he might also decide to rid himself of that annoyance by terminating the Euripides project, dismissing her brother and evicting her father from the only home he possessed.

And at the very heart of the matter was the project itself. Even if Alex could reconcile the Duke to his marrying her, how could she live with him with the intimacy of a wife and not sooner or later inadvertently reveal that she was the true author of the work? He could well feel the loyalty he owed the Duke required him to reveal the truth. Placing Alex in an impossible position between protecting her and lying to Farisdeen.

He might be dismayed and angry himself if he discovered her secret, feeling he too had been insulted and deceived. After all, she had in fact deliberately misled him about her true role.

Virgil had just recently warned her again about being more vigilant, saying he'd thought he'd heard Alex lingering outside the library at Edge Hall one day when they'd been working. He'd been upset for a week, until enough time had passed without Alex saying anything that he was reassured that his suspicion had been in error.

No, she'd had no choice but to refuse Alex—no matter how much it hurt. No choice but to break off their friendship at once, knowing if he continued to see her and decided to press his suit, her longing for him might make her weaken. Putting *her* in the impossible position of choosing between her attachment to Alex and the careers and reputations of her family.

There hadn't been any alternative to sending him away—had there?

She'd made the circuit of her room so many times, arguing and debating with herself, she had likely worn down the nap in the carpet when a knock came at the door, followed by a jiggling of the door latch.

'It's Mary, miss. Why did you lock the door? Are you all right? Won't you let me in?'

Sighing, Jocelyn walked over to unlatch it. 'I had the headache and wanted to lie down for a time undisturbed,' she told Mary as she entered. 'I'm feeling better now.'

Which was hardly true, but the maid offering to

bring her cold compresses or a sleeping draught wasn't going to cure what ailed her.

'Are you sure you're better, miss? Lord Darnsby has called and is waiting for you in the parlour. I said I'd fetch you, but if you're still feeling poorly, I'll tell him to call again later.'

Jocelyn was sorely tempted to have the girl tell him just that. But she wasn't likely to feel better any time soon. She might as well see what the Baron wanted. He'd already warned her he was persistent, and if she avoided him now she'd just have to deal with him later.

After the disastrous scenes she'd already experienced with the Duke and Alex, today was already ruined. Rather than defer until later a meeting that might potentially ruin another day, she might as well talk with the Baron now.

With a sigh, she tossed the shawl back over her shoulders and walked out of her chamber.

Chapter Nineteen

As she entered, the Baron was standing in the parlour by the hearth, hands linked behind his back. At the sound of the door opening, he turned, then advanced towards her with a smile.

'I took a chance that you might be finished working! I'm so glad I did.'

'We decided to end a bit early today. I've been suffering with a headache.'

A heartache, more like, but no need to tell him that.

'Oh, dear! You are feeling better, I trust? I wouldn't wish to drag you from your chamber if you are still feeling ill.'

'No, I had a bit of a rest and am much better.' And when had lies begun to slide so easily off her tongue? Maybe when she claimed to Alex that she had outgrown her girlhood infatuation?

Whatever name she put to the strong emotion she felt for him, it had certainly not yet begun fading.

'As I told you last night, before I was forced to leave your charming company,' Darnsby was saying, 'I will not be much longer in London. In fact, I received a message from my estate manager this morning, indicating problems have arisen with the construction of the new cottages. Tolliver is a good sort, but for difficulties with a project of this magnitude, I prefer to oversee things myself. So I will be leaving London tomorrow.'

'I'm sorry to hear that,' she made herself say with a smile. 'I've enjoyed getting to know you.'

'I'm pleased to learn that! Because for the first time, I don't intend to remain at Waverly Park after my short yearly sojourn in London. Once the project is back on track, I will return here. When I do, I hope very much to see more of you.'

'A pleasant prospect! I shall look forward to it.'

He reached for her hand and, reluctantly, she let him take it. After raising it to his lips, he gave it a lingering kiss. 'I hope to make it much more than "pleasant"! I'd like to share gallops in the park, walks in the garden and endless stimulating talks about Greek literature. And in the process, I very much hope I will be able to convince a beautiful and talented lady that one day, when her important work is completed, she should take on a new role—with me.'

Pulling back her hand, she held it palm up, wordlessly telling him to stop. She knew he'd hinted of his interest, but this was too much, too soon, and in her present state of agitation, she couldn't deal with it. 'Please, don't ask me anything now. I've only just met you!'

He held up both hands, acknowledging her request. 'I know we haven't been acquainted long. Once again, I'm being precipitous. I'm not formally asking anything of you, now. I just wanted to assure you again of my deep regard, my serious intentions and my promise of being willing to wait until you are ready. I didn't want to leave London until I was sure you understood all that.'

She nodded, hoping now that he'd said what he came for, he would leave. Her head was throbbing again, to the point that she simply couldn't make polite or even very coherent conversation. 'I do understand.'

'Knowing my ultimate goal, you won't…forbid me to see you again? For I can tell I have distressed you.'

'Anything that might interfere with my work distresses me!' she cried, finally able to give an honest answer. 'I simply can't be distracted by envisaging plans for the future right now—not until the work is much closer to completion.'

'And what if I promise to offer not distraction—only friendship?'

Friendship. The word immediately brought up the image of Alex's face, filling her with bittersweet longing.

After terminating that relationship, she stood in dire need of a friend.

'I suppose it would be foolish to ban seeing someone who could become a friend. As long as you recognise that friendship may be all I could ever offer.'

'I don't deny I aspire to more, but I won't ask for anything warmer than that…for now.'

She probably should discourage that aspiration. The cold dead ache at the centre of her chest, where her heart used to beat, hadn't indicated with as much as a flutter any inclination to transfer her tumultuous feelings from Alex to anyone else.

But she was too tired and dispirited, and her head hurt too much, for her to find the words to dissuade him.

Fortunately, he didn't seem to require a reply.

Instead, he kissed her hand again. 'I won't keep you any longer. I need to finish my preparations, so I may leave London at first light. I expect to be gone no longer than a fortnight. You do plan to remain in London at least that long?'

'Probably, though I am not certain of Lady Bellingame's exact plans.'

At the moment, she'd be relieved to leave London at first light herself and flee to the solitude of Edge Hall—as long as Alex was not there.

'I shall hurry back, then. Thank you again for seeing me. Best wishes to you and Virgil for your work to prosper! Please give my regards as well to Lady Bellingame and tell her I will call again as soon as I return.'

With a bow, to which she returned a curtsy, Darnsby walked from the room.

One hand on her aching head, Jocelyn wandered back up to her room, to find Mary waiting for her. After one look at her face, the girl said, 'You've not recovered, have you, miss? Don't you worry! My ma gave me her recipe for the best tisane! Just you lay yourself down on the bed. I'll make it for you and be back in a trice.'

Unprotestingly, Jocelyn let the maid help her out of her shoes, eased herself up on the bed and leaned back against the pillows.

Maybe she ought to seriously consider the Baron's proposition—sooner rather than later, she thought dully, fingers pressed against her closed eyes. Accepting him would put an end to the temptation still nagging at her to recall Alex and accept his proposal. Darnsby could provide her a handsome home, a respectable position, intelligent companionship and encouragement to continue pursuing her scholarship even after her project ended.

Could she trust *him* with the truth of her involvement?

No, she could not. And she did not want to enter a marriage in which she had to hide who she really was.

Besides, if Darnsby were truly fond of her, it wouldn't be fair to marry him unless she could reciprocate his affection.

After she barely formulated the words, her heart emphatically rejected that possibility. Just considering the prospect of sharing her life and her thoughts and her body with Darnsby made everything within her revolt.

She smiled a little sadly, marvelling at how impossible it seemed that she could give herself to anyone save Alex. Until the truth she'd been resisting for so long finally resonated deep within her.

She couldn't imagine belonging to anyone else because she *loved* Alex and always would.

From the moment Alex had revealed his changed destiny to her, she'd been trying to convince herself that what she felt for him was just an intense girlhood infatuation. A friendship she'd always cherish, but an attachment that would fade over time. Not the sort of deeply committed, intense, everlasting love a woman feels for a man.

She'd been wrong.

Now that she'd sent him away and tried to push herself to consider the possibility of marrying someone else, she was forced to admit what her heart had been trying to tell her for some time. That the instant attraction she'd felt for Alex when she met him at the age of sixteen had over the years deepened into a true and lasting love.

Was there any way she could have it all?

She made her aching head run through the possibilities one last time, but the ultimate answer didn't change. There wasn't…unless she were prepared to risk the welfare of those closest to her.

At that conclusion, she lowered her head on to her hands, her eyes leaking silent tears.

She'd known that sending Alex away would hurt.

She'd only just realised she would be devastated for a lifetime.

In the late afternoon three days later, Jocelyn finished the final words of the verse and put down her pen. 'I think we've done enough for today, Virgil,' she told her brother, who was as usual pacing the room, scanning the Greek original of the Euripides play on which they were working.

'What?' he replied abstractedly. 'Oh, yes, a fine session,' he continued before she could repeat her remark. 'I wanted to ask Papa about the next section anyway before we begin work on it. The theme is very similar to the last translation he did.'

'He's having tea with Aunt Bellingame in the salon, I believe,' Jocelyn said.

'Excellent! I could use a hot cup. Will you be joining us?'

'I don't think so. I've been sitting in this chair long enough to grow roots. I believe I'll take a stroll in the garden. Tell Aunt Bellingame I'll go up and change in good time to be ready for dinner.'

Nodding, her brother closed his book and walked towards the door. On the threshold, he halted, looking back at her. 'Do you really think you should go out tonight? You've been looking rather tired. Maybe you ought to stay in and rest.'

'I'm fine. A nice long walk in the fresh air is all I need.'

'I'll save you some tea, just in case.' With a nod, her brother walked out.

She must really look peaked, Jocelyn thought, if her normally oblivious brother had noticed there was something wrong. Gathering up her shawl, she walked down the passage and out into the garden.

Though it was more the long sleepless nights than the late evening entertainments that had made her weary and out of sorts, she thought as she walked down the path, the spring colours of the bulbs and flowering shrubs muted under a sky of grey scudding clouds that promised rain.

Sleepless nights wondering if she'd done the right thing by refusing Alex Cheverton—and not firmly discouraging Lord Darnsby. Sleepless nights hoping the dull ache that throbbed in her chest would ease. Sleepless nights coming to realise that the work she'd thought so vital to a fulfilled and happy life was not able to fill the ragged, gaping hole left by losing Alex.

Not until she'd sent him away for good had she fully realised how huge a part of her life he'd become. How much she'd come to rely on seeing him almost daily, bantering with him, trading opinions and exchanging information—and lately, those thrilling kisses. Thinking of a future without him meant envisaging a world like today's, only with the sun permanently obscured by a thick dark layer of clouds. Leaving her to plod along in a grey universe devoid of colour, excitement and anticipation.

Denied the passion of being held and kissed by the man she loved.

And she'd thought she known herself and what she needed so well!

But none of her endless analysing through those long sleepless nights had produced an alternative that would allow her to recapture the warmth, laughter and passionate fulfilment of a life that included Alex.

He would have to marry soon—and she could not.

Even if she decided after this project was complete not to undertake any more, by that time Alex would doubtless be married and there would be no possibility then of trying to recapture the closeness of the time when he'd asked for her hand.

But neither could she risk confessing the truth to him, thereby endangering her brother and father in order to secure her own happiness.

Besides, there was no guarantee, despite Alex's protests, that he would be able to marry her, even if she were prepared to navigate the tricky business of living with him without divulging her secret. Alex was determined to chart his own path, but wedding her in the teeth of the Duke's opposition would create difficulties even his determination might not be able to overcome.

A marriage between them was impossible, just as she'd told him. She should just resign herself to the crater blown into her heart and life and force herself to move on.

Apparently he had.

She had to admit, as the awful reality of life without him had grown painfully clearer, she'd hoped he might return and try once again to persuade her. Although it was good that he hadn't, since after fully realising the bleakness of life without him, she wasn't sure she could have withstood the compulsion to accept him if he had.

But as the days passed and he did not call, she was forced to conclude that though he'd rashly asked her to marry him, losing her had not left as unfillable a gap in his life as it had in hers.

Maybe she ought to think again about the possibility of wedding Lord Darnsby…some day, if the Euripides project ended and she did not go on to others. If he were willing to settle for mutual respect and a life built on shared interests.

An immediate, instinctive resistance told her that prospect wasn't any more palatable now than it had been when she'd first considered it.

Reaching the brick wall at the far limit of the garden, she closed her eyes and leaned forward to rest her aching head against it, listening to the sigh of the wind through the trees, the muffled bustle of activity on the street beyond the wall.

She would weather this. She would put aside her heartache and redouble her efforts to make the final translations the best she'd ever done. Once the project neared its end, she would look about in earnest for a companion's position. If Virgil persisted in refusing to co-operate on further projects, somehow she would figure out a way to continue on her own.

'I wouldn't have thought communing with good English brick would help your Greek translation.'

It took an instant for the softly spoken words to penetrate her dull abstraction. But once they had, she whirled around so quickly, she almost lost her balance.

'Alex?' she whispered incredulously as he reached out to steady her.

'You should have known I wouldn't be dismissed that easily. I just needed to arrange some things first. I hope you missed me.'

'Oh, Alex!' Before she could consider the wisdom of it, overwhelmed with relief and joy, she launched herself into his arms.

He hugged her close, rubbing his chin against her

hair. 'I missed you, too,' he whispered—and then leaned down to kiss her.

Her response was fierce and instantaneous. Wrapping her arms around his neck, she crushed herself against him, until she could feel the rapid beat of his heart against her chest while her lips met his with a desperate eagerness. And when, at his urging, she opened to him, a flood of desire surged through her as his tongue sought and stroked hers.

Binding her even closer, he deepened the kiss, tasting her, teasing her until she felt she couldn't get close enough, kiss him deeply enough. Heat built in her blood and seemed to melt the core of her, until her whole body sparked and fizzed with an urgent energy.

Had she breath enough, she would have gone on kissing him for ever. But at length, with them both gasping, he broke the kiss, though he kept her in his arms.

'Don't even try to tell me again about your fading girlish infatuation,' he murmured against her ear. 'You kiss like a woman passionately in love.'

She needed to resist his insidious appeal, but that kiss had left her reeling and her wits too scattered for clever argument. Before she could try to cobble together a denial, he put a finger against her lips.

'You can't kiss me like that and then claim you don't care about me. And before you abuse me, I agree, I should have not been so precipitous in my proposal. I should have wooed you in earnest, given you time to be sure of the depth of your feelings. It's just, once I fully recognised the depth of my own, I could think of nothing but how much I wanted to make you my wife. You do love me, don't you, my heart?'

He still held her loosely in his arms. She ought to step away—but she just couldn't make herself. Not when she'd missed him so dreadfully and being here, in his arms, felt so very right. 'Very well,' she said on a sigh. 'I won't try to deny it. But what I feel for you doesn't change the facts. I am still committed to finishing the project with Virgil, and cannot allow myself to be distracted.'

'Like this?' he said and kissed her again.

Her body argued that this might be the last time he kissed her and she should therefore enjoy it. Pushing aside the reprimands of conscience and good sense, she kissed him back just as passionately as she had the first time.

'Definitely too—distracting,' she managed to say disjointedly when he let her go. 'Besides which, the Duke would be furious if you defied him and married me.'

'Let me worry about the Duke, won't you? And you know I won't stand in the way of your translations of Euripides. We can be married at the old church in Edge Hall village and live at the Hall while you finish it. I promise to satisfy you so completely every night, you will begin every new day refreshed and ready to work.'

While she sputtered to summon words to explain why that would not be a good idea, he moved her to arm's length, so he could look into her eyes. 'You don't need to be afraid any more, Jocelyn. I know you are the true author of the translations. I'm enormously proud of you and I would never betray your secret.'

Shock rippled through her. 'You *know*? But how? I didn't think I ever said anything to give you—'

'You didn't,' he interrupted. 'That day in the garden, when you tried to send me away? I came back inside to argue with you. While I was standing outside the library, debating what to say, I overheard you working with Virgil. Once I began to listen more closely, it soon became obvious which of you was composing the verses and which one just making suggestions. I'd had vague suspicions before and after your masterful museum tour, it made perfect sense. What a gift you have! If, after the Euripides finishes, you want to take on another project, I'd be delighted to sponsor you, with or without Virgil. So you see, since you've completely failed to convince me that you don't love me and have been assured that I will support and safeguard your work, you have no remaining reason to refuse me. Do you?'

Alex knew…and was *proud* of her. Not just proud, but ready to protect and promote her translations indefinitely. If she didn't already love him, that fact alone would have earned her complete devotion.

But it didn't solve all their problems.

'There's still the Duke…'

Chuckling, he kissed her hands. 'What do you think I've spent the last few days doing?'

'I thought you were finding a replacement bride.'

'For you, Jocelyn? Surely you know there isn't another woman in the world who could replace you. Not for scholarship and never in my heart. I love you. I suppose I've loved you for years, blinding myself to the fact by telling myself you looked on me only as a brother. However we began, you've become so much a part of my life and everything I love that I cannot imagine living without you. I do not intend to live without you. So stop being so contentious and tell me you'll marry me.'

'But the Duke!' she persisted. 'Yes, I love you, too, but loving you means I can't bear the thought of ruining your life.'

'I've spent the last few days coming up with a solution to the problem of the Duke's objections. Do you trust me, Jocelyn?'

She didn't need to think that one over. 'Yes.'

'Then believe that I can deal with the Duke. And even if all my plans to persuade Farisdeen fail, leading to a permanent break, we could still marry and live at Wynborne. My estate doesn't boast a ducal mansion, but it has a comfortable, rambling old manor house with plenty of room to house us, as well as your father and brother. There's a tolerable library to entertain your father while you work with Virgil. Granted, it wouldn't be the best of options. I'd much prefer to continue earning income to supplement the estate's revenues. But I really don't think it will come to that.'

'But if you break with the Duke—what will you do when you finally do inherit, having established none of the contacts and received little of the instruction you should have to properly perform all the duties?'

Alex shrugged. 'I'm a reasonably intelligent man and you are brilliant. We will manage just fine. If Farisdeen chooses to send me away, he's cognisant enough of his duties as Duke to hire competent managers to oversee his various properties. He's already trained me to run them, so picking up those reins again when the time comes will pose no problem. As for the duties in Parliament, my good friend Gregory Lattimar has a brother-in-law in the Lords, whom I'm sure I could call on for assistance. Now, I know you have no desire whatsoever to become a duchess, but have pity on me! I never wanted to become a duke, either. Surely, if you care for me at all, you won't condemn me to face that thankless task alone. Surely you will marry me and love me and help me carry that burden—won't you, my darling Jocelyn?'

While she stared at him mutely, wanting desperately to accept, but still not sure she should do something that would cause such an upheaval in his life, he sighed. 'I see you are determined to be that tiresome brat. Very well, I shall do it again—properly.'

With that, he dropped to one knee before her. 'Jocelyn Sudderfeld, my heart, my life, will you lift the crushing burden of my future by promising to stand by my side? Will you race hunters with me and, heaven help us, practise equestrian tricks with me to catch you when you fall? Will you argue with me and bandy insults every day—until I stop your lips with kisses? Will you marry me and make me the luckiest man in England for the rest of my days?'

If he promised to protect her secret, she *could* trust him. And if he believed having her at his side was worth whatever tumult it would cause, how could she continue to resist?

'Yes, Alex, I will marry you.'

With a triumphant cry, he bounded up and kissed her again, deeply, passionately, until they were both dizzy. Breaking away at last, he said, 'No more of that until after the wedding! When I can finally claim you as my own, I want it to be in a chamber with a soft bed and hours of uninterrupted time—not a hurried encounter in a chilly garden.'

'Oh, I don't know. The garden seemed rather...warm, just now.'

He held up a hand. 'Please, no more temptation! I'm too close to breaking as it is. Instead, let me go seek out your father and secure his approval. Then it's off to confront the Duke—so I may know where we will live to have the banns called. I don't want to wait an instant longer than necessary to marry you and demonstrate just how much I need and want you.'

'You will return to confront the Duke after you speak with Papa? You are sure Farisdeen is at home?'

'Yes, I made sure he would be there all afternoon before I came to see you. I don't want to lose any more time before I proclaim you before the whole world as my future wife.'

'If we are to be partners, then let me go with you. To tell Papa and to face the Duke. And don't worry, he can't insult me any more than he already has. In fact, I should like to look him in the face and let him know I neither fear him nor have any interest in currying his favour. Besides, I should very much like to watch you implement whatever "plan" you've devised to outmanoeuvre him.'

'My ferocious love,' he said fondly, kissing the tip of her nose. 'Very well. Let us speak with your father, and we'll seek out the Duke, as we will do everything from here on—together.'

Chapter Twenty

After obtaining the approval of their wedding plans from Jocelyn's shocked but delighted father, Alex led Jocelyn into the hallway. 'Are you sure you want to come with me? Farisdeen can be cold and cutting—as you know. I don't want him to hurt you again.'

'He can't touch me now. Knowing you love me and that Papa and Virgil are safe is all that matters. Let him say his worst—it will make no difference.'

'Very well. Let's be off to confront the beast in his lair.'

Disdaining a hackney, they walked the short distance to Grosvenor Square, Jocelyn clinging to Alex's arm. But as they reached the front steps of the town house, she halted.

'What is it?' he asked, looking down at her. 'If you've changed your mind, I wouldn't blame you a bit. I'll walk you back home and come back alone.'

'It's not that. I wouldn't turn coward and abandon you. It's just—are you *sure* you want to do this? Once you've announced you intend to marry me whether Farisdeen approves or not, you've set in motion events that cannot be halted or reversed. Are you sure you are willing to risk all that—for me?'

Warmth filling him at the anxiety in her eyes, he said, 'What I cannot risk is losing a lifetime of happiness in order to retain an approval I never sought. Yes, Jocelyn, I am completely sure.'

She nodded. Taking a deep breath, she squeezed his arm. 'Then let us walk into our future—together.'

'That's the spirit!' Confident that whatever happened, with Jocelyn as his wife, he would have all he needed and desired, Alex led her up the entry stairs.

Thurgood opened the door to them, his eyes widening at the sight of Jocelyn on Alex's arm. 'Would you inform the Duke that I would like to see him?'

'Will the young lady be accompanying you?'

'Yes, but you needn't announce that. He will discover soon enough that I have come with Miss Sudderfeld—who has just done me the honour of agreeing to become my wife.'

Shock briefly registered on the butler's face before he schooled his expression. 'Allow me to offer my congratulations, Mr Cheverton. I hope they won't be...premature.'

'Thank you for your concern, Thurgood, but I have the matter well in hand.'

'I do hope so, sir. If you will follow me?'

The butler led them up the stairs to the library—scene of Jocelyn's angry interview days earlier. Casting her a quick glance Alex whispered, 'Don't worry. This visit will end much differently than your last one.'

She gave him a wry smile. 'I don't suppose Farisdeen will try to throw us down the stairs, in any event.'

'Certainly not. A duke never exerts himself in such unseemly ways. He would ask Thurgood to do it. Fortunately, I'm thirty years younger and four stone heavier, so he'd probably not risk the attempt.'

Encouraged to see her smile, he pressed her fingers. Then heard her deep intake of breath as he breathed deeply himself and walked her into the library to the sound of the butler intoning his name.

His attention focused on the ledgers open on the desk in front of him, Farisdeen didn't look up as they entered. 'I'm fully occupied with estate business at the moment, Alex. Could you come back later?'

'I'm sorry, Duke, but I'm afraid this will not wait.'

'What could be so—?' the Duke began saying, breaking off when he looked up. 'Miss Sudderfeld? What is *she* doing here?'

'We've come to inform you that Jocelyn has just agreed to marry me.'

For a moment, stony silence reigned. Then the Duke said quietly, 'So you intend to defy me in this?'

'I do. My life, and my happiness, are at stake and I cannot allow you to interfere in those.'

'And how much will it interfere in your "life" and "happiness" if I cut off your funds and terminate all contact with you?'

'That would be regrettable. I understand that my decision will come as a…disappointment and that you might no longer wish to tolerate my presence. I propose to return to Edge Hall and resume managing it. Reducing your irritation by keeping out of your sight, for the rest of your life, if that is what you prefer.'

'In the face of such defiance, why would I allow you to reside in comfort at Edge Hall? Did I not warn you that disregarding my wishes would carry consequences? I will cast you off completely! See how well you can support a wife on the pittance your own estate earns you!'

'And *you*, Miss Sudderfeld!' the Duke continued, turning to Jocelyn. 'Are you truly so selfish and ambitious that you would see Cheverton ruined and virtually penniless for ten or twenty years, so he can eventually step into my shoes and make you a duchess?'

'I have every confidence that Alex can provide for us, whatever you choose to do,' Jocelyn said calmly. 'Though I would be sorry to be the cause of a breach between you, since he has assured me that I am as essential to his happiness as he is to mine, that is all that matters to me. I would just as soon not become a duchess eventually, but being Alex's wife would make even that tolerable.'

'Not want to become a duchess?' the Duke scoffed. 'You might at least do me the favour of speaking the truth.'

'I understand how impossible it might be for you to believe that, but it is true none the less. I neither seek your favour nor fear your displeasure.'

His eyes sparking with anger, Farisdeen switched his gaze to Alex. 'You truly intend to marry this...this mannerless harridan? She will be a disaster as a duchess!'

Alex laughed. 'If you are holding up Lady Anne as the model for a proper duchess, then I'm counting on it. Thanks to you, I have extensive experience in running a large estate. If you choose to terminate all contact with me, which is entirely your right, I've already made enquiries about obtaining another position. You may remember Mr Orrel? He owns various mining interests.'

The Duke curled his lip in distaste. 'That cit? A miner's son who enriched himself dealing in collieries? Yes, I know *of* him, though we are certainly not acquainted.'

'I wouldn't think so. Else you would know that in addition to making his fortune in mining, he now owns all the victualling and trading concerns in Chichester—which is where I first met him, while arranging supplies for Edge Hall. A year ago, he purchased a large estate in Devon. When I next saw him, he asked me to recommend a good estate manager since, not having been bred to the land, he knew little about managing it. He added that should I ever tire of working at Edge Hall, he'd hire me at twice whatever you were paying me. I'm sure he'd be delighted to honour that offer.'

'You would leave my protection to work for *Orrel*?' the Duke asked incredulously.

'He would be thrilled by the prospect of hiring me. Not a very subtle or genteel character, Mr Orrel. I imagine he wouldn't wait an instant before going off to boast to all his friends that he'd have the heir to a dukedom working for him.'

Alex waited for the ramifications of that comment to sink in. By the look of distaste on Farisdeen's face, he knew precisely the moment the Duke realised what the *ton* would say when they heard Farisdeen's heir was working for a miner's son.

'You wouldn't,' the Duke said flatly.

'It wouldn't be my preference. But I don't intend to let my wife live in striated circumstances. I would prefer to continue managing Edge Hall. But that is your choice.'

Alex watched as the Duke, his pale face red now with anger, once again turned towards Jocelyn. Before he could speak, Alex broke in. 'And please don't demean yourself by attempting to threaten Miss Sudderfeld. Should you try to punish her by terminating her brother's project and evicting them from Edge Hall,

I've already contacted the Duke of Portland to see if he would be interested in assuming sponsorship. His Grace, you may remember, has already received acclaim for the translations of Aristotle done by his rector, Reverend Owen.'

Farisdeen's red face now went pale again. After a long, silent moment, he said, 'I suppose you believe you have checkmated me.'

'This isn't a game, Your Grace. It's my life. My happiness. If you are accusing me of scheming to secure those, I plead guilty. It is not my intent to defy you in anything else. I'm perfectly resigned to accepting the burden of a title I never wanted and to being schooled by you in its duties. But I've no interest in becoming a leader of society. I wish to return to Edge Hall and continue managing it as before, coming up to London only as you think necessary to attend Parliamentary meetings and become better acquainted with those peers you feel I need to know. But I will do it on my terms. Those terms include making Jocelyn my wife.'

With a growl of frustration, Farisdeen jumped up from his chair and paced back and forth in front of the hearth. Squeezing Jocelyn's hand for encouragement, Alex waited calmly for the Duke to make his decision.

Banished or accepted made no difference. He would have Jocelyn and, as she had told the Duke, being together was all that mattered to them.

At last, Farisdeen swung to face them. 'I cannot make a mockery of myself and my ancient title by having it become known that my heir is working for a *coal miner's* son. And I wouldn't give Portland the satisfaction of telling the scholarly community that I didn't have enough interest or funds to complete Sudderfeld's project. I suppose I have no choice but to allow you to return to Edge Hall. I'm not sure when or if I will wish to see you again.'

'I didn't set out to alienate you, but I understand your anger. I shall leave this house as soon as possible and return to Edge Hall with the Sudderfelds. We will have the banns called at the parish church, with our wedding to follow immediately afterward. We would be honoured if you chose to attend.'

At that, the Duke stared at him with disbelief. 'You are an impudent rascal, aren't you? Get out of my sight before I change my mind and cut you off after all!' With that, he stomped back to his desk, threw himself into the chair and looked back down at his ledgers.

'I appreciate your forbearance,' Alex said quietly. Taking Jocelyn's hand, he bowed while she curtsied. Eyes fixed on his ledgers, the Duke didn't look up.

Jocelyn remained silent as they walked downstairs and out the entry door. But once they reached the park at the centre of Grosvenor Square, she turned to face him and laughed out loud.

'You are the most complete hand! Threatening to work for a coal miner's son? Did Mr Orrel really offer you a job?'

'You doubt my honesty?' Alex slapped hand to his chest. 'I'm stricken!'

'Well, did he?'

'I'm appalled that my future bride has such a low opinion of my veracity. Yes, Madam Doubter, he did. Not recently, of course, but he did make the offer last year. And I can promise you he would definitely broadcast to the entire world his glee at having a duke's heir as his employee.'

'And Portland! You must have listened well those

evenings when Papa told me there'd almost been a bidding war between Portland and Farisdeen over who would sponsor the Euripides translations! Apparently the two have been rivals in everything since they were young men at Oxford.'

'I told you to trust me, didn't I? You're not the only one, Miss Translator, who can figure out plot and motivation. I might have been dealing in shades of meaning less subtle than those you work with, but I do know what matters to a duke.'

'I did trust you. And you claim I am the intelligent one! You were masterful!'

'I'm so glad that my future wife thinks me "masterful". It's a welcome change from the scrubby brat who was more likely to abuse me.'

'No more scrubby brat. This fiancée believes her future husband is brilliant. Handsome. Irresistible.'

'I don't think I'm going to miss that scrubby brat at all,' Alex said, laughing. 'But before she vanishes for ever, let me apologise to her for acting out of turn, displaying my preference to Farisdeen at that soirée without first informing her or making sure of her feelings. I'm profoundly grateful that my rashness and arrogance didn't destroy what we had before it could begin.'

'Nothing could destroy my love for you. It only took a few hours of examining what my life would be like without you for me to realise that. So the scrubby brat accepts your apology. Her future husband is very persuasive, you know. And did I ever tell you how well he kisses? Oh, how I love those kisses!'

Then right there, in the middle of square, heedless of pedestrians strolling the paths and carriages passing by, Jocelyn rose up on tiptoe and gave him a resounding kiss.

'I can hardly believe it!' she said when he released her at last. 'To return to the countryside I adore with my project to work on, my family safe—and the love of my life to cherish for the rest of my days. You really will let me practise equestrian tricks?'

Chuckling at her delight, Alex nodded. 'As long as I ride beside you, ready to catch you if you fall. And as long as no one else is around. I'd have you ride more safely, in breeches. No side saddle and skirts.'

She gave him a provocative look. 'Tight, clinging knit breeches that reveal every curve?'

At that mental image, Alex's body immediately tightened. 'There'd better be no one around.'

She reached up to run a tender hand down his face. 'Indeed. You may have cavalierly rejected the possibilities of a deserted garden on a chilly day, but I find the prospect of the open countryside…alluring.'

Groaning, Alex took her hand and kissed it. 'Minx! If you continue in this vein, I may need to ride to Doctors' Commons for a special licence. I'm not so sure now I can wait to claim you for long enough to call the banns.'

'Then I shall have to stop teasing you. The tenants and villagers admire you so much. I cannot deprive them of the joy of sharing our wedding day with us.'

'So you are ready to come back to Edge Hall with me, have the banns called, and marry me in the village church?'

'You wouldn't prefer St George's, Hanover Square, or Westminster Abbey, as befits a duke's heir?' she teased.

'The parish church will do just fine for an estate manager. Although with you at my side, I feel more blessed than a king. The Duke will probably not grace our wedding with his presence, but with your family and mine looking on, and my best friends from Oxford, it will be a true celebration. I can't wait for them to meet you—and you to meet them.'

'I shall love to meet them. What an event it will be, with family, the villagers and everyone from estate to share it with us!'

'Our private celebration afterwards will be even more joyous and thrilling,' he promised, knowing the desire blazing in him must be clear in his eyes. 'Can you be ready to return to Edge Hall tomorrow?'

Tucking her hand back on his arm, she said, '*I* could, but so hasty a departure would be discourteous to Aunt Bellingame. She's already accepted invitations in our names for the next several days. Let us give her a week to accustom herself.'

'I might need a moment to compose myself before we go in to tell her of the collapse of her hopes that you'll marry someone else. I must say, I dread that interview more than I did facing down Farisdeen.'

She shook her head at him. 'You needn't worry. She only disapproved of you because she never thought there was a chance you could actually wed me. *I* might care nothing about the title, but I assure you, my aunt will be over the moon about having her great-niece become a duchess. She'll boast of it as far and wide as your Mr Orrel would have, if he'd succeeded in hiring you!'

'Shall we go back to Upper Brook Street, then?'

'Yes, I am ready!' With a giggle, she gave a little hop and skip before turning back to seize his arm. 'Oh, Alex! I can hardly believe the world can hold such happiness!'

His own heart aglow, Alex said, 'It's just beginning, my love. We'll have each other for a lifetime.'

A month later, Alex stood in the kitchen at Edge Hall, checking with the Cook, the housekeeper and the butler about the preparations for the wedding breakfast for the villagers and tenants to be held after the marriage ceremony this morning. Having heard nothing from the Duke in the weeks since their acrimonious interview in Grosvenor Square, before purchasing provisions for the feast, he'd checked again with the Duke's London solicitor to see whether or not his access to Edge Hall's household accounts had been cut off.

To his relief, the solicitor informed him he was still able to authorise whatever purchases were necessary to run the estate. Nor had the Duke terminated the personal allowance he'd bestowed on Alex when he announced him as his heir.

Perhaps the Duke's anger had cooled somewhat. In any event, Alex had jumped on the chance to use those personal funds to buy the necessities for the celebration, so that the Duke could not later accuse him of stealing from estate resources for his own ends.

The final preparations overseen, he went back upstairs to the parlour where his friends Gregory Lattimar and Crispin d'Aubignon, Viscount Dellamont, waited to escort him to the church. Where, in just a short time, his family and his bride would greet him.

'Everything up to snuff downstairs?' Lattimar asked as Alex walked into the parlour.

'All in readiness.'

'Are *you* ready?' Dellamont asked. 'Quite the dark horse, wasn't he, Gregory? Not a whisper to either of us about his interest in any female and then an invitation to his *wedding*? I thought at first it came from you, playing a prank on me!'

Gregory laughed. 'And I thought mine must have been from you, playing a prank on me! With all your family milling about last night, we didn't have a chance to speak privately, Alex. So tell us more! Else we shall both remain highly offended that you dishonoured our long friendship by saying nothing to us about this.'

'It was all…rather sudden,' Alex admitted. 'I almost confessed my interest in Jocelyn at that dinner we shared several months ago. But I didn't believe anything would ever come of it—and didn't want either of you quizzing me about her.'

'Would we do that?' Gregory asked Dellamont. 'Poke and prod if he were evasive? Keep at him until we tricked him into revealing everything?'

'Not us,' Dellamont answered with a straight face. 'We've always respected each other's privacy in matters of the heart.'

While Gregory made a choking sound, Alex said, 'I hadn't intended to shut both of you out. None of us was in a hurry to marry. When we met for dinner that night, I thought it would be years before I'd have to consider finding a wife. Then Penlowe died. Suddenly I was heir, with the Duke's vastly increased concern about the succession, and with him pushing his favoured candidates at me. I should also point out, neither of you were in London for me to consult.'

'Unfortunate. We could have lent you a sympathetic ear.'

'Or at least provided the necessary quantity of liquid assistance to your deliberations. Naturally, you could have revealed all your agonising. We being the souls of discretion.'

Alex laughed. 'Oh, yes. Like that time at Oxford when the two of you crept up to the bedroom of the daughter of the Earl of—'

'No need to remind us of past misdeeds,' Gregory interrupted. 'Now, tell us more about the lady. A scholar, I understand. Her father seems to be an amiable, learned man. She assisted him with his translations and then has done the same for her equally learned brother?'

Though Alex yearned to boast to his friends of his bride's true brilliance, he didn't dare take the chance that they would find her authorship as objectionable as the scholarly community undoubtedly would. 'Yes.'

'Never thought you'd end up with an intellectual!' Gregory said. 'The ladies that interested you when we were at Oxford were skilled in...other arts.'

'But his bride is so lovely, he's probably able to over-look her being a bluestocking.'

'She is beautiful, isn't she?' Alex agreed. 'And clever and unexpected. I can never predict what she might do or say.'

'Sounds more alarming than alluring to me,' Del-lamont said with a laugh. 'More to the point, what did the Duke have to say about it? I can't imagine he fan-cied having his librarian's daughter as the next Duch-ess of Farisdeen.'

'He wasn't pleased,' Alex acknowledged. 'We haven't spoken since I informed him I would marry her, whether he approved or not.'

'Did he threaten to cut you off?' Dellamont asked. 'My father threatens me with that all the time and I've never even hinted at marrying a woman he couldn't accept.'

'He did, but ultimately I...persuaded him not to take that action.'

Dellamont studied his face. 'It's almost time to leave for the church, but some day, when we have more lei-sure, you must tell us over a good bottle of port just how you engineered that persuasion.'

'I'd made contingency plans in any event that would

have allowed us to marry, even had he chosen to cut me off,' Alex assured them.

'Good manager that you are, I'm sure you did,' Gregory said. 'But Dellamont is right. We must get you to the church now, lest your bride believes you've left her at the altar.'

'Nervous?' Dellamont asked as they walked down the stairs and out to the waiting carriage. 'I would be. Marriage! It's so...permanent.'

Nervous to claim Jocelyn as his bride, to delight and bedevil and love him the rest of his life? 'Not a bit. Anxious.'

Gregory laughed. 'Then climb in the landau and let's get you married.'

And so, a short time later, Alex stood at the front of the ancient stone church, the vicar before him, and gazed down the aisle to await the appearance of his bride. His breath froze and his heart pounded in his chest with joy and anticipation as he saw her on her father's arm.

A burst of sunlight through the old windows gilded the burnished curls pinned beneath the circlet of early roses adorning her head. Her gown of deep green satin hugged her curves, the voluminous sleeves emphasising her delicate neck and shoulders. And the joy that shone in her dark eyes and lit her smile resonated deep within him.

Soon after, he claimed her hand and recited with her the words of the wedding service. And then he was leading her down the aisle, out the door past the cheering villagers, to help her into the flower-bedecked phaeton.

Followed by his friends and family in their carriages, accompanied by boys from the village and the estate who ran beside their carriage, shouting, he drove them back to the grounds behind Edge Hall, where the wedding breakfast had been set out.

'Happy?' Alex asked, turning his attention from the horses long enough to kiss Jocelyn on the nose.

'Delirious,' she answered. 'The only thing better will be when you take me up to your room later. Thinking of that, shall we skip breakfast and go right to dessert?'

He chuckled. 'Don't tempt me! Having waited this long, though, we can wait a bit longer. The tenants and villagers would be so disappointed not to be able to toast the bride.'

'Or personally thank the Duke's heir for the sumptuous feast he has set out for them.'

Pulling up the carriage, he tossed the reins to a waiting groom and went over to lift her out of the carriage. To the huzzahs of the guests who'd already reached the banqueting tables, he gave her a long, lingering kiss.

As he tucked her hand on his arm to lead her to their place at the head table, a tall, silver-haired figure caught his eye. Jocelyn must have noticed him at the same moment, for she stopped short. 'Farisdeen?' she exclaimed.

It was indeed the Duke, who was heading towards them. Not sure what Farisdeen intended—to sow discord or harmony—Alex felt himself tense. If the Duke meant to berate them, Alex would deflect the lecture in short order.

After bowing to Jocelyn's curtsy, the Duke held out his hand to her. Hesitantly, she offered her own, which he carried to his lips and kissed.

'Let me offer my congratulations on your marriage, Mr and Mrs Cheverton.'

'Thank you, Your Grace,' Jocelyn replied. 'I am

pleased you decided to attend the festivities. Does that mean we're forgiven?'

Alex winced, but that was Jocelyn—blunt and unafraid. Holding his breath, he waited to see how the Duke responded.

After initially stiffening, the Duke let out a reluctant chuckle. 'I do hope you don't count diplomacy in your future, Mrs Cheverton. You certainly are direct.'

'Yes, Your Grace. But I prefer to know at once where I stand, rather than try to decipher the meaning from a paragraph of obscure phrasing.'

'As your brother does so well in your work? It's true, I was angry for quite a long time about your husband's defiance. I am not accustomed to having my wishes disregarded. But ultimately, that anger faded...leaving behind the ache I still feel at the loss of my son. I realised then that fate and chance had offered me another son, a man of honesty, character and strength. A man worthy of being my heir. I could allow pride to deprive me of his company and pique at being outmanoeuvred keep me from giving him the insight and encouragement he needs to one day take my place. Or I could bow to reality and accept his right to control the most intimate aspects of his life.'

'A handsome concession, Your Grace,' Jocelyn said. 'So you will stay and celebrate with us?'

'I will.'

'Thank you, sir,' Alex said.

Gazing at Jocelyn, the Duke shook his head. 'Did she tell you I'd offered her money to give you up? An offer which she threw back in my face.'

'You did?' Alex exclaimed. Looking at Jocelyn incredulously, he said, 'Why didn't you tell me?'

'I didn't want to do anything that might further in-flame the disagreement between you.'

'How much did he offer?'

'He didn't name a sum. I probably should have asked. It might have been worth it to give you up,' she teased.

Listening to the banter between them, the Duke shook his head. 'She may make a duchess after all.'

'Good heavens, I hope not!' Jocelyn exclaimed, making Alex laugh and even eliciting a rare smile from the Duke.

By then, most of the guests from the church had arrived and were taking their places at the tables set out on the lawn. Striding over to the head table, the Duke raised high a glass of the wine a servant poured for him.

'To the future Duke of Farisdeen—and his Duchess.'

'To the Duke and Duchess!' the guests echoed.

'Oh, dear,' Jocelyn murmured as Alex walked her to her place. 'Now that Farisdeen has publicly acknowledged us, I don't think we'll be able to avoid the Duke-and-Duchess roles.'

'I'm afraid not,' Alex murmured back. 'Discouraging as the prospect is, I already promised him I'd go through with it. But I promise *you* I'll make it up to you. Soon. Tonight.'

'Tonight and every night…or afternoon…or morning?'

'At every opportunity, my impatient wife. And that's a promise I look forward to keeping!'

And to the cheers of the assembled guests, Alex gave his bride another lingering kiss.

* * * * *